I0673198

VENOMOUS VALENTINE

By Michael Jameson

Published by Piscataqua Press
An imprint of RiverRun Bookstore
142 Fleet Street
Portsmouth, NH 03801
www.ppressbooks.com

ISBN: 978-1-944393-82-3

CHAPTER 1

LOVE LINK. That was all it said.

Written entirely in uppercase letters mind you, but that could be completely irrelevant. The E and the L were separated with just enough distance to convince a certain Homicide Detective it had to be two words. But that's all he could figure out. He didn't have the first clue as to whether it meant an unknown suspect wrote it trying to say: Love, Link. Besides that, the only other things that came to mind were words like Lifeline or Love Line. The latter is supposed to be two words, the only difference were the letters K and E. This basic, or elementary, stuff came to him very quickly as always. But he tried not to think about that. It just brought back a dark memory of being four years old and how exciting it was writing the entire alphabet on a chalkboard in the right order in uppercase letters.

Unfortunately, opportunities were rare for him to

express his enthusiasm to anyone. Granted, you can't expect a four year old to anticipate reactions from others. Maybe some of them do, but this guy wouldn't bet on it. He would hope not, for the sake of innocence alone.

That's Chauncey for you. That's how he feels.

He never said much about this to anyone. Perhaps holding on to this idealistic notion of childhood innocence helped keep things in perspective. But that's an unusual combination, especially if it's coming from the mind of a Homicide Detective. Fortunately, these thoughts would come and go in a matter of seconds, and Detective Chauncey could concentrate on the case.

Another all-nighter most likely, he thought.

Then again, it hadn't been declared a murder investigation. So why was he here? Simple, he heard it on his old Police Scanner and lived only a short distance from the University. He'd get called to check things out anyway. The Boss knew where to find him, not that he ever had to look very hard. Chauncey would often arrive at the scene beforehand. Meaning before Boss Bobby Burrell did, as would be the case tonight.

Chauncey hadn't done anything yet. Obviously, he wasn't in a position to do so. As a Homicide Detective, he knew he had to wait until the case was officially declared a Homicide. It probably was, but he knew he'd have to wait. Which was fine, just the nature of the business. Chauncey knew not to touch anything. All he'd done so far was kneel down quickly, thirty seconds tops, to get an idea of what he'd be getting himself into.

Nothing stood out, just those words Love Link written on the outer part of the right arm, maybe a few inches above the wrist. It wasn't a tattoo. Chauncey had seen enough writing from countless Magic Markers and Sharpies throughout the years to know what he was looking at. What he found disturbing was not seeing any sign of physical injury. No marks of any kind, which meant no sign of strangulation or head trauma. That meant no lacerations or bullet wounds could be found either. This definitely wouldn't be an open and shut case. Exactly where it would go from here this particular Homicide Detective honestly had no idea, and Chauncey wouldn't kid himself or anyone else about it otherwise.

Strangely enough, Chauncey didn't really notice all the loud commotion he was surrounded by. Be it the loud sirens from police cars, ambulances, or fire engines. A helicopter flew overhead with a searchlight shining far too bright for anybody to handle. Luckily that occurred during his quick examination of the fresh new corpse that lay before him. To whom did he owe his thanks to for such an incredible sight on this beautiful evening?

Sarcasm: Chauncey's personal savior.

Something he usually kept to himself. The way he saw it was that some people like to pray for the best outcome. Others saw the craziness of the world on a daily basis, and nothing could alter the damage that was already done. The best thing anyone could do was try to figure out who caused it. You may never learn why but at the very least the culprit was apprehended, which offers some closure. To somebody you hope.

The Boss didn't mind the sarcasm, but no boss would want to complain about their best man showing up at the scene before they did, especially if it's the County's best Homicide Detective. Still, there is something that The Boss doesn't know: The best guy on the force had a very specific reason for arriving at the scene early. It had nothing to do with eagerness or efficiency, but simply to get his act together before applying himself the best that he could. The majority of his cases occur at night, or at least that's when the body is discovered. This made it all the more interesting. A number of the murderers he captured could hold jobs, but he couldn't recall if they were the 9 to 5 ones. You would think if that was part of the pattern he'd remember. However, it boiled down to the kind of job they held and the type of personality they had.

Profiling it was called, created by the FBI.

Unfortunately, there was more to it than most people realized. Chauncey knew that better than anybody. The majority of his cases didn't require a phone call to the Feds, but if Boss Bobby Burrell thought it was necessary he wouldn't question that approach. More often than not it made things easier, but the times they got involved were few and far between. And Chauncey still preferred to keep it that way.

The Homicide Detective was waiting for the boys in blue, or as he liked to call them uniformed brothers-in-arms. Don't worry sisters get accounted for also, no one ever needed to question him on that one. He just had his favorite sayings. Granted, this is also something he wouldn't share very often. In this line of work, there wasn't time to worry about political correctness, not as far as he was concerned. There may have been others in law enforcement who strongly disagreed, but he never took the time to find out who they were. For Chauncey, that was small talk. To anyone and everyone he was Detective Chauncey, or simply Chauncey. Be it personally or professionally.

The yellow Police Line Do Not Cross tape was starting to be put up. It wouldn't be long before the white tape would be on the cement sidewalk surrounding the body. No identification yet, all he knew for sure was he had a white male, probably in his early to mid-twenties, with the words Love Link written on the outer part of the right arm. The Campus Police might know who the poor guy was. He had no idea who called this in, but he recalled that a fire alarm had been pulled first. At least that's what was stated over the airwaves. However, it was shortly afterwards that a body had been reported found lying face up on a cement walkway approximately thirty feet before the main entrance of one of the dormitories. What originally caught Chauncey's attention was there being no mention of a fire, making him assume it was a false alarm. He also had to keep in mind if any part of Prime State University had gone ablaze there would have been a countless number of people roaming outside the campus. The entire student population for starters and a lot more fire engines and ambulances. But the worst part is the reporters from every news station in the county sticking their noses in the investigation before having the slightest clue. That wasn't far off, and barely fifteen minutes had passed since there had been any mention of a body discovered. Chauncey could always remain one step ahead of the hottest game in town with the old-fashioned Police Scanner. He relied on the internet as much as anyone else did these days, but the scanner worked best for local excitement.

Chauncey stepped further away from the body so the boys in blue could finish blocking off the crime scene. Shortly afterwards he heard a familiar voice behind him.

"Chauncey," said Boss Bobby Burrell. "As usual you make me think we should switch positions."

"Triple B," said Chauncey. "What's happening?"

"Not much. I just got a text from the Campus Police. They've got a name for the poor guy."

"Who is it?"

"Roy Cumberland, age 24, grad student. No criminal history. Pretty sure he pulled the fire alarm before he went."

"Any medical issues, like heart disease in his family?"

"That's being looked into as we speak, but I don't think so. The family will be notified as soon as possible."

"Too bad it can't wait until tomorrow morning."

"I know, but this will be all over the TV and internet within the next hour. The parents live about two hours north of here. If a cop in their town doesn't notify them right away a random friend or acquaintance will call them at 3am. That'll be a thousand times worse. This poor guy's mother will probably be hysterical."

What Boss Bobby Burrell, or Triple B, was talking about is a part of the job that Chauncey didn't like to think about. Having to show up at someone's house unannounced to tell them a loved one is dead, most likely a result of foul play. Then again, telling the parents that their son or daughter is dead of a drug overdose wasn't any easier, or a car accident for that matter. Bottom line: It's not an easy task period. Sometimes it's referred to as doing the dirty work, but no cop would ever want anyone outside of law enforcement to know that.

It's a weeknight, Chauncey thought to himself. No sign of a keg party anywhere. That's something you'd expect to see over the weekend, and Prime State didn't have the reputation of being a big party school. But what college doesn't have them?

"Any ideas?" asked Triple B.

"Not really," said Chauncey. "More than likely he pulled the fire alarm. We'll see if the prints match, that won't take long. Poor bastard knew something was wrong with him. But everything else with forensics, autopsy, toxicology report, that will take time."

"What else is new?"

Triple B's cell phone went off. He checked the number that popped up.

It was the Campus Police.

"Burrell here." he answered, listening to whatever was said for about two minutes. "Okay," he said, before hanging up.

"What's up?" asked Chauncey.

"They got some poor kid down at the station in tears."

"Downtown?" he asked.

"No," said Triple B. "At the Campus Police office."

"At least we can walk there. What have they got?"

"They just gave me the kid's name. Paul Raymond. Guess he was a good friend of Roy's."

"Name doesn't ring a bell. Is he a student here as well?'

"Probably," said Triple B. "I'm sure we'll find out the minute we get there."

CHAPTER 2

IT WAS THE DEAD OF NIGHT, so to speak, and getting much closer to the midnight hour. This Roy Cumberland guy's body remained exactly where it was supposed to for the time being. Strangely enough, the Prime State Campus Police Office also remained quiet considering everything that was going on right now. The only exceptions here were Triple B engaging in a serious one on one discussion with Sergeant Matheson, who usually worked the graveyard shift during the week or got called in whenever an emergency occurred, along with Chauncey dealing with another poor guy trying to hold back tears and obviously on the verge of hysteria.

There was something different about this poor guy, at least as far as Chauncey was concerned. He immediately started thinking of this Raymond character as a poor kid. Right from the get-go he sensed something a little off about young Paul, a little slower than most people he questioned. Granted, that's not what he was doing, not yet anyway. They'd only been speaking for a few minutes, not a lot of questions so far. Perhaps Paul had a learning disability, like attention-deficit-disorder, or just really immature. Chauncey didn't want to jump the gun, however. In all fairness, it probably hadn't sunk in for Paul that a good friend was dead. Go easy he thought to himself.

"When did you last see Roy?" asked Chauncey.

"Tonight," answered Paul.

"What time tonight?"

"A little before eight," said Paul.

"Did he seem okay?"

"Yeah," said Paul. "He wasn't sick."

"So he didn't say he wasn't feeling well for any reason?

"No, he was going to see Jane."

He immediately paused because this was a good start. He got a name right away. Take it slow with this kid.

Chauncey wanted to take a minute both for himself and Paul. He made his way over to the front desk. Both Triple B and Sergeant Matheson had made themselves comfortable by sitting in the chairs behind it. He motioned to Triple B to get a coffee for him. All he had to was nod to his Boss, who knew exactly what he meant by it, as well as how he liked it. It took twenty seconds tops to get what he wanted, coffee with extra cream and no sugar. In no time he made his way back over to Paul, who was sitting in a chair the waiting area which was maybe fifteen feet from the front desk. He didn't want to be in a private room out back and grill this kid. That would create more grief panic-stricken outbursts, and no one was considered a suspect yet. He didn't know anything about this Jane either.

"Who's Jane?" asked Chauncey. "Is she a friend?"

"Yeah," said Paul, very slowly. "Well, kind of."

"What kind of a friend?"

"She works with my Uncle, in the lab."

"Does your Uncle work here?"

"Yeah," said Paul.

"Does Jane have a last name?

"Newton."

"Sorry I didn't catch that," said Chauncey. "What is it?"

"Newton," said Paul. "Jane Newton."

"Why are you guys talking about Wayne Newton?" Triple B asked, just blurting it out.

"SHUT UP!!!" yelled Paul. "It's not funny!"

So much for avoiding an outburst, Chauncey thought. Maybe bringing this kid in a backroom wasn't a bad idea. He gave himself a few seconds to concentrate again then motioned to Triple B with his right hand to indicate he had everything under control.

"So she works for your Uncle in a lab," said Chauncey.

"Yeah," said Paul.

"Where exactly?" he asked.

"Here."

"Okay."

He decided he had enough information to start with. It would be pretty easy to learn exactly who Jane Newton and Paul's Uncle were right away. The Uncle is most likely a Science Professor of some kind, his first guess in regards to Jane Newton's job title was a lab assistant or an intern. With any luck Sergeant Matheson might have the files on these folks already. Still as a Homicide Detective he never counted on luck whether he believed in it or not.

Chauncey couldn't get over how quiet it was. He expected a good amount of the students living in the dorms would be outside right now checking things out, taking a ton of pictures with their cell phones and posting it on Facebook seconds later. He was also curious if it was just himself, along with Triple B, Sergeant Matheson, and Paul were the only ones here in the Campus Police Office.

"Matheson," said Chauncey. "Are you the only one on duty tonight?"

"Yeah," answered Sergeant Matheson.

"You're not going to call anyone else in?"

"Probably not, since you guys are here you'll be taking over the investigation, right?"

"Yeah," said Chauncey. "But we're definitely going to keep you in the loop. That much I'm sure of."

There was something the great Homicide Detective couldn't shake: Why weren't a mob of students gathering outside? In some ways that wasn't a bad thing, that meant less pictures leaking onto Facebook or YouTube. But the combination of a dead body and the lack of crowds or onlookers made it seem even more lifeless than it already was. He didn't care to deal with the media right away, but sometimes having civilians present created some kind of energy in the air. It was hard to describe but it helped, a little.

"So where is everybody?" he inquired.

"What do you mean?" asked Sergeant Matheson.

"The students," answered Chauncey. "You would think a murder would be enough to get everyone in the dorms out of bed!"

"Not tonight," replied Sergeant Matheson.

"Why not?" asked Chauncey.

"The spring semester hasn't started yet. Things won't start up again until a week from Monday. You won't see a lot of folks back here until the Saturday or Sunday before that. Most students are celebrating Christmas or Hanukkah, and New Year's is right after that. Are you telling me you forgot about the winter break?"

"Of course!!!" declared Chauncey rolling his eyes. "Hell, I've lived here long enough you think I'd remember!"

When he shouted out loud like this it always meant that he was frustrated and angry, with himself. The winter break may not be the best thing to call it, he thought to himself. There's never an inch of snow here, not in this part of California. Then again it was unusually warm tonight, especially for this time of year. It still got as cold as a bastard some nights. This may have been an exception, but he wore his jacket anyway. Not that it would have been that big of a deal if he hadn't, since he always kept it in the car.

All of a sudden it hit Chauncey: What was Roy Cumberland doing here? He was obviously connected to this Jane Newton, and probably Paul's Uncle, whoever that was. Sergeant Matheson had obviously kept up on current events at Prime State University or the lack of them right now, time to get some more info.

"Matheson," said Chauncey. "How familiar are you with this kid's Uncle and Jane Newton?"

"Very familiar," answered Sergeant Matheson.

"Great," said Chauncey. "I love you already."

Sergeant Matheson smiled, trying not to let out a laugh. It might not be appropriate for a homicide case, but it was a lot easier dealing with other constituents on the police force who had a sense of humor, especially in the middle of the night.

"Paul Raymond's Uncle is Professor Stanley Horace," said Sergeant Matheson.

"Go on," said Chauncey.

"Definitely the most well-known of the faculty here at the University, and the most talked about."

"Why's that?"

"His background is the most unusual, without a doubt the most exotic. A few years back there wasn't anything like this in the Science Department, at least not to the extent that it is now."

"His background," said Chauncey. "Which is?"

"He's a Herpetologist."

"Okay, I know what that is. So he study's reptiles and stuff, right?"

"Yup," said Matheson. "But that's only half of the equation."

"What do you mean?" asked Chauncey, even more curious.

"Not only does he teach here but he's also the assistant to the Head of the Science Department, who's retiring next year. I'm sure you can guess who's next in line for that position."

"Is there more?

"You bet, he worked for Widen Laboratories for a number of years. Still does kind of."

"That's factored into the equation, right?" asked Chauncey.

"Absolutely," said Matheson. "You got a multibillion dollar industry there. That's how Professor Horace came to our attention. No real teaching experience when he came here. His qualifications, however, were more than enough. A PhD gets you in when there's an opening here, know what I mean?"

Chauncey knew there was more to tell, and was ready to hear it.

"There's more," continued Matheson. "The big folks who run Widen Laboratories also have a big influence."

"The money men," said Chauncey.

"You're damn right!"

"I bet there's still a lot more to tell," said Chauncey.

"Widen Laboratories now finance everything at Prime State University. Not only did they build a lab for Professor Horace, but they officially own this place."

"Seriously?" asked Chauncey. "How come there was nothing in the press about it? That's a big deal! Especially around here! A grant from anyone or any corporation for Prime State is front page news, you know that."

"It's not a big secret," said Matheson. "But they kept it out of the press. Widen Laboratories being who they are power does what it wants, know what I mean?"

"It sounds like a nice touch of fascism, at least as far as I'm concerned. Except in this case it's just sugar-coated by building brand new labs and grants for anything and everything, convincing both the teachers and the students the sky's the limit. Am I heading in the right direction?"

"Yeah, and since their buyout was never heavily publicized everyone associated with Prime Stare University is convinced that miracles happen here, a Utopia so to speak."

Not anymore, Chauncey thought to himself. Now it's time to dig deeper.

"What do you know about Jane Newton?" he asked.

"Works for Horace in the lab," answered Matheson. "Started out as an intern a few years back, but I use the word intern loosely. The internship was financed by Widen Laboratories, which became the standard procedure for everything around here. I know you've already put two and two together."

"What are her relationships like with everyone here?"

"Not much to tell. She'll occasionally do some substitute teaching if it's necessary, that's the only reason why her name's on the payroll. She's a full-time employee at Widen Laboratories, so she's really just a familiar face on campus. I have to say, however, nothing bad is ever said about her."

"That Roy Cumberland lying dead out there," said Chauncey.

"I have a feeling she was more than a familiar face to him," concluded Matheson.

Chauncey still wanted to get more information out of Paul Raymond, but that could wait. Give the kid time, right now he had enough to work with. He sat down next to him to make it easier.

"Go home, okay?" said Chauncey. "I'll get back to you in a day or two. We'll take care of everything, try to get some rest."

"Okay," said Paul, who slowly stood up and exited

through the front entrance. He head remained down, and didn't so much as glance at Chauncey, Triple B, or Sergeant Matheson.

Before getting back up again, Chauncey looked outside and made sure the kid wasn't getting bombarded by reporters. No sight of one yet, if any had they'd be at the crime scene. But it wouldn't be long before a whole slew of them would come barging in.

"Time for more coffee," he said.

"You got it," answered Matheson.

Chauncey had just muttered that to himself, or so he thought. Instead he was thinking out loud, perhaps he's more alert tonight than he realized.

CHAPTER 3

IT WAS NOW THE FOLLOWING MORNING, a little after 11 am. Chauncey actually had a good night of sleep, considering he didn't get to bed until four in the morning. He got up about an hour ago, which gave him plenty of time to get it together and make his way back over to Prime State University.

He was glad he handled the reporters as well as he did. But he needed to give credit to Triple B and Sergeant Matheson too. It was just the three of them in the office last night, which might have helped the question and answer sessions with multiple interviewers go by quicker and more efficiently. The lack of students on campus meant there wasn't a huge mob scene. Not many locals showed up either. Granted, their presence was obvious but because the murder took place in the middle of the night during the week the majority of the residents were sleeping. Chauncey himself was just amazed that he didn't have to start the case by doing an all-nighter. It may not be in the books as a standard procedure, but most of the time it was how things went. How did he get so lucky? He knew it was pointless to ask that particular question, luck never had anything to do with it.

Chauncey wanted to be alert for his meeting with Professor Horace. Getting some shuteye before the sun came up helped him considerably. He was a night person by nature, but preferred to fall asleep while the sun was down. He only drank two cups of coffee last night. Small ones mind you. Special thanks to the one and only Sergeant Matheson, who probably needed it more than he did. He didn't ask Sergeant Matheson if this Professor liked coffee, but hadn't thought that far ahead. He just knew he'd be seeing him this morning. At least the repeat drives back and forth from his home to the campus would be short and sweet. Hopefully he'd have a small siesta before returning tomorrow.

There was no problem finding parking. Chauncey pulled into the nearest available space that didn't require a handicap or faculty sticker. The Detective couldn't find an indication of requirements needed in the space he pulled into, causing him to briefly ponder if the students could park here as well. The parking lot was located in front of the Widen Science Building, which naturally made him assume the name had something to do with Widen Laboratories taking over. Regardless, he wasn't about to enter this place with an expectation of optimism or enlightenment, like going to Epcot for the second or third time and slowly beginning to appreciate it as a learning experience.

Chauncey exited his car and headed to the front entrance. The doors were unlocked, not surprising as Professor Horace was supposed to be there waiting to be interviewed. Obviously death, especially homicide, is something that most people would consider a very important reason to talk. However, he didn't know anything about this guy. Granted, Sergeant Matheson did a very good job briefing him he had no physical description of the Scientist. Other than that he just knew this was some important Herpetologist who had a nephew named Paul Raymond.

Chauncey finished his coffee when he entered the building. A large trashcan was located at the left side of the double doors. Perfect timing, he thought to himself. Then it occurred to him, he forgot to get an extra cup for Professor Horace. Granted, he had no clue if the guy even liked coffee but it was a good way to break the ice. Worst-case scenario would leave him drinking it, something he had no problem with whatsoever.

The directions to the Professor's lab were simple. He wrote them down on a small piece of paper he'd left in his car. All he had to do was take a left down the first hallway and go up a set of stairs to the top floor, which was technically the second floor, meaning he didn't have to climb any higher. The lab was located directly in front of him. Things were going pretty easy so far.

Chauncey just hoped that this Professor Horace would be a half-decent conversationalist. The last thing he needed to deal with was a preoccupied know-it-all with eyes glued to a textbook or conducting a chemistry experiment where the slightest distraction would burn down the building.

He was about to find out.

The Detective stood in front of another set of double doors. He listened for any sounds of productivity that might be occurring inside. He couldn't hear anything except a generator, and there's nothing unusual about that. Be it in a public building or a house or whatever. Chances are in a place like this everything would have to be operating on all cylinders with a type of lab not commonly seen in this area. Especially if dangerous, possibly venomous, reptiles are kept here on a twenty-four hour a day basis.

For some reason, Chauncey expected to see an intercom or a buzzer of some sort. He forgot to ask Matheson for a number to reach the Professor at. Surely this guy had to have a cell phone or a private extension in the lab. Probably, he thought to himself, too late to worry about that now. He went ahead and knocked on the door. Four times to be exact and not very hard either. A voice far off in the distance, faint but clear, granted him permission to enter.

"Come on in," it said. "It's open."

If that's Professor Horace the guy can probably hear an entire conversation through a wall. Chauncey remained optimistic. At least he didn't have to wait. He turned the knob and pulled the door open, which was pretty heavy. Then again these weren't the glass doors he went through at the front entrance, it didn't take a genius to figure out there would be far more safety issues in this kind of environment compared to the lobby downstairs. By law these doors were probably installed, allowing The Detective to think of terms like biohazard and OSHA.

Still, Chauncey didn't think he needed to put on a radiation suit.

Upon entering, there was no sign of Professor Horace. Chauncey displayed common courtesy by waiting for the door to shut completely. The sound of a click was the cue for him to move forward. Slowly mind you, but forward. The first thing he noticed was the pallets on the floor against the walls on both sides of the room with brown boxes on them, most were covered with bubble wrap.

Nothing unusual, Chauncey thought, probably stuff that gets shipped back and forth from Widen Laboratories to Prime State University, most of the time anyway. All kinds of procedures had to be followed in order to allow exotic reptiles and various chemicals go through customs for delivery. Other than that, it was a brightly lit room with white square-tiled floors and white walls.

Next was a large-sized entrance with no doors leading into the large laboratory Chauncey anticipated, the moment he set foot in there he noticed the width of the place was far longer compared to the room he exited with pallets stacked on each side. Up against both walls he saw glass booths with all kinds of wildlife, most of which were reptiles naturally. Despite the distance and no real expertise, it was very easy to determine that the majority of them were venomous snakes. This didn't stir up any fear or anxiety, but he did not want an up close and guided tour.

Not unless he had to.

Chauncey also noticed the same kind of white walls in here as well. The only difference was a little more than halfway up there were large windows surrounding the entire place. After that was maybe a foot and a half of the walls again before reaching the ceiling, which had a big glass window fixture right in the middle of the room. He didn't try to estimate the length and width of it, but if you were scared of heights you wouldn't like it up there, even with a ladder or safety net.

For some strange reason, he felt very isolated.

That wouldn't last long.

After quickly glancing up at the glass on the roof again, the sound of footsteps could be heard on the right. Chauncey looked over to the sight of a black man in a white lab coat with very short hair and a trimmed beard, who extended his hand and smiled.

"Chauncey Winfield?" he asked.

"Hi," said Chauncey, shaking his hand. "I can't remember the last time anyone used my full name."

"You know I've been expecting you. I do my homework if I'm expecting visitors, especially if it's law enforcement."

"So you're?" Chauncey asked, pausing.

"Stan Horace."

"That kid Paul," said Chauncey. "You're his Uncle?"

"That's right," said Professor Horace. "He wasn't adopted. I married a white girl, his aunt specifically."

"That gets that out of the way then."

"Don't worry about it," said Professor Horace, laughing a bit.

Chauncey knew this would be easy, for now anyway.

"First thing I have to ask," said Chauncey. "What was Paul doing on campus? The school's been shut down to students. Did you know he was here?"

"Of course," answered Professor Horace. "That nephew of mine is always here."

"Why? Don't tell me it's because he loves doing homework throughout the entire year Does he assist you in the lab?"

"He helps me out occasionally. But Paul's not a student here at Prime State."

"He's not? But you said he's always here."

"He lives here."

"Seriously?" asked Chauncey. "I'm sure he doesn't camp out here in the lab. Does he sleep in an available dorm room?"

"In all honesty," said Professor Horace. "He does live in this particular building, but you won't find him sleeping here in the lab."

Chauncey thought for a second before saying anything. He quickly replayed in his head the act of coming into the building just a few minutes ago. He didn't closely examine the layout upon entering, but like many colleges most of Prime State University's dorms were separate from the academic buildings, and it was very unlikely that any of the downstairs offices could be converted into luxury suites, or even cheap studio apartments for that matter.

"I have a feeling he's not planning to spend the rest of his life crashing on a couch in an administrator's office," he stated.

"You got that right," said Professor Horace. "He lives on the bottom floor."

"Bottom floor, basement I assume?"

"Exactly, but don't get it wrong. You're not going to find him sleeping in the boiler room."

"That would almost justify free rent!"

"Absolutely, but he still doesn't have to pay anything. It's actually pretty nice down there. It is considered a maintenance area that is very well-maintained. Maintenance has its own building, but you probably know that."

"That I do."

"Believe it or not," continued Professor Horace. "After you open the door just walking down the stairs it's very easy to sense how nicely kept it is. Nothing like a basement that you would think has been abandoned since World War II. As soon as you reach the bottom floor there's a nice well-lit and clean hallway that contains four large rooms on the left. Three of them are used as storage facilities by the maintenance crew, both for school equipment and personal belongings."

"Must be a bit of a pain in the ass to search through all those rooms to find something you need."

"You'd think so, but no."

"Seriously?" asked Chauncey. "Everyone I know hates going through stuff, be it a basement or garage or whatever."

"This is true," said Professor Horace. "But this is one of the very few occasions where you'll find it's not the case."

"I'm listening."

"Everything that goes in and out of there is kept on file, both on paper and computers. Each item is placed in a specific area in the room it will be put in or taken out of, and the computer is who makes the decision as to the designated locations. I must also tell you that whoever has access has fingerprints in the system, along with identification badges, which must also be processed. So the employee, item, date, and time are on record whenever stuff goes in and out. Last but not least, it's very well-organized in all of the rooms with plenty of space to move around. If there's a way to keep a tractor-trailer down there it will be discovered."

"I'll have to see it at some point," said Chauncey. "I'll write everything down later. Everything you've told me is pretty easy to remember. I take it the fourth room is where Paul stays?"

"You got it," said Professor Horace. "Would you like to go down there right now? I'm sure Paul's up now, watching reruns of The Man from U.N.C.L.E. or something."

"That won't be necessary, not right now."

"I can call him."

"No," said Chauncey. "He's dealing with enough problems at the moment. I want to wait another day or two, let him calm down a bit."

"Very thoughtful of you," said Professor Horace.

"I'll take that as a compliment. But I got to ask, where do his parents fit in to all this?"

Professor Horace remained silent for a moment, but the guy was pretty straight-forward as far as he could tell.

"Nowhere," he said. "They're long gone."

"What do you mean by that?" asked Chauncey.

"You didn't look into his background at all, did you?"

"No."

Chauncey stayed silent. He had a feeling it was a long story. Far more complicated than Professor Horace's connection to Paul due to an interracial marriage. In his mind, and in this day and age, there was no reason to give something like that much thought. But for some reason people still took notice and the majority of these folks were not detectives.

"They've been dead and gone for quite some time now," said Professor Horace. "Up in Seattle where they raised Paul."

"What happened?" asked Chauncey.

"Murdered, brutally I should add by Paul's older brother Steven. You want the gory details I suggest you look it up yourself, Detective Chauncey."

"This is obviously a sore subject and I don't blame you one bit, Professor Horace."

"That's the icing on the cake with that story. I can tell you what lead up to it. Steven Raymond is doing life in prison because of what he did along with a lot of other things, especially for what he did to Paul."

"No offense," said Chauncey. "But when I talked to the kid he seemed a little off, and not because of what just happened to that Roy Cumberland friend of his."

"You're right," said Professor Horace. "My poor nephew may have been a candidate for major depression or mental illness. Those traits are definitely in the father's side of the family. Steven Raymond I will only describe as a sociopath. I can't picture that guy having a conscience before or after killing Paul's mother and father. He physically and psychologically abused poor Paul during childhood, and molested him as well."

At this point Chauncey did not want to hear the long story, he wanted the Professor to stay in a brighter mood, which had been the case throughout the entire interview, so to speak.

"We don't have to discuss the matter any further," said Chauncey. "That Roy Cumberland guy, did you know him well?"

"Just acquainted," said Professor Horace. "He was a

student in one of my classes last year. He wasn't a science major, just took the course either as a prerequisite or just to add credits. Most likely the latter, I think he was a graduate student. Paul talked about him a little bit, but nothing stands out. The best person to talk to works with me a lot here in the lab, and occasionally substitute teaches as well."

"Is her name Jane Newton?"

"Yeah, that's the one. It may take a little while to reach her, I don't expect her back here until sometime next week. You can call Widen Labs and ask for her extension, I'm sure she'll get back to you. But she's taking some vacation days."

"Paul said something about her being here last night, meeting with Mr. Cumberland."

"That's very possible you'd have to ask her about it."

"Don't you see it as a strange, or even morbid, coincidence that she's taking time off just after meeting with Mr. Cumberland?"

"Not at all," said Professor Horace, very confidently. "It's been confirmed for weeks, at least to me."

"Okay," said Chauncey. "That makes sense."

The Detective had to keep in mind that he hadn't seen or said a single word to this Jane Newton. So he knew better than to jump to any conclusions about her character, much less her involvement. There's a good chance she's out of the area if she's on vacation, and he also had no idea if she's the type of person who keeps up with local news or current events on a daily basis. The scientist types, you could never tell. Professor Horace seems like the kind of guy who has enough sense to stop and smell the roses once in a while, but quite often that's the exception instead of the rule. He decided to approach this situation as if she wouldn't find out what happened for at least another day or two.

"Tell you what," said Chauncey. "Just have her call me

when she comes in."

"Are you sure?" asked Professor Horace. "I'm not expecting her back until next week."

"We still don't know anything yet," said Chauncey, "There's no reason to chase her down right away. This is just the beginning of the investigation."

"She might call in a day or two, should I tell her anything?"

"I'm sure she'd rather hear from you what happened to this Roy Cumberland guy. The local police in his hometown had to send out an officer to inform his parents of his death. That's never easy. I know she's not a relative, but it's better for her to find out from someone she knows."

Chauncey knew suggesting this approach was unprofessional, but he also had to keep in mind that he knew almost nothing about this case so far. Professor Horace had been easy to interview, even after being very blunt about Paul's upbringing. That was definitely something he didn't want to learn more about unless he absolutely had to, and he sure as hell didn't want to drudge up early childhood trauma the next time he talked to the poor kid, which was probably going to happen in the very near future.

Before saying anything else he decided to take a quick glance around the laboratory for a second time. Despite there being some fascinating wildlife contained everywhere the place had a strange vibe about it. The white walls and large windows made him think of two things: psychiatric units and glass houses used for growing plants. The latter made a lot more sense, but if this place had been empty a mental patient could easily blend in wearing a white gown or straightjacket. The Detective wouldn't forget this sight anytime soon. A mental note was unnecessary, no pun intended. Nor did he intend to say anything to Professor Horace about it. The situation so far had been very good, so insults were out of the questions. He also kept in mind this guy seemed really good-natured and might see the humor in it, but he didn't want to test that theory.

Leave well-enough alone, he thought to himself.

Unfortunately the moment Chauncey came to this conclusion he realized that Professor Horace had disappeared from sight. This definitely spooked him a bit. He had been lost in a train of thought just for a moment and everything changed. He took a quick glance around the room, thinking the interviewee might have had to tend to one of the reptiles on short notice which prompted the vanishing act.

The answer was no.

This scenario would have justified an instant Amber Alert if Professor Horace was a small child. Chauncey definitely knew this wasn't the case, but it spooked him a bit. The most logical thing to do was call out the Professor's name, but his gut instinct told him otherwise. The quick glance around the room let his eyes catch an entrance with no doors on the right rear side. Chauncey had actually viewed it from his left side but also considered the angle he walked in from. When he first walked into the laboratory it was located on the right, and he turned back to face the other entrance he came in from.

Law enforcement's explanation from a technical standpoint instead of plain English, Chauncey thought someone like Professor Horace might be impressed by this. Then again, he had no way of knowing since the disappearance prevented him from asking. What should he do now? Well, there's no reason not to take a guided tour of the downstairs section of the laboratory if this guy's just going to leave me here by myself.

Without hesitation, Detective Chauncey slowly headed to the entrance with the staircase leading to the downstairs part of the laboratory. The Professor hadn't said anything about it during the interview, but didn't need to. In this case, Chauncey also did his homework. Perhaps it would've been smart to wait another couple of minutes, but for all he knew maybe the Professor had something that demanded his immediate attention down there.

He was about to find out.

After taking the first few steps a strange sensation flowed throughout his entire body. The only thought that came to mind was darkness, but couldn't determine in what way. He didn't feel any fear but at the same time he wasn't thinking about any scenario meaning literally a "lights out" approach. However, he noticed the lights in the stairwell were very dim, feeling unusual considering the look of the upstairs laboratory with the white walls all around it. Perhaps that contributed to the state of mind he was beginning to develop. Logic would make anyone think if it had to do with the darkness light a match. But if that was the case Chauncey wouldn't have liked it. Even though he knew in this type of laboratory it was unlikely there were chemicals of any sort that were flammable when exposed to the air, then he recalled he wasn't carrying any matches. He did have a lighter on him, but the last time he tried to use it there was no spark. No fluid, no flame, no lighter. Almost no point to claiming you have one if that's the case.

Chauncey began to take notice of these racing thoughts going through his head. Not unusual for him, but too much while walking down a flight of stairs. Was he supposed to feel this way? He asked himself that because he considered how everything had been set up so far. With the white walls, large windows, and dimly lit stairwell he had no idea what to expect next. Scientists could be preoccupied and passionate simultaneously, making him think Professor Horace wanted to create a certain energy or vibe for everyone to pick up on while visiting.

You never know, he thought to himself.

At the same time the Detective inside told him not to fill his head with these crazy ideas. Thinking was definitely a requirement for this kind of work, along with common sense. Philosophy 101 did not play a big role here. Maybe for coping with the situation or trying to stay positive but that's it. However, the positive aspects of philosophy always played a role in his life somehow. Be it Zen stuff or Mr. Miyagi's content vibe in The Karate Kid.

Chauncey arrived at the bottom of the stairs and took a few steps forward. Whatever he initially saw or heard off the bat didn't process right away. That happened sometimes. Once in a while he would just space out or go blank the first time he heard or observed something important. Not just when it came to the job, either. This also occurred when he read simple directions how to operate a new household appliance he bought. This Detective was one of the few guys that would actually tell you that real men do need directions. Of course he never shared this information with anyone, including Triple B. He wouldn't want anybody to question his abilities as a Detective. He also knew not to be so tough on himself. You can't expect everything to work out right away.

Even Albert Einstein flunked math the first time around.

Chauncey started to think about similarities that Einstein and Professor Horace might have, intelligence-wise at the very least. In academia both of them would soar through the stratosphere. Their IQs alone would impress anyone. Chauncey concluded Professor Horace was completely aware of the world around him, seriously doubting the same could be said for Einstein. What gave this away was calling the Detective by his full name. Chauncey never heard anyone do that throughout his entire career.

"There you are," said Professor Horace standing behind the Detective.

"Yeah," said Chauncey, slightly startled. "I didn't know where you went. I only came down here to find you."

Detective Chauncey was too good in his line of work for anyone to sneak up on him like that, or so he thought. He just hoped this guy didn't get the sense that he spooked him.

"That's alright," said Professor Horace. "Did I startle you?"

"No," he responded.

Bad liar, he thought. This time anyway. The Professor didn't display any signs of suspicion or hostility, quite reassuring while staring at each other straight in the eye.

"If you want," said Professor Horace. "I have to set things up for a special project I'm working on. You can help out. It's pretty easy. Then I'll give you a very exclusive tour where you will see anything and everything beyond what your imagination can hold. Stuff you never thought existed. I can guarantee you will not find anywhere near the information online compared to what's here."

"That's okay," said Chauncey, making up his mind quickly. He was definitely interested, but knew the frame of mind he was in wouldn't allow him to process everything the way he wanted to.

"You sure?" asked the Professor. "You're already down here, not many people get to see this part of the lab. That includes most of the student body and faculty."

"Another time," said Chauncey.

"Alright," said the Professor.

Both of them quickly headed back upstairs with the Professor more or less escorting the Detective all the way outside. Some light conversation continued until they arrived at Chauncey's car. At the last second the Professor remembered to give him Jane Newton's extension was at Widen Laboratories. He should've written it down considering the state of mind he was in. No big deal. Most companies you just had to call the main number and give the name of whoever you wanted to talk to. A pretty easy tack created long before the internet and cell phones were invented. Who's to say we were completely in the dark ages before that? Not entirely!

Chauncey wasn't worried. This guy was not a suspect. But he hadn't interviewed everyone necessary, be it the extended circle of friends and colleagues the Professor would have, definitely a long list.

Best place to start: Jane Newton.

Not now, he needed to recharge the batteries.

CHAPTER 4

WHEN CHAUNCEY ARRIVED HOME he immediately pulled into the first parking space available, a standard procedure for anyone living in the building even though he didn't like thinking about it in those terms. He resided in a duplex, basically two townhouses that are stuck together. It was just him and the landlady Mrs. Watson, who had been widowed for some time now. Her husband served in the U.S. Army for twenty years as an MP. She respected Chauncey for his background as a Detective, influencing her decision to take him in as a tenant eight years ago.

Granted, Chauncey and her late husband's personalities had very few similarities, but since both of them worked in some type of law enforcement she thought she could trust him. Of course she knew with cops there was always a chance of being dirty or corrupt in some way, but she felt safer renting to this Detective more than anyone else.

Mrs. Watson's car was in her usual spot. It wasn't a parking space specifically for her. But being the owner of the property she could claim it if she chose to, even Chauncey had no problem with that. There was no need to, however, since the only two cars you'd see on a daily basis belonged to them.

As he passed the first unit, specifically Mrs. Watson's place, everything was okay as far as he could tell. She was quiet and kept to herself most of the time. Strangely enough you'd think with her being the landlady she'd be keeping tabs on him, definitely not the case. Chauncey wouldn't even define it as a case considering the line of work he's in, and if he told her that she would probably agree with him.

Since there was no need to check up on the landlady it was time to see the other lady in his life. Not the girlfriend, but Lady meaning his dog. One living creature on the planet he could always look forward to spending time with. Just knowing he had someone in his life who always looked forward to seeing him. She would be super-happy and excited the moment she saw him walk through the front door. Of course after a few minutes she would be content and want to snuggle with him if he decided to lay down, which he was pretty sure he would do. Mrs. Watson was getting ready to take her for a walk when he left to go to Prime State University to interview Professor Horace, so there wouldn't be a dire need to take her out again right away.

Lady's breed of dog was one he didn't know anything about when he took her in. A Finnish Spitz to be precise and interesting sounding enough to add a little humor to it. Coming from Finland meant a nearby neighbor would be Norway, making him think of Valhalla and all that stuff. Spitz is a Jewish last name, as far as he knew anyway. He liked saying her full name was Lady Jane Spitz a.k.a. Thundermutt! The Jewish Viking!!!

Mel Brooks would have been proud.

Chauncey often wondered if creating this persona for

the dog came from a musician he'd heard of from the New York area. Specifically a bass player named Dave "The Beast" Spitz, who appeared on the album Black Sabbath featuring Tony Iommi: The Seventh Star back in 1986. This particular album always remained in his head because he always referred it as the first solo effort by Black Sabbath's guitarist Tony Iommi which explains why his name is billed directly under the group's name on the front cover.

What also stuck in Chauncey's head even more was the video made for the single from that album called "No Stranger to Love." The most amazing thing was remembering seeing the premiere on MTV, back when they actually played videos! Years later he found out the actress portraying Tony's "Love" interest was the one and only Denise Crosby, best known for her roll as Tasha Yar on Star Trek; Generation. She also starred in Pet Semetary, from a Stephen King novel using the same name and incorrect spelling.

Another movie she starred in he remained very fond of was the rarely seen cult classic Eliminators, released around the same time as the Black Sabbath video. Lightning struck twice for the young actress in 1986 even if she was just a familiar face and not a recognized name until the end of the decade. If the Detective had gotten into showbiz and only had stuff like that attached to his name he'd be happy, even if he never got any real recognition. Then again, he'd never attempted to get into showbiz so he really didn't know.

What also stayed stuck in his mind about the so-called Black Sabbath album and video was the other musicians. Singer Glenn Hughes did a phenomenal job on the recording, which was usually the case despite supposedly having bad drug problems at the time. Chauncey loved the Deep Purple album Burn which featured both Hughes's vocals alongside David Coverdale. Think whatever you want about what Coverdale did later on with Whitesnake, but when he first appeared on the rock scene he was amazing.

Of course one musician on the Sabbath/Iommi/Seventh Star album impossible to forget was Eric Singer, the amazing drummer who also appeared on Black Sabbath's next recording The Eternal Idol. After that he was able to land a phenomenal gig touring with the late great Gary Moore. All thanks to Bob Daisley, who worked with him in Sabbath, which lead to a countless number of gigs for many years afterwards with groups like Badlands, Alice Cooper, and eventually KISS. The latter two Chauncey got to see with Eric behind the kit, he did not disappoint the audience. Not as far as this Detective was concerned.

You might ask what prompted Chauncey to think about stuff like this. These trivial facts may not be important to world issues or have very little use in the majority of the Detective's cases, but remembering this stuff helped get his concentration back. This was very helpful when suffering from a lack of sleep, and wouldn't get it any time soon. Right now that wasn't the case. But he was very frustrated because he felt so well-rested when he went to interview Professor Horace just a short while ago. Could something in the lab trigger how he felt? That was far-fetched, and there were no distinctive smells he picked up on while he was there.

Chauncey headed up the front steps to his place and unlocked the front door. As soon as he opened it and stepped into the kitchen he looked straight ahead into the living area, where his little Lady was lying on the mattress in front of the TV. Quite often he took the mattress from the single bed from the upstairs spare room and brought it down there. The main reason is because he had cable hooked up to that particular television set and had way more choices of channels to choose from. The other reason was so Lady could lie down and snuggle with him, feeling like a kid again thinking of sleepovers with friends while growing up.

Little Lady wasted no time getting up and trotting over to see him. Her tail wagged fast and in a slightly circular motion, kind of like a propeller. She usually didn't bark when he got home, instead she'd breathe heavily and look up to stare him straight in the eye, with a look on her face than can only be described as a huge smile.

At least he liked to think so.

Chauncey wasted no time getting his shoes and jacket off, in a matter of minutes all he had on was a short-sleeve shirt and some sweat pants. His regular outfit if he thought he'd be home for more than a couple of hours, or if he was in for the night. Right now he didn't know what the case might be, nor did he care. All he wanted to do was lie down on that mattress with his most faithful friend and companion from the animal kingdom.

As soon as he placed himself on the mattress he looked to the left and found the remote to turn on the television. He felt instant gratification because he found it where he remembered leaving it. Of course the only other place where he would usually find it was on the small table next to the recliner. Not that it would have been the end of the world if he had to get up again to get it.

Strangely enough when he turned the television on the movie being shown was Eliminators. He could record it if he really wanted to, but it would be nice if it came out on DVD. However, you could watch it in its entirety on YouTube which he'd done at least once or twice. This actually gave him the initiative to turn it off which was fine considering it was near the end, specifically at the part where Crosby's costar Andrew Prine who portrayed the adventurer/explorer Fontana started getting riled up and going off about being surrounded by cavemen, kung fu, and robots with the bottom line being he had no idea what was going on. Sometimes in these types of low-budget films you're not supposed to understand what's happening, be it the characters or the audience, at least as far as Chauncey was concerned.

In Eliminators the character name Fontana was taken from a screenwriter and novelist involved in the Star Trek franchise D.C. Fontana. Chauncey read at least one or two of her Star Trek novel spin-offs over the years, but for the life of him couldn't remember which ones they were. Not that he would have made any effort to do so. He liked Star Trek only to a certain extent. Star Wars was a bit more up his alley. Now he started thinking about episodes of a very short-lived TV series from the late 1980s he viewed online called The Highwayman. Tim Russ had a supporting role as D.C. Montana, obviously derivative. He also saw this particular actor in a small role in the Charles Bronson vigilante picture Death Wish 4: The Crackdown and if he remembered correctly eventually found big success as a regular on Star Trek: Voyager.

How does he remember all this? Or for that matter why? The Detective himself couldn't fully explain it. But hoped in the long run it was more helpful than hurtful, at least in terms of his career. He barely paid attention to Voyager, and the only thing that stood out in his mind was Kate Mulgrew starring as the first ever female captain in the history of the series, other than that catching a late rerun of an episode with Sarah Silverman. Perhaps someday he'll track down a serial killer who will leave clues only Trekkies would know, or showbiz trivia for that matter. Chauncey wouldn't view himself as an expert with this stuff, but knew enough that he could solve the case a lot quicker.

Andrew Prine's name came to mind again, who also played a Deputy in another one of his favorite cult movies from the mid 1970s The Town That Dreaded Sundown. For some reason he kept forgetting the actor had significant roles in both pictures, and most people would agree this particular film displayed a higher quality to it even if it's only to a certain extent. What really stood out was the performance by Dawn Wells, despite just a brief appearance. She definitely proved she could do a lot more than play Mary Ann Summers on Gilligan's Island, typecasting had to be frustrating back then. A hot TV series guaranteed you would be a star in the public's eye back then, but good luck didn't come very often when cancellation time came.

Now the musician's name John Prine came to mind, causing the song "Way Down" to run through his head. Not a bad tune, but he definitely didn't want to listen to it online. Not right now, time to open up the laptop, which was on the floor by the left side of the mattress where television and DVD remotes were also located. As he did this, little Lady slowly crept back onto the mattress and laid down, snuggling up against the right side of his body. It didn't take long to get on Google all he had to do now was type in what he wanted to look for.

"Widen Laboratories," Chauncey said to himself. "Let's see what we can find."

All he needed was their main number and extension for Jane Newton's voicemail. This information should be easy to find, that was the reason why the internet was invented. As far as Chauncey was concerned and... Bingo! An instant search displayed Widen Laboratories main website at the top of the screen, specifically the California division. When he clicked the mouse to get on the main page he clicked the Contact icon. The main number for their nearest facility popped up immediately, which would obviously be the one located in town. He soon found where he needed to log on for employee extensions, but surprisingly found that none of them could be displayed onscreen. Instead he would have to listen to an automated voice provide every single three digit extension number available.

This was going to take a while.

Chauncey took his sweet time searching for his cell phone. He didn't have to look very far (or get up off the mattress) because he surprisingly remembered to put it in the right pocket of his sweatpants before lying down. Thankfully the dog was resting next to the upper part of his right chest. Otherwise he'd be hearing beeps when pushed up against it, possibly pushing the call button and accidentally reaching out to someone he didn't need to speak to right away, be it Triple B or the girlfriend or whatever.

The Detective found his cell phone and went to the Add Contacts section right away. He immediately put in the main number for Widen Laboratories listed on the main page, which was easy enough. He briefly considered calling and asking for this Jane Newton's voicemail. Whoever answered would more than likely transfer him directly to it, but wasn't sure if he could get her actual extension. He also had to keep in mind with this particular case he didn't have much to work with yet. Just this Roy Cumberland guy who pulled a fire alarm before dying, with a very distraught friend whose Uncle is a well-respected scientist connected to both Prime State University and Widen Laboratories. He hadn't met this Jane Newton yet, and had no idea what to think of her.

"One step at a time," he said to himself.

Chauncey doubled checked the volume on the laptop to make sure it was all the way up. He'd been on YouTube for a little while the last time he went online, which you usually wanted to have the sound on for regardless of what you might be watching. Other than that there really wasn't any other reason to, not in his case. A quick click on the volume control indicated a definite yes. Now he'd just sit back and listen to a long list of names and numbers one by one. This would be the most redundant thing he had to do in who knows how long, the worst part being connected to the job. Something he actually cared about.

A somewhat dry, female-sounding voice stated to Chauncey, or whoever was listening:

"Welcome to the list of Employee Extensions from A to Z."

Thankfully, this wasn't as dull sounding as a lot of other automated voices out there. Not compared to the other ones heard when dialing information, utility, cable, or credit card companies. Then again, Chauncey vaguely recalled the last time he called the credit card place. That sounded alright.

As long as they get their money, he thought to himself.

This time around the automated voice sounded like someone who was in a half-decent mood giving driving directions, even more pleasant compared to most of the GPS devices he'd heard, tolerable at least.

Now boys and girls it's time to start the alphabet:

"Abbott, Anderson, Barry, Blake, Butler...."

The Detective immediately noticed he only heard the names and not the numbers. He looked at the screen and quickly realized the extensions were simultaneously listed next to the names but not stated. The worst part, however, was how slow the process was taking. It would probably take a few minutes before arriving at the letter N. He also knew it wasn't a low signal or slow internet. This was how Widen Laboratories wanted it.

"Not exactly a roadblock," he said, quickly glancing over at the dog. He liked acting like she was part of the conversation. "But a lot like slow traffic. Still I'd rather be stuck with this than behind the wheel and going nowhere."

When he said that, however, his patience had worn thin. He turned the TV back on to see how much closer it had gotten to the end of Eliminators. Not that he would pay close attention to it, just kill some time. He lowered the volume way down on the TV so he could hear the Widen Laboratories employee names stated until it reached the letter N.

"Edwards, Evans, Freeman, Gillen...."

"More than halfway to the halfway point," Chauncey said in a humorous tone, looking over at his little Lady. What he meant by that was G was the seventh letter of the twenty-six in the alphabet, so M was thirteenth and smack in the middle of it so N would be next in line.

"Keep the eyes on the movie and the ears on the laptop," he said. This was his idea of multi-tasking. More names he heard over the internet indicating he was reaching his destination point.

"Lane, Lawton, Leonard, Mahoney......."

At the halfway point, he thought to himself, finding it funny Mahoney was the first name listed under M. How could he forget all those Police Academy movies with Steve Guttenberg playing that role with Michael Winslow as Officer Jones who could do all of those funny sound-effects? He needed to pick up those on DVD sooner instead of later. Now were at the home stretch!

"Mann, Martin, Murphy, Newton, Norton..."

Chauncey immediately looked back at the screen and caught the three digits over her extension right before it disappeared. He was pretty sure he could use the mouse to scroll up the page to double check but didn't think it would be necessary. The extension was 978.

He entered Jane Newton's initials and extension under Widen Laboratories cell phone number since there was a good chance that might be her personal number. Working for a large corporation like this meant she had to have access to her voicemail. How often she checked it or returned calls was another matter altogether. The Detective couldn't begin to speculate on that theory since he knew nothing about this person. Without thinking about it he pressed the call button, the instant the company's automatic answering service kicked in he accessed Jane Newton's number. It rang at least eight times before her voicemail turned on, with a typical response you expect from just about everybody on these things.

"Hi you've reached Jane Newton at extension 978. Just leave a message and I'll get back to you. You can also reach me at Prime State University......."

He didn't play close attention to exactly what had been said as soon as the college thing got mentioned. It wouldn't be difficult to track her down at Prime State if she was there, but he probably should have written down the exact day and date she said she'd be returning.

No big deal, he thought. He had all the information he needed for the time being and just waited for the beep, which was anything but short and sweet. Should he leave a message? It wouldn't hurt to wait on that, the beep got the last word in there. This prompted shutting the volume off on his phone and setting it so it could only vibrate while he was napping.

Chauncey didn't have a problem leaving the phone on all the time, even when charging it. Being a Detective meant it's in his best interest to do this. But he didn't like being disrupted by loud rings or beeps for that matter, especially while relaxing. He found it much easier to respond, allowing him to ease into an assignment and focus better instead of launching into a panic mode. His line of work is stressful enough already.

Now for the biggest decision of all: Should he catch the end of Eliminators again?

The quickest answer was no. He hadn't watched the

movie enough times to remember every detail, but knew enough where he didn't feel any desire to. The rest and relaxation mode had kicked in to the point where some shuteye was in demand, and Lady was snuggled up next to him indicating it was the best idea for both of them.

Then again, could he ever think of a time when his little Lady didn't want to chill with him? No way. She never so much as attempted to complicate the process of decision making, and why would she? Any time spent with him was the best time in her mind.

If only most people thought like that, of course the Detective knew that usually wasn't the case.

Pun intended.

Now he just had to exit out of Widen Laboratories phone directory, bringing him back to the main page. The same process was required to get off the company's website and back on Google again. One click on the tiny x in the upper right corner shut down the Google page instantly. The signal strength for the internet was really high at the moment, but he just wanted to turn everything off and close up shop for the afternoon.

The icons disappeared and the screen went completely blank, which takes a little longer than turning off the television. Maybe that's why he preferred watching regular TV and DVDs instead of sitting through some movie that's hard to find on YouTube. In all honesty he was pretty sure he enjoyed kicking back in his recliner or lying on the mattress with the dog viewing anything enjoyable on a big screen over sitting through something online, which made him feel like he was in an office environment.

The last place he wanted to be.

Here and now is what's important.

Right now he simply wanted to snooze.

The dog lying beside him encouraged that feeling even more so. Yet something sparked in his mind, despite being on the verge of dozing off.

Tim Russ.

Chauncey felt tempted to open the laptop again and learn everything about him, and there was probably a website due to such a devoted following from Star Trek alone. Not to mention the IMDb page that would list every role he ever played.

Should I? Chauncey thought to himself.

Fuck it.

CHAPTER 5

Chauncey slowly began to awaken from his siesta. Thanks to a particular alarm clock so to speak. His little Lady lifted her head and began barking while still lying next to him. When this happens it's usually because she heard a faint noise outside.

"Shut up," he said, but not sounding aggressive or hostile. He never took that tone with her. If anything it was acknowledging her reaction to whatever got her attention.

"Be quiet." Almost always the second response from him, He didn't want her to worry. Most likely it was nothing, probably just Mrs. Watson out front or the mailman doing a late delivery, which happened periodically.

However, Lady stood up with her tail wagging and continued barking. Okay there was more to this than he thought. He heard the front door open in the kitchen, prompting him to sit up and turn his head. He knew exactly who it was, the other "Lady" in his life if you will.

Ali.

Or Ali Wilkens, the Detective's longtime girlfriend and Lady's other best bud, foster mother, even babysitter whenever Chauncey was on a case bound to become an all-nighter. The three roles are in no particular order when it comes to importance. She barely got through the door and he knew right away what she'd been up to. The spandex pants, tank top shirt with an unbuttoned and light-colored jacket over it meant she'd been on the job as well. However, he didn't want that to be brought up first.

Little Lady was already standing up on the mattress yet quickly got off it and ran over to Ali. The barking had stopped but that didn't keep her from feeling as happy as always with her tail wagging and panting heavily which made it look like she had a big smile on her face. Next she stood up on her hind legs and put her front paws up near Ali's waist.

"Hello my precious!" said Ali, petting the dog's head. "Did I wake you? I hope both you and Papa Chauncey got a lot of rest in before I got here. I can't wait to chat with you two!"

"Hi there," said Chauncey, not with a lot of enthusiasm but still sounding very pleasant. He'd just woken up so it would take a few minutes to focus. He never displayed a bad mood or got vicious after waking up, so in his mind it seemed perfectly alright.

"I heard about what happened at Prime State," she said. "I'm surprised you didn't call me."

"About what?" he asked.

"Looking after Lady of course!" she said with a big smile growing on her face.

"Oh right. I thought I'd be pulling an all-nighter too. Luckily it's the winter break so no students are around, which would have created a major shit show if it happened during the semester."

"Wasn't that Roy guy a student himself?"

"Yeah," he said.

"Did you find out why he was there?"

"Kind of," he answered. "I still have a few people I need to talk to more in-depth, one I haven't even met yet."

"So it's more or less just baby steps at this point?"

"Pretty much," he said, albeit casually.

"Slow and steady wins the race."

"Very true," he stated. "Especially when you need extra sleep and have to look after the little baby!"

Of course he was referring to the dog, something he couldn't live without. Being single he could manage, but the longest period of time he went without a dog was about a year and a half at the most. In hindsight he couldn't believe how depressed he'd gotten during that time. Ali knew that long before they even started dating. Maybe she'd forgotten, or she embraced that quality.

Judging by the sight before him, he was pretty sure it was the latter.

"How'd class go today?" he asked.

"Which one?" she responded. "I had four."

"Made it a busy day I take it."

"You got that right."

The same old question racked his brain, but he always felt the need to ask again and again.

"Do you sleep alright when I'm gone and it's just you and the dog?"

"You know the answer to that!" she responded. "Why do you always have to be reassured that's the case?"

"I don't know," he said. "I guess I feel bad when it happens and you have a full day planned the next morning and I don't know about it."

"Like I said," she stated in a very straight-forward tone, but not too serious. "You can rest assured that's the one case that is already solved. There's no mystery involved!"

"Sounding like a poet who doesn't know it!" he answered.

"You got me there!"

The Detective was glad he had someone in his life outside of work who could paint the big picture for him, which often made it easier to iron out the small details.

Whatever, he thought to himself, great to have her here regardless.

Chauncey fully stood up and stretched his back before getting off the mattress then walked over to Ali and Lady. Both of them were still in the kitchen, each focusing on the other. In Ali's case he would say about ninety percent and Lady was definitely over the one-hundred mark, but that would change when he was face to face with his significant other and the dog sitting upright between the two lovebirds, yet she could hardly be considered an obstacle or hindrance of any kind.

Chauncey didn't feel fatigued which meant he wouldn't have to take another shower, definitely some more coffee but not right away. Ali might need to relax a bit but probably wouldn't need any sleep. She may not have a rigid personality but she usually stayed on a normal schedule, somewhere in the 9 to 5 realm. Not exactly during those hours but that's the basic idea, the exception might be occasionally substituting an evening aerobics class in the middle of the week, which only happened about once a month.

The two exchanged a light kiss, it would have been better to embrace each other instead. Neither of them had a problem doing that, but they always remembered when the dog was stuck in the middle and didn't want to crush her, the unconscious cautiousness between father, mother, and child. From their point of view anyway, perhaps some advocates from Planned Parenthood could learn something from them. But neither of them ever had children. None were being "Planned" for, not as far as Chauncey knew. Ali never so much as discussed it with him As far as he was concerned he reached an age where it wasn't in his best interest. He didn't see himself as being too old, but felt that he'd gotten too used to living and working on his own time that he should not consider taking on that kind of responsibility. Dogs were the closest thing he wanted to having children of any kind.

Chauncey turned his attention to putting regular clothes back on. He and Ali weren't planning to go out later but he felt more alert and he didn't want to brew another batch of coffee just yet, funny how thinking about caffeine and Keurigs felt like a mission in and of itself. But right now the main objective was exchanging wardrobes, which was immediately within reach, specifically being on the kitchen table. The jacket was placed neatly on one of the chairs, but his pants and shirt were on the table. He hadn't thought about where he left all this stuff. He didn't recall very much about his usual routine, practically a ritual at this point. Amazing he'd remember to put the cell phone in the pocket of his sweatpants.

For a split second Chauncey felt like he was taking a more methodical approach. He removed the cell phone from his pocket and placed it on the table. Logic dictated that should be done first. He slightly turned away from Ali even though light conversation was still occurring between the two of them. He didn't necessarily feel shy or bashful, but most of the time she'd only see his private parts under certain circumstances. Naturally while getting it on, or during very rare occasions when they showered together, the last time being about four months ago give or take a week. Granted, he didn't feel the need to make a mental note every time it happened, or mark it on the calendar, so to speak. Their sex life was frequent enough that it left no room for complaining, not on his end.

Perhaps there was a bit of a macho thing on his part. He was used to her only seeing him aroused with his clothes off, with those places almost exclusively being in the bedroom and once in a blue moon the shower. He never gave it very much thought but he knew how small it got when not in the heat of the moment but that's how it's supposed to be! Everybody knows that! It means everything's functioning normally. The Detective started to wonder if the main reason most guys were getting prescriptions for Viagra was because of insecurity and paranoia instead of having an actual problem with intimacy. Nowadays the mentality seemed to be that of having a hard-on 24/7. That would probably get uncomfortable after a day or two, especially while changing your clothes or trying to fall asleep. However, even Chauncey had to admit it was okay to wake up with one every now and then, the best times being when Ali spent the night and she took notice.

Very little imagination is required to figure out what happens next.

Of course Chauncey had to focus on the current situation, and after undressing and redressing he could put all his attention back on Ali and Little Lady.

"Did you see her?" asked Chauncey, glancing at her before briefly looking down at the dog.

"Who?" asked Ali.

"Mrs. Watson," answered Chauncey. "I thought you might have talked to her for a minute or two before coming in."

"Nope, didn't catch a glimpse of her on the way in. Come to think of it not a single sound when I walked by. Usually you hear her TV about now but there was none of that, didn't see any lights on either."

"She might have gone out, was her car there?"

"I think so, I'm not sure."

"She probably dozed off on the couch again. A light will go on the second she wakes up."

"I'm surprised she never got that thing where all you have to do is clap your hands," Ali said in a slightly humorous tone.

"You've got to give her more credit," said Chauncey. "She's not that old."

She wasn't completely serious when she said that, but he was just starting to refocus and put things into perspective. He also had to keep in mind that both of them socialized with Mrs. Watson enough over the years they considered this nice woman to be both a friend and a good landlord.

Chauncey always paid the rent on time. Barely a week passed since the new month and the New Year had started, making it easy to recall paying on January 1st. Granted, Mrs. Watson could not cash the check until the following day but he liked to stay on top of those things. The Detective's motive here was common courtesy, nothing more, nothing less. She very rarely rushed out to the bank after receiving the payment, but she was the first and only landlord he ever had that decreased his rent. He never knew anybody with a landlord as generous as Mrs. Watson. In every case he'd heard of when the rent changes it means it's going up!

Chauncey realized he didn't know what the current balance was on his checking account. Come to think of it he hadn't looked at it since the New Year began. He didn't have the first clue if his rent check had been cashed or not. Then again, all he needed to do was ask Mrs. Watson if she had taken care of it, most likely the answer would be yes. He started to imagine how great it would be if he could have an ATM machine inside his place. It could not get any more convenient than that. The only problem is how quickly cash runs out. There's no point in having money extending beyond whatever his balance is, maybe Ali's too, but that's about it. Other than that it would only be helpful if Mrs. Watson wants him to start paying the rent in cash. Perhaps he could place it outside the front door at the bottom of the steps, and have an automatic fee for everybody who uses it that would go directly to him. Anyone who has to stop at a private residence at all hours of the day and night to make deposits or withdrawals has to be really desperate, who cares if you have to pay an extra $2.00 to get what you need?

Wishful thinking and Chauncey knew that, even if it happened he'd be no better than all the other cutthroat businessmen practicing the not so fine art of fascism. Perhaps he'd become a bit neurotic contemplating these ideas. Is it wrong to put an idea to the test with the sole purpose of making a profit? Of course not, yet he also realized he'd always been used to receiving a paycheck every week. Stuff like taxes, health insurance, and retirement benefits were taken care of and he didn't have to think about it, or concern himself with paying someone else. It wasn't his job, possibly that was the issue for him. He didn't like to think of his profession as a Detective as just a job. To a certain extent Chauncey could always consider himself a free agent or contractor, but he was exclusively signed on to the local Police Department who were responsible for paying him. He called the shots, but on paper technically Triple B was the Boss a.k.a. Boss Bobby Burrell.

Chauncey got so wrapped up in his thoughts he started to feel like he blacked out. Not in the sense that it felt like everything had literally gotten dark, but after changing back into his regular outfit he realized he'd become oblivious to whatever Ali was saying. Not that he purposely tuned out the conversation but for a split second he couldn't even hear what she said, much less anything else for that matter.

The Detective could only describe his current state of mind as turning the volume of your television or radio all the way down, then slowly turning it up again to decibel one, which is only a faint sound to most ears. Chances are you wouldn't be able to decipher a single word. Chauncey owned a handful of DVDs where the sound could be all the way up and he still couldn't hear the dialogue. He couldn't figure out if a connection between the television and DVD player might be the cause or something to do with the specific disc. Probably the latter, whatever it was caused a lot of frustration. Yet he still got some enjoyment out of it, especially when he would lie on the mattress with little Lady and the fan was on at maximum speed. Logic dictated fans make it more difficult to hear things, he knew that. Remember it was only specific DVDs, and normally he only wanted subtitles when he viewed foreign films in the theaters. But the situation made him appreciate the dialogue and script more in regards to whatever he might be watching.

A few more seconds passed and Chauncey's hearing returned to a normal level, whatever that might be. An estimate somewhere between decibel one and full blast, not quite even keel. But for the Detective the minimum level is seven, maybe eight. Definitely not eleven leave that to Spinal Tap! He was glad Ali hadn't picked up on it otherwise she would have waved her hand in front of his eyes. That only happened once a few years ago, if it happened frequently she would have called him out on it a long time ago. With aerobics being a top priority in her life she wouldn't let it slide.

"Time to make the coffee," he said.

"Are you sure?" she asked.

"I think so," he answered.

When he first said that he was talking to himself, but went along with what she asked him. He needed to be more alert, even if he planned to stay in for the night. However, with everything he'd dealt with these past twenty-four hours, actually less, he should be ready for anything. A gut feeling surfaced. Something he couldn't explain to anyone, especially at the moment it occurred. This was probably a phenomenon common with people in his line of work. If you're investigating a crime where a wrongful death takes place it might help, but Chauncey wasn't sure why the sensation began to grab hold of him. Perhaps some leads would present themselves early on with this case, who knows? The Detective wouldn't bet on it but right now it seemed like a good idea to keep his mouth shut and his eyes and ears open, the exception being interacting with Ali and Lady.

"Want me to make it?" asked Ali.

"No, I'll get it," answered Chauncey. "You and little Lady are long overdue for some quality time together."

"Very true," she said. "We can never have enough of that, can we?"

"Damn straight, at least as far as she's concerned."

Ali and Lady made their way into the other room where the mattress was, thinking the dog would lay on it again. But when Ali sat down on the recliner little Lady just stood at her feet. It looked like the dog was really looking forward to having company and conversation. This suited Chauncey just fine. He quickly started brewing up a new batch of coffee. Mainly for himself but he would always make sure he had some extra in case Ali wanted some. She usually drank it first thing and the morning, but what he called the common courtesy factor kicked in.

The cell phone rang. Chauncey looked over to find out it was exactly who he thought it would be.

None other than Triple B, most likely with more information about last night's homicide.

He was about to find out.

"What's up Triple B?" asked Chauncey, albeit casually.

"I'm down by the swamp," answered Triple B.

"What the hell are you down there for?"

"We found another body. Name is Stacy O'Connell, used to work for Widen Labs."

"Used to, huh? Sounds like there could be a connection to the Roy Cumberland guy we found last night."

"It's possible. Coroner says she's been dead at least eighteen hours."

"There wasn't a big gap of time between the two, and both of them are connected to Widen Laboratories in some way."

"You got that right," confirmed Triple B. "Do what you need to do."

"I'm on it," said Chauncey. "I'll see you soon."

Ali came back into the kitchen. She knew already Chauncey had to go out again.

"Where do you need to go?" she asked.

"The swamp," he answered.

"Did they find another body?"

"Yup, most likely there's a connection."

"Take all the coffee you need. You know I hardly ever drink it at this time of night."

"Thanks. What time is it?"

"Seven of Nine," she answered, checking her watch.

"Okay."

Seven of Nine, he thought to himself. It was kind of amusing since it made him think of Star Trek: Voyager yet again. He didn't have the first clue why except that it was more useless information.

He had no idea who played the part, either. Perhaps this and the coffee about to enter his system will spark his mind which will get him focused on the case.

Who was he kidding? Of course it would!

"A new episode of The FBI Files will be on in a few minutes," said Ali. "Do you want me to record it?"

"Definitely," said Chauncey. "Don't wait up!"
"I know by now, believe me."

CHAPTER 6

THE DRIVE TO THE SWAMP wasn't much farther than traveling to Prime State University. At least twice the distance, but that wasn't a whole lot as far as Chauncey was concerned. Perhaps he'd been living in the area too long, but if you're in law enforcement in the city or town you reside in it's definitely a good idea to know every part of it, especially if you want quick results.

The swamp itself was known on record to be a part of Chase Conservation Land, which was connected to the neighboring town of Samson. A lot of people were unaware of it, but when you're a Detective it's your job to know, even if no one called it that. All you needed to do was mention the swamp and everyone knew what you meant. Regardless if Chauncey got a call from Triple B to get out there as soon as possible or it got mentioned online or over a police scanner, it only got called the swamp.

Another name did exist for the swamp, but not many people knew about it, only a handful of cops who'd worked in town for at least a decade would know what you're talking about.

It got called Badlands.

The Detective had been informed years ago it got that name because dangerous fugitives, including the ones you saw on John Walsh's show America's Most Wanted often ran and hid out there when being chased. In the dead of night the Badlands was the best place to go if you didn't want to be found, thick marshes along with forever growing vegetation, bushes, trees, and everything else you could imagine made it the perfect cover. It didn't matter if a Police Helicopter with the best surveillance equipped for nighttime searches got sent out there. The end result was a lost cause. The worst of it, however, was dealing with the paparazzi when these situations occurred. Law enforcement couldn't tell anyone searches for dangerous fugitives were ineffective under these circumstances.

The only thing Law Enforcement Officials could do was put up a front and the reporters and the public were told what they wanted to hear, which was usually that the best and most qualified folks were out there combing every inch of the swamp, with high confidence that the individual would be captured within hours. Then again, anyone with half a brain who read the papers each day or followed the news regularly online or on television could figure out the same thing happened over and over again. The fugitive on the run always got captured a few days, at the most a week, after the search of the swamp had supposedly started, but miles away from it. Even if John Walsh himself gave an in-depth explanation as to why there was no point in carrying out this task, which he did understand and knew little could be done, no one could get past the fact that a very dangerous criminal was out there. At one point he told a lot of the guys he knew it was tougher than searching for a needle in a haystack but recognized and appreciated the best effort being made.

The official name for the swamp Chase Conservation Land was very contradictory. If more people were aware of it, especially criminals, most likely they would never attempt to hide out there. The Detective thought it sounded like the perfect playground for a cat and mouse scenario, an invitation for cops and robbers to set up shop. Obviously it wasn't, so maybe it wasn't such a bad thing that most of the locals knew nothing about the Chase name. Chauncey thought Badlands was more appropriate. The only other times he heard Badlands before was Ozzy Osbourne's guitarist Jake E. Lee's short-lived band with that name which featured Eric Singer on drums, who spent the least amount of time in it, and supposedly not by choice. It didn't matter since his career was the opposite of every drummer's fate in Spinal Tap. Like the title of the first KISS record he played on, success was his best Revenge.

Chauncey also knew about a feature film called Badlands. It came out in the late seventies or early eighties. Martin Sheen was in it. Sissy Spacek might have had a role as well. This surprised him. He had no idea what it was about, and was positive he hadn't seen it. He most likely glimpsed at copies of it while spending countless hours browsing video stores during his youth and had no relevance to the case, which was okay because this got the thought process in high gear, something he needed to concentrate in order to work better.

Driving out to the swamp seemed to take less time compared to going to Prime State University, which was slightly ironic since Chauncey could walk to the school if he absolutely had to. Perhaps it was due to less traffic on the road, maybe because it was a only a short drive down Route 21 after driving on Main Street through the downtown district, not very far from where Prime State

University is located. So it didn't make sense that he practically passed by it to get where he needed to go.

Chauncey should've suspected he'd feel a little off. First with having to go to Prime State University last night investigating that crime scene there, with no way of figuring out right away what the deal was with this Roy Cumberland just dropping dead. Staying up way past the witching hour drinking too much coffee as usual and talking to that poor kid Paul Raymond didn't help much, but he did what he had to do. He probably should've seen to it personally that Paul got home safely, but he was positive Matheson stayed on top of that. He also had to consider the interview he had the very next day with Professor Horace. If something bad happened to Paul he would've found out about it by now.

Back to the train of thought required to remain on the rails of reason and rationality. Despite racing thoughts retracing the events of the past twenty-four hours it helped Chauncey to recognize the state of mind he possessed at that moment, it doesn't take a genius to realize a steady diet of coffee beginning last night at Prime State while investigating something that most likely was a murder. He also needed to consider the fact that he only got a small amount of restless sleep when he made it home. He did feel refreshed the next morning when he went back there to interview Professor Horace, but that wouldn't last long. All he really did after that was go back home and nap again for the remainder of the daylight hours, woken up by the dog's barking when the girlfriend arrived. He definitely went too long without digesting a full meal. The Detective wasn't a Doctor, but he didn't have to be to come to this conclusion. Maybe a trip to the Lucky Dog Diner was appropriate for later on tonight. They stayed open late, at least until midnight during the week.

It would be another minute or two before Chauncey

arrived at the swamp. Route 21 was a narrow road taking you out of downtown Prime toward Samson. He was a bit surprised to see another car pass him in the opposite direction. He appreciated the fact that their high beams went off before he turned at the next exit. At least there were still some considerate drivers out here in the dead of night, no pun intended. If only this was the case out in Los Angeles in the middle of the day! The Detective knew places like Prime and Samson were the boondocks compared to L.A. even if they were technically defined as cities.

Upon reaching the bottom of the exit ramp he took a right on Hobson Road, a quarter of a mile from there was the swamp. Even from a distance he could see flashing blue and red lights, especially since Hobson Road was similar to Route 21 in the sense that it was a straight ride down to the swamp. Perhaps if more bodies turn up there it could be rechristened as Badlands. A good suggestion, one Chauncey would keep to himself. There probably were more dead corpses out there, but no one ever volunteered to put together a search to see party to find out. You didn't have to watch America's Most Wanted to know that the live ones were much more valuable, cash rewards were always a good incentive. Volunteering sounded too charitable venturing out into the Badlands.

When Chauncey arrived on the scene he realized there wasn't a huge crowd of people there. Not yet anyway, not much more than the amount of people who showed up at Prime State University last night. Practically nobody the entire time while investigating, which makes things a lot smoother. People may not be correct in defining exactly who was at the swamp. Technically yes a bunch of human beings for sure. However, none if you mean regular civilians who didn't work in law enforcement or assist them in some, along with local citizens or townies.

Thank God there were no reporters here, but it wouldn't take long for them to start coming out of the woodwork. The Detective hoped to assess the situation and get out as quickly as possible. He realized the moment he pulled in that the police officers closed off the area, a good sign. Hopefully the body could be removed before a million news vans with bright lights and cameras made an entrance. A million is an exaggeration, but it doesn't feel that way. Especially around Prime, where there aren't a lot of murders yet plenty of hype having a swamp frequented by dangerous fugitives whose faces are displayed on America's Most Wanted on a weekly basis.

Along with various emergency vehicles like police cruisers or ambulances Chauncey saw everyone he expected to see whether it was regular uniformed officers, emergency medical technicians, even a fire engine. Yet a bit surprising that Fire Chief Fernandez was there, he honestly couldn't recall the last time he saw the guy. Months maybe close to a year ago. A nice guy, very approachable, but not known for being very talkative. Not somebody who tries to be the center of attention. It didn't seem necessary for anyone from the fire department to be here, but finding a dead body needs to be taken seriously by everyone, not just law enforcement even if it's not the result of a murder. So he knew best to simply appreciate the fact that Fernandez would take the time to check things out and not use credentials as an excuse to just sit behind a desk.

Of course Triple B was there, waiting for him naturally. He was just glad a name and occupation had surfaced for the newly discovered body. Pun intended in his mind but would keep that to himself. Her name was Stacy O'Connell, who until recently, had been employed by Widen Laboratories. She knew too much. What did that mean? He had no idea. Just that it wasn't a coincidence for two people connected to Widen Laboratories in less than twenty-four hours.

Probably the most important guys present at the scene were the ones connected to the Coroner's Office. Chauncey liked to call them Morgue Men, or better yet Forensic Folks, which he thought was the most appropriate terminology. Best said just in case a few lovely ladies were around, especially those present who worked in that particular field. Then again, if the Return of the Living Dead actually occurred wouldn't it sound more appealing to blame it on the Morgue Men? Food for thought, just not human flesh!

Right away Chauncey could see the main guy from the Morgue Men. Not in terms of authority, but who would be present at the majority of crime scenes, specifically ones with dead bodies, most frequently. This guy's credentials identified him as Mickey Dolan, M.D., but everybody called him Frosty. As far as Chauncey knew no one ever asked why. The surprise part, however, occurred the moment Frosty looked up and walked over to Detective Chauncey right away.

"She's been dead about eighteen hours," said Frosty.

"Anything else?" asked Chauncey.

"Due to strangulation," answered Frosty. "She also had the words Love Link written on her neck, looked like it was tattooed on there at first, but no."

"Just like the last guy."

"Roy Cumberland wasn't strangled."

"I meant the Love Link thing."

"Right," responded Frosty.

At least this Frosty guy caught on quick, Chauncey thought to himself, he really needed to give the guy more credit for getting on the same page right away. Perhaps their conversations should be a bit more in-depth, both on personal and professional level, but he really had no idea if Frosty was much of a conversationalist.

"Have you talked to Triple B?" he asked.

"Yeah," said Frosty. "He told me to report straight to you."

"Thanks."

That explains that. Now he had to find out if Triple B knew everything already. Right after Frosty walked away Triple B would approach him and he'd get the answer he was looking for.

"You got briefed on everything?" asked Triple B.

"Pretty much," answered Chauncey. "What did he tell you?"

"Nothing, I told Frosty to report to you first. I figured you'd pick up on the connection instantly with that Love Link thing."

"I thought he didn't tell you anything."

"All he mentioned was that Love Link thing and something about strangulation. I haven't even looked at the body, as soon as he told me those two things. With that first thing I knew it would be best just to wait for you to get here, treat it the same way we did with that Roy Cumberland guy."

"Did Cumberland's family get contacted?'

"Yeah, I got confirmation first thing this morning."

"Were the parents able to shed light on the matter?"

"As for any useful information, no, Roy Cumberland did say something to them about Widen Laboratories, but nothing in detail. I guess he was somewhat liberal, but not an over-the-top, heart on his sleeve kind of guy. Not the type who immediately jumped to conclusions by attracting attention to himself. He didn't stand outside city halls with protest signs, much less go on strike at work unless he didn't get paid, according to his mother."

"You did learn something useful!" declared Chauncey.

"What do you mean?" asked Triple B.

"The type of personality this Roy Cumberland had. Don't you see? He looked into things before taking action! He obviously wanted to learn what the deal was before doing anything about it!"

"You think so?"

"I know so! He stumbled onto something he wasn't supposed to know about, and I'll bet he learned it from Jane Newton!"

"That's a possibility," said Sergeant Matheson, who seemed to pop up out of nowhere next to Triple B.

"What brings you out here?" asked Chauncey.

"I found out this Stacy O'Connell was a former employee of Widen Labs. Everything we've found out so far, whether it's about Roy Cumberland or this poor young woman there's a connection between the two. Since it started at the campus last night, by law I have to get involved, unless the U.S. Marshals or the Feds barge in and take over."

"Haven't heard from either of them," said Triple B.

"Not yet," added Chauncey.

"For now we should just treat it like we won't," concluded Sergeant Matheson. "With any luck we'll be out of here before the news nuts show up."

"I know you're not a big fan of that," said Chauncey.

"You know how glad I am this isn't happening while school is in session? It's bad enough what I've had to deal with these last twenty-four hours. The phone calls and emails will be nonstop as soon as the spring semester starts!"

"It won't be just news nuts either."

"I know! Then again, I've never met John Walsh. I'll talk to him, something you guys have done. He can call and ask as many questions as he'd like instead of producers or agents!"

"At least you're sounding optimistic!" said Triple B.

"Thanks, I guess."

Chauncey quickly nodded to Triple B and Sergeant Matheson and headed over to where the body was located. Frosty stood about fifteen feet away talking to fellow constituents, people he assumed were most likely Morgue Men. The Detective recognized the other faces, certainly not the names, but enough where it triggered some type of recollection. Yet it was dark enough out where he wouldn't take the time to get a closer look at them. These Morgue Men were alive and well, Stacy O'Connell wasn't. A quick glance at her body had to be the most important task at hand.

He took out a small flashlight, turned it on and kneeled down. This Stacy O' Connell certainly wasn't wearing anything unusual, just a black long-sleeved shirt and jeans with the same color, kind of simplistic. He didn't want to coin the phrase Plain Jane for her outfit. Luckily she wasn't a Jane Doe, and he still hadn't gotten in touch with that Jane Newton as of yet. Right now that was the only person he wanted to call Jane until he talked to her.

The moment he noticed her shoes were also black he shined the flashlight on her neck. The words Love Link were located at the bottom right of it with the same color and shape of the letters found on Roy Cumberland's right arm. The only difference being the size of the letters, which were significantly smaller. Whoever's behind this, Love Link is definitely their calling card, and wants to make sure everybody knows that.

Oddly enough, Chauncey didn't look at the marks on the neck very closely. Obviously the result of being strangled, which he knew, yet it seemed odd that it was all at least two inches above the Love Link lettering. Definitely the calling card!

The Detective got back on his feet and walked back over to Triple B and Sergeant Matheson. He had an idea only to be shared between the three of them.

"Guys," said Chauncey. "How much information do the news nuts have?"

"Not a hell of a lot," answered Triple B.

"Tell me more."

"We haven't confirmed or denied if that Roy Cumberland was murdered."

"Do they know about the Love Link thing?"

"No," said Triple B. "I even told Frosty he didn't need to put that in the official police report and we'd look into it."

"Is he alright with that? He doesn't see it as being a little too sleazy?"

"For now it's okay since we haven't put together enough information about either of the victims. Remember, I told you Roy Cumberland's parents just found this morning, and they won't be able to come down here until tomorrow to see the body."

"Alright," said Chauncey. "No one talks about the Love Link thing, you got that?"

"Okay," said Triple B.

"No problem," confirmed Sergeant Matheson. "You think we should run that by Frosty, too?"

"You definitely need to remind him," said Chauncey. "Right now he'll keep it safe, we haven't searched too deep into the case yet."

"That's enough for him to keep quiet," said Triple B. "We've worked with him long enough to know he'll be alright with it."

"Alright," said Chauncey, again. "I'm out of here. I'll leave it to you guys to talk to him before the night is over. I'm betting the news nuts we'll be here in about sixty seconds! I'll take off like a thief in the night!"

"Don't let them hear you say that!" said Sergeant Matheson, amused.

"They'll turn you into a suspect," said Triple B, laughing.

"You guys can vouch for me," added Chauncey. "So can John Walsh! I'll see if I can get him to call you, Matheson!"

"I'll see to it Frosty keeps his mouth shut."

Those were the last words he heard from those guys

when he left the scene. Matheson began to laugh with Triple B after making that last statement. Chauncey started his car and drove off. Timing was impeccable. Only seconds after turning onto Hobson Road the first news van passed by. He didn't take the time to find out which television station it came from. He was just grateful to avoid these people or parasites for that matter. However, he should have made a mental note of it, just to be professional. Granted, all he had to do was call Triple B to find out. The Detective knew better than to give any indication he was slacking, despite the fact that Triple B knew Sergeant Matheson had a tougher time dealing with the press than he did.

It wasn't long before Chauncey arrived at the exit he needed to take to get back on Route 21. Less than a minute passed during the time he drove up the ramp and started driving down that particular road. He reminded himself that the Lucky Dog Diner was still open and located at the bottom of the ramp on the right side of the exit he needed to take to get back to downtown Prime. He nixed the idea altogether, deciding he'd rather be at home with the girlfriend and the dog. There was enough food in the house that he could make something half-decent for himself. He also needed to consider the possibility that he might be able to get some quality sleep out of the deal, too.

Chauncey drove a few miles down Route 21 when he took notice of a place located off the exit he just passed. The Woodward Hotel, which had been vacant for years, meaning you wouldn't see any customers, much less owners or anyone attempting to run the place. The Detective was surprised there were no takers yet. Then again, he never saw it posted for sale in the classifieds either.

Something caught his attention out of the corner of his eye, however. He wasn't looking very closely at the

Woodward Hotel. There was no reason to, not at first. A person was standing out in the front of the hotel, just a short distance from the road it was located on, which could easily be seen while driving on Route 21. Chauncey could tell it was a woman, standing statuesque. The only way he could truly describe it, and if he didn't know better he would've mistaken it for a lawn decoration or a scarecrow, which was unnecessary for a place like that.

The Detective felt what he saw, a piercing sensation flowing through his entire body. A deadly stare from someone who seemed to be glowing, were they seeing eye to eye? Or possibly worse, in his line of work he often had to worry about scenarios where the "eye for an eye" mentality got carried out. In this case he wouldn't attempt to kid himself. It was a distinct possibility.

The name Stacy O'Connell entered his mind, instinctively it seemed. Somehow believing that's who he'd laid his eyes on. But that's not possible, he thought to himself. The poor woman's body had just been found at the swamp, Triple B confirmed that over the phone. Chauncey didn't need to get to the scene of the crime right away, but that got him thinking. Maybe whoever was behind all of this wanted to make these murders look easy to solve. So far the only connection was the Love Link signatures, if you will. He didn't know what else to call them, they definitely weren't tattoos. He still loved the old expression calling card but no one else in his line of work said that very often, not that he could remember.

Chauncey started getting a sinking feeling, which literally felt like was heading to the bottom of his stomach. The Detective knew somehow this would be a tough one. Was the killer intentionally using different methods on the victims not wanting to establish any kind of pattern? First impressions would make anyone believe Roy Cumberland had a heart attack, but tonight

Chauncey got the proof he needed to think otherwise. Whoever he was looking for wanted him to know the first victim's death was no accident!

Suddenly and without warning Chauncey just snapped out of it, exactly what he had no idea. However, no statuesque figure of a woman was standing out in front of the Woodward Hotel. Nothing was glowing either, it was dark out and it would have been obvious if that was the case. The only sensations he could compare to what he had just felt were an eerie dream-like state or a deep hypnosis. The strangest part being that he was still in the same spot on Route 21 when he first spotted who he thought was Stacy O'Connell, even more bizarre was sitting behind the wheel of his car which never felt like it stopped moving.

The Detective didn't want to think about it any longer, for better or worse or right or wrong.

"I have no clue what's going on here," he said to himself. "I have to get some real fucking sleep!"

CHAPTER 7

TWO DAYS HAD PASSED since Chauncey had checked out the crime scene at the swamp. Technically a day and a half is more like it. The time was shortly before eleven in the morning, meaning the quick examination he did on Stacy O'Connell's body occurred the night before last. Whatever, he was glad he had all of yesterday to himself. The most helpful part was being able to fall asleep shortly after returning home from the swamp a.k.a. Badlands. He could relax even more knowing he'd avoided the news nuts in the nick of time.

The Detective played the cards right without really putting a lot of thought into it, giving him all of yesterday to work the kinks out of his system. Time was on his side. However, the Rolling Stones were the ones who said that, not the Kinks.

He was appreciative of getting to bed at a normal hour, or what many people consider to be a normal hour. He couldn't help being a night person, and didn't enjoy not being able to rest his head on a pillow after the sunrise came. If he was on an assignment he could deal with it. Other than that: Forget it!

Strangely enough, only a little more than twenty-four hours passed since yesterday began and he already started reminiscing about how great it went. The first thing he and Ali did was have a half-decent breakfast together with the AM radio on at a very low volume, the reason being he wanted to keep the police scanner on simultaneously at a higher volume just in case anything happened around Prime he needed to know about.

By midday Chauncey and Ali took Lady for a long walk on several blocks through many neighborhoods in the area, eventually winding up in Downtown Prime. He couldn't remember the last time he brought the dog that far into town, the stranger part being able to stop thinking about work almost entirely, at least for a little while.

This reminiscing distracted him in a good way. He wasn't putting much thought into driving back to Prime State University, which was exactly what he was doing at that moment. Not that he needed to considering how short the drive was from his place. Ten minutes tops with traffic, and at this time in the morning very little was expected. In another hour that would definitely change, but not drastically compared to when school was back in session.

Enjoy it while you can was Chauncey's thought about all of this.

Everything should be easier this time, specifically returning to the Widen Science Building to conduct another interview. Paul Raymond was the guy in question, and should expect Chauncey to arrive any minute. The Detective did leave a message on the guy's voicemail to verify he was on his way. Maybe the phone had been turned off. Or perhaps Mr. Raymond hadn't woken up yet. Either way he'd find out shortly.

Chauncey arrived at the Widen Science Building yet again. He was pretty sure he pulled into the same parking space from the last time he was there. A small detail like that hardly mattered, but being a Detective for so many years he never knew what might be useful regarding any case he was working on. Something as trivial as that might jog the memory, even if it seemed like it had nothing to do with the current assignment.

Now the gears started rolling which put Chauncey back into work mode. No hunches or cop-like instincts entered his thoughts while walking into the main lobby of the Widen Science Building for the second time. There was no reason to have those feelings, at least not yet. Everything looked exactly the same compared to his first trip here the other day. Professor Horace had also given him directions to Paul's place, which weren't complicated. He left the piece of paper he'd written them down on in his car, showing how little he was worried about it. The door to the basement/storage area where Paul stayed would be unlocked when he arrived.

The Detective felt tempted to stop in and have a talk with Professor Horace but first things first. He knew Paul Raymond was expecting him, maybe afterwards. Then again, he thought better of it. He'd rather have extra coffee with him if whenever he stopped in on anyone unexpectedly, and he hadn't brought an extra cup of it for the drive over. Very rare for Chauncey no matter how much of a caffeine fix he may have had at home, and oddly enough he'd only consumed one before leaving.

It couldn't have taken Chauncey more than a few minutes to find the entrance to the basement, storage facility, or whatever you wanted to label it as. Just as promised he was able to get in without incident. He already knew this particular door wasn't kept under a traditional lock and key. Professor Horace told him when they first met that both identification badges and a fingerprint analysis were required. When visitors like Detective Chauncey are expected the Campus Police get notified by Professor Horace or Paul Raymond or whoever connected to Prime State University is expecting a guest under important circumstances, and a murder investigation definitely qualifies. An override is conducted by the officer who is in charge, possibly Sergeant Matheson, on the shift the guest is arriving and/or the meeting is occurring. The override registers into the main computer's central processing unit, which carries out the procedure requested then remains on record in the memory banks of the computer's files permanently. At least that's how Chauncey would try to explain something that complicated in Plain English!

All those thoughts went through the Detective's head right as he was about to open the door. A lot for sure but he understood all of it. He always tried to think everything through with complicated technical stuff like computers or science whenever possible. With the exception of a basic electronics guide he didn't want to get into every little detail of something with the schematics involved if it wasn't necessary no matter how interesting it might be.

The moment Chauncey opened the door and took the first step downstairs he couldn't believe his eyes. He had never seen a staircase leading down to any basement so immaculate, much less a garage or storage facility for that matter. The most unusual part was the thin, blue carpet he set his feet on. If he didn't know any better he'd be convinced that steam-cleaning was conducted every twenty minutes, and this was just the stairs mind you.

Forget about odds and ends of any sort left on the sides of the steps most people would expect to see. Items no one had touched since their grandfather served the country during World War II were not going to be found. No coat racks with old winter jackets or extra flannel shirts had a place here either.

Not now. Not ever.

The white walls on either side of the staircase retained a plain but pleasant vibe as far as he was concerned. Whoever constructed this definitely had vision, when was the last time you saw a reality show about the best staircases and the walls surrounding it? If this was just the beginning he couldn't wait to reach the basement and get sucked in by the beauty of that.

Right he was.

Whatever would be a typical response for him regarding Cleanliness being next to Godliness, maybe now he understood the meaning behind that.

There's a first for everything, right?

The Detective took his first step on a light, tan-colored tiled floor. On the right side were white walls with windows at the very top which he estimated the length and width of them to be four feet by one and a half feet. He was pretty good at approximate guesses with that kind of stuff.

Never knew how or why.

The light shining in from the late morning sky he could only describe as breathtaking. Chauncey would always remain a night owl by nature, but if he hung around here more often he wouldn't mind taking in a beautiful sunrise every now and then despite being inside a so-called basement. This would definitely be the exception and not the rule.

On the left were the four doors Professor Horace had talked about. Not much to see unless you planned on entering one of them to get stuff you needed and since Chauncey did not work directly for Prime State University that possibility was completely out of the question, the only exception being if a warrant's obtained and Triple B assisted him in the case. Of course the Campus Police did do an override so he could come down here but in no way would that grant him access to see what kind of prizes were hiding behind door number one, two, or three! They weren't stupid. He knew Paul Raymond would be behind door number four, hopefully anticipating his arrival.

Chauncey wondered if the Prime Housing Authority offered anything similar to what he'd seen so far. Whenever he had to visit someone's place, the elderly or a renter in possession of a Section 8 voucher through the city, most of them lived in digs that seemed average at best. That's not a bad thing, but you'd think anyone who worked forty-plus hours every week for the majority of their adult life could rightfully have more money saved and live off a bigger budget instead of being forced to wait for a small social security check to come in every month and pinch pennies on a daily basis!

That's enough of that, Chauncey thought to himself.

The Detective slowly made his way to door number four, Paul Raymond's pad as far as he knew. Oddly enough, it was unlocked and opened about an inch or two. He heard familiar music playing on the inside but couldn't pinpoint the artist or the song, other than being a very recognizable instrumental piece on a guitar. Chauncey knocked and got no response, the second time he pounded on the door harder, hoping that could be heard over the music.

Not happening.

Chauncey slowly pushed the door open, only a few inches in so far and he recognized a certain smell already. He instantly knew what to expect, and it probably explained why this kid didn't pick up the phone when he tried to call him earlier. The entire interview would be a waste of time.

Chauncey pushed the door approximately halfway open and looked inside. Paul Raymond was sitting upright on his bed with his back leaned up against the wall behind him. This scenario was something Chauncey had seen played out countless times. The kid placed a tiny wooden bowl in his mouth with his left hand, with his right hand holding onto the lighter needed to smoke the bowl every few seconds.

The Detective decided to wait for young Paul to have one last hit before saying anything. He thought the kid glanced over at him very briefly.

"Is this a bad time?" asked Chauncey.

Paul Raymond responded by quickly turning his head toward the Detective, the bowl immediately fell out of his mouth hitting the edge of the bed and landing on the floor.

Definitely, Chauncey thought.

"I can come back later," said the Detective.

"No! No! That's alright!" said Paul, naturally sounding very wound up thanks to the grass he smoked, the only truly negative side-effect of being one with nature using this stuff. The paranoia creeping in when you get stoned by yourself, not that big of a deal to Detective Chauncey, yet still illegal in many places in the U.S. and controversial enough where you always have to look over your shoulder before sparking it up.

"Paul Raymond, right?"

"Yeah," Paul responded, still sounding a little tense.

"It's not a big deal," said Chauncey. "I'll come back in a few hours."

"Look," said Paul, trying to calm down. "I just took my first hit when you popped your head inside."

"I don't know about that."

"I mean," said Paul, talking a bit slower. "I just packed my first bowl. I haven't had much yet."

"Fair enough," said Chauncey.

Paul quickly moved over to the side of the bed and placed his feet on the floor then leaned over to pick up the bowl he dropped moments earlier. He put it on a nightstand then slowly stood up and walked over to Chauncey and shook hands, deciding there's no point trying to hide anything now.

"How have you been feeling?" asked Chauncey. "You were having a pretty rough night when we first met, understandably, of course."

"Thanks," said Paul.

"Where are you at now?"

"Been keeping it together since you saw me that night at the Campus Police Office," he answered.

"How so?" inquired Chauncey, very gentle.

"Haven't been as hysterical since then, sorry about the weed it relaxes me and takes the edge off a bit and much needed after all of that."

The Detective liked where this was going, he sensed the kid was trying to be on the level with him. He didn't think it possible when they first met, justified considering the situation, not exactly normal when a friend gets murdered. Chauncey needed to remind himself occasionally to never underestimate anybody regardless of first impressions. The two of them looked at each other straight in the eye for a few seconds. Best to say something so it wouldn't feel like an interrogation.

"It might have helped Reagan with his Alzheimer's Disease," he said, sounding a bit spontaneous.

"Yeah," laughed Paul as he raised his bowl, as if making a toast. "You never know!"

"Something was off about that guy. Way back when he made it so pot possession only got you a ticket around here. Then when he ran the country he declared the war on drugs!"

"Jerry Lewis should have run for Governor after old Ronnie left, maybe George Carlin!"

"Are you kidding? You couldn't put someone like Carlin into office he would've made sense of everything!"!

"Politicians aren't supposed to make sense," said Paul. "They just tell people what they want to hear!"

Chauncey started to feel a little more relieved. The kid didn't have to struggle be on the level with him. This conversation could go on for quite a while. Hopefully they wouldn't get into a subject like fascism, who knows how long they could carry on about that?

Nevertheless, just roll with it.

"At least Schwarzenegger got back to doing movies again! He was honest enough to compare his position as the Governor to the Terminator. What do you think is worse? Being collected from or getting terminated?"

"Depends on how much he's collecting from you, who needs a reason? Power does what it wants!"

"True," said Chauncey. "I always wondered why he never used Conan's name at all. Conan is one of the good guys despite being a barbarian or destroyer. He could have called himself King Conan!"

"I don't know about that" said Paul. "He didn't have much of a wardrobe in those movies, remember? Even if you compare it to what little he had on in Pumping Iron."

"Ever do any physical fitness yourself?"

"Here and there but I never could get into it the way guys like Schwarzenegger could."

"I hear you there," said Chauncey. "It's not appealing to look at another guy's physique, right?

"Yeah," said Paul. "But I'm not homophobic either!"

"It doesn't mean you are."

"Right, I don't even think about my image much when I look in the mirror."

"You just want to look presentable."

"Exactly!" declared Paul.

"You're just a regular guy!" stated Chauncey.

The Detective now knew for sure they got off on the right foot. The small talk worked very well in their favor. Make this kid feel as comfortable as possible, which defined where his head was at the moment. The brief pause in conversation allowed Chauncey to hear the music playing on Paul's radio again. He'd almost tuned it out trying to get this kid's full attention slightly complicated by the weed factor. Like the thought he had to himself earlier it felt like he was on the right track, his quick glance at the radio on the small table next to the bed caught Paul's eye as well.

"If you want I can turn this off," said Paul.

"What station is it?" asked Chauncey.

"It's a CD," answered Paul.

"I've heard this before," said Chauncey. "Countless times, it reminds me of the old surf guitar music."

"You're right about that. The song is called Rumble by Link Wray."

"Link.......Wray?"

"Yeah, heard of him?"

"I have," answered Chauncey. "The memory is starting to come back a little, it's been a while."

"I take it you've heard of Dick Dale too?"

"Absolutely, actually that name is easier to remember!"

"Agreed, most people would probably say that!"

Both Chauncey and young Paul smiled slightly, allowing the conversation to become more relaxed. Chauncey actually smirked more than he smiled. Yet one thing stood out in his mind after the name Link Wray had been mentioned:

Love Link, the words written on Roy Cumberland and Stacy O'Connell, the two murder victims. Now Link stands out big time, but is it meant to be a name or a term? Does this kid seem like the type that would be involved in a homicide? Chauncey didn't think so, but an alarm went off in his head. Maybe it was a trivial thing, like taking notice of parking in the same spot again. He didn't feel the need to write anything down, but this Link Wray's name would remain in the back of his mind for quite some time. Not necessarily in a bad way, he felt tempted to go out and find a compilation CD or something, maybe go on YouTube and find videos created using surf guitar music with Link Wray, Dick Dale or whatever.

"I have to admit I'm kind of impressed with this place," said Chauncey. "Your Uncle told me it was nice down here but I didn't expect anything like this."

"Most people don't," said Paul.

"You'd give Prime Housing Authority a run for the money!"

"You think so?"

"Definitely, I didn't take coming down here seriously but the staircase alone had hints of beauty, along with seeing the sun shine in through the windows! I understand why you want to stay down here. The term comfort zone is an understatement."

"Okay," said Paul. "But I should probably be more careful if someone in law enforcement is at the door."

"It would be a smart move," stated Chauncey. "A lot of other guys I work with might bust your balls a bit more."

"I'll keep that in mind."

"Good idea, but you don't have to deal with any slumlords, right?"

"Definitely not," said Paul, sounding humble.

"And I don't have to term this place as something owned by the B.B.A."

"What's that?"

"The Bargain Basement Association," said Chauncey, being sarcastic.

"Never heard of them," said Paul.

"Of course not!" said Chauncey, laughing a little bit. "I made it up, they don't exist!"

"If you happen to find a cheaper basement apartment to rent give me a call, maybe we can suggest that the landlord should use the name! He might get more business!"

"You're probably right!"

They both laughed together for another minute or two until Paul picked up a remote to turn on the television. Chauncey turned his head to see if anything worth watching was on. He didn't know which station it was, but he recognized the movie right away: The Town That Dreaded Sundown.

"I like this one a lot," said Chauncey.

"Same here," said Paul. "I thought Dawn Wells was great in this even though she only has a small part. She could definitely do more stuff than Gilligan's Island. Did you ever see her in another movie called Winterhawk?'

"Yeah, I'm pretty sure she did that one around the same time she did this. I think it was the same director who did both of those movies."

"You're right. I have the DVD around somewhere which has an interview with her. I think the director called her up at the last minute to do the part."

"That's right," said Chauncey. "A lot of people are convinced the movie inspired the second Friday the 13th movie with the killer having the potato sack over his head. Maybe that's the reason why the hockey mask came about in the third movie."

"Could be," said Paul. "It obviously worked out for the better since most people remember Jason for the hockey mask."

"True, but the second one has maintained a loyal following."

"I can't argue with you on that one, so has The Town That Dreaded Sundown!"

"Damn straight," said Chauncey. "And Jason never attacked anyone with a trombone!"

"This is true," said Paul, smiling more. "Maybe in the next movie he should shove a clarinet up someone's ass!"

"That's something he hasn't done yet! I think he's

getting too comfortable with machetes and axes!"

This conversation keeps getting easier and easier, can't call it an interview. At least not yet, might as well stick to the subject at hand.

"By the way," said Chauncey. "Have you ever seen a movie called Eliminators?"

"You bet," answered Paul. "The one that Denise Crosby was in right before she made it big on Star Trek, it's just a cheesy low- budget adventure flick yet you can't help liking it!"

"That's the one! A little trivia for you, there is a connection to Eliminators and The Town That Dreaded Sundown."

Paul paused for a moment, but it didn't take long to come up with an answer.

"Fontana," he said. "Am I right?"

"Tell him what he's won!"

"Don't expect me to remember the actor's name!"

"Don't sweat it," said Chauncey. "You're the only guy I've met who knew that, then again I don't remember asking anybody else. I don't remember that most of the time!"

"That means you have a life!" stated Paul, very positively.

They smiled simultaneously. Both of them were on the same level as far as a sense of humor was concerned.

"I do occasionally," said Chauncey.

"That makes one of us," responded Paul.

"Don't be down on yourself, kid. You got a pretty good setup down here, I wouldn't complain."

"It definitely beats the Bargain Basement Association!"

"Like I said," added Chauncey. "It gives the Prime Housing Authority a run for their money!"

The Detective started thinking he might be in the wrong line of business but he was pretty sure you didn't qualify for anything if you worked for any housing authority, easier to keep talking about old movies.

"Something else came to mind," said Chauncey. "Have you ever seen a movie called Badlands? I think it came out in the late seventies or early eighties."

"Was Martin Sheen in it?" asked Paul.

"Yeah," answered Chauncey. "That's the one."

"It came out in the early seventies, 1973 I think."

"It goes that far back?" asked Chauncey.

"I think so," Paul responded. "But I'll have to watch it again, I don't remember much about it."

"Same here, I'm not sure if I've ever seen it."

"I thought Badlands had to do with something around here."

"The swamp area off Route 21," said Chauncey.

"Okay," said Paul. "But I don't think either one of them are connected in any way."

"Probably not, but the swamp would make a great place for a horror movie combining both fact and fiction!"

"I'm with you there, they say you can run but you can't hide, except in that swamp!"

"That's why it got called Badlands," confirmed Chauncey.

"Ever been out there? I mean the general vicinity, not too many people will venture out there unless they want to disappear."

"Not really," answered Paul, not a definite yes or no, but more than satisfactory as far as Chauncey was concerned regarding the subject matter.

"Seems like the perfect place for the reptiles in your Uncle's lab," stated Chauncey. "Both for finding and releasing them, oddly enough I never hear about sightings of exotic reptiles, or any kind of nuisance complaints."

"I've never heard of anyone going fishing out there either," added Paul.

"True," said Chauncey. "The body we discovered out

there was hidden in plain sight if you catch my drift."

"Did you figure out who it was?" asked Paul.

"Stacy O'Connell," answered Chauncey. "Have you heard of her?"

"I met someone named Stacy a little while back, I think she was a friend of Jane's and had an accent, Irish maybe."

"Jane," said Chauncey. "Would that be Jane Newton?"

"Yeah, she works with my Uncle in the lab a lot."

"Thought so, can you tell me anything else?"

"Like I said I only met her once, I'm not entirely sure about the accent either."

"Do you think she had connections to Widen Labs?"

"Probably, I mean if she was with Jane that would more than likely be the case."

"Okay," said Chauncey. "Did your Uncle know her?"

"Possibly," answered Paul. "I mean he's a lot more involved with stuff here than at Widen Labs, Jane's the one who keeps him up to date with what happens over there."

"In a way he doesn't really work for Widen Labs anymore, I know the company owns this place but his job here is considered to be educational, research he seems to do on his own, right?"

"You just reminded me of something, he still has an official title for researching stuff at Widen Labs."

"What would that be?" asked Chauncey.

"Independent Research," answered Paul.

"Is that what he was doing before coming to Prime State?"

"I think so, I'm pretty sure Jane Newton is in charge of that at the Widen Labs facility here in Prime."

"That would make sense does she talk about it at all?"

"About what happens there? Not really, I mean the research with reptiles isn't a secret, I think she's out of town on assignment because of that."

"Did she specify in any way exactly what she'd be doing?"

"Not at all except there'd be a small group of them going with her, not necessarily people who worked for Widen Labs. Maybe contractors. Consultants, some guys from the military for sure."

"She told you that?" asked Chauncey.

"The military people for sure," he answered. "I do remember that, it sounded like an exciting adventure. I wish I could've gone, but I don't think I'm qualified."

"Where were they headed?"

"Overseas, either the Middle East or Africa, I'm pretty sure it's somewhere in Africa."

"It's probably some intense research she's involved in," said Chauncey. "That explains why I haven't gotten in touch with her."

"What's that?" asked Paul.

"Nothing," answered Chauncey. "I thought your Uncle told me she was on vacation."

"She usually takes a vacation around this time every year, but she said she was on a mission of some sort."

"A mission explains the military guys and the exotic reptiles, but wouldn't your Uncle know about it?"

"She told me it was classified and not to mention anything to my Uncle."

"Does he know what's going on?" asked Chauncey. "If it's confidential and classified he might not be allowed to discuss any of it, especially if he wants to keep his job."

"Most likely," added Paul.

"All he could talk about is everything you just told me!"

"So he's not in any trouble?" asked Paul.

"You're both off the hook."

"What about Jane?"

"I haven't had any contact with her as of yet, I won't

have a clue until I talk to her."

Jane Newton should be able to point me in the right direction, Chauncey thought to himself. But I only have the option of waiting for her to return from her expedition or safari or whatever it might be.

"She knew a little about the swamp," said Paul.

"What?" he asked.

"Jane," answered Paul.

"Sorry," said Chauncey. "I wasn't paying attention."

"Jane did talk about the swamp a few times."

"What did she say?"

"Not much, just that it was the place to go if you wanted to disappear, and that Widen Labs should utilize that area more since the land isn't used for anything."

"I don't know how far they'd get trying to do that, most of it is protected. Conservation land, it's the Chase Conservation Land to be precise."

"I think she said something about that, maybe she could find a loophole to use it for experiments in nature."

"I'm sure that would get a lot of scrutiny, even if the studies being conducted were only observational. You know someone will accuse them of dumping chemicals out there, if it hasn't happened already."

"I've never heard anything like that," said Paul.

"Neither have I," said Chauncey.

That doesn't mean it hasn't happened, the Detective thought, especially considering the fact that he had no idea Widen Labs officially owned Prime State University until the other day.

"Reptiles could be put out there," said Paul.

"What do you mean?" asked Chauncey.

"Who would know?" he suggested. "I mean no one goes out there anyway, and the ones that do want to disappear, who cares if they're never found?"

"That's Jane Newton talking."

"Right, how'd you guess?"

"Just a gut instinct," confirmed Chauncey. "Before I go, who was that we were listening to again?"

"Link Wray," answered Paul.

"Right," said Chauncey. "I'll have to find one of his CD's the next time I go shopping for something besides groceries."

"You want to borrow mine?" asked Paul, turning his head and reaching out with his right hand to pick up the Link Wray disc and handing it to the Detective.

"You don't mind?" asked Chauncey.

"Not at all, I have a feeling we haven't seen the last of each other."

"You're probably right, I know I'll have to talk to your Uncle again, and Jane Newton. So I'll be making more appearances here at the Widen Science Building!"

"Great," said Paul, nodding simultaneously while Chauncey turned around to make an exit. Seconds after entering the corridor he contemplated the CD the kid let him borrow:

Love Link, Link Wray, he thought. Am I reading into it too much? Possibly, Paul Raymond's not the type to get involved in a murder, not intentionally.

CHAPTER 8

A FEW HOURS HAD PASSED since Chauncey had met with Paul Raymond. Or interview technically speaking, at least that is what someone like Detective Chauncey would have to label it as. Part of the job, but the kid seemed like someone he could eventually strike up a friendship with, maybe Professor Horace as well, but that will depend on the outcome of the case. Good vibes radiated from both of them, so to speak, hopefully the same is true with Jane Newton.

It was about 2:30 p.m. Chauncey was sitting at a small table by the window at Cameron's Coffee Café, or Triple C some folks called it. Chances are most of their loyal customers didn't know about Triple B, the only name seen in the local press was Boss Bobby Burrell, but not the nickname used regularly by Chauncey or his other colleagues.

Only a few other customers were present besides Chauncey. The majority of the crowd from lunchtime had been gone for quite some time now. There were some familiar faces that Chauncey had recognized who exited the place when he stepped inside about an hour ago. He wasn't sure if he knew their names but the majority of them probably worked in Downtown Prime. The shop is located on Main Street and at least a handful of them worked at Prime State University.

That much the Detective was sure of.

One glimpse outside displayed an overcast sky, the sun had disappeared completely, and Chauncey had no idea if it was going to rain or not. In his line of work a smart move would be to check the weather forecast for the day as soon as he woke up, despite the fact that it wouldn't impact his very loose itinerary, except maybe a hurricane or tornado taking him to the Land of Oz. Detective skills might come in handy both on and off the yellow brick road, but they sure as hell won't tame lions, tigers, or bears. Everything had gone smoothly, specifically meeting with Professor Horace and Paul Raymond, but it might not stay that way.

What starts off as baby steps could lead him to a very bizarre battleground. There has to be a connection, whoever is responsible for the deaths of Roy Cumberland and Stacy O' Connell wants the Detective to know that. Otherwise Love Link wouldn't have been written on either one of them. Tattooed is not an appropriate term, even if it's the first thing everyone thinks of, but technically that's not what it was. The handwriting was exactly the same, definitive marks like a tattoo artist. Perhaps it wasn't a good idea to keep that information out of the press, maybe someone can identify the style of writing as a friends doodling. But who in the world would want to recognize it as evidence in a murder case besides the killer?

Too many questions were already going through Chauncey's mind. Spontaneous theorizing might not be the best idea right now. Keep it simple, everything had gone smoothly up until now. There is no point in complicating things until it actually gets that way. He wouldn't have to wait long. His phone rang and it was none other than Triple B, maybe the Boss might have some definite leads.

"What's going on?" asked Chauncey.

"I'm at the Woodward Hotel," answered Triple B.

"What the hell for? No one is planning on moving in there in our lifetime!"

"You're right about that, another body's been found there,"

"What???"

"Not inside the hotel, right on the front of the property where everyone can see it!"

Chauncey paused for a moment, he thought about the notion of a corpse being out in the open. Someone might have spotted it driving down Route 21 in broad daylight, a far worse scenario than discovering Stacy O'Connell's body in the Badlands. He hoped a mob scene hadn't gathered there yet.

"Who called it in?" asked Chauncey.

"Just get down here," said Triple B.

"Alright," he promised. "Can you at least give me a little bit of information?"

"Female, approximately in her mid-twenties with dark hair and an unusually pale complexion, that's all I can tell you."

"You're kidding!"

"What do you mean?" asked Triple B. "Of course not!"

"Never mind," said Chauncey. "I'll get down there as fast as I can!"

Chauncey paused a moment, both physically and mentally. It felt like time stopped completely, just like the other night when he drove by the Woodward Hotel and saw what he saw, quite clearly considering the distance from Route 21 and the property itself. He almost forgot that Triple B was still on the line.

"Does she look anything like the last girl?" asked Chauncey.

"Kind of," said Triple B.

"I'm leaving right now, alright?"

"Okay."

Chauncey chugged down the last of his coffee out of a small cup with maybe half an inch left at the most. He placed a dollar on the table along with some loose change he took out of his pocket. Everyone who worked there always told him not to bother since he was a semi-regular with very minor demands, but he wanted them to know he appreciated their service no matter what, even though he didn't make the kind of money a lot of the other customers did. The two employees behind the counter were preoccupied. One was on the phone while the other had just finished making a coffee for a customer standing in front of the cash register appeared to be in a deep conversation, another reason to leave a tip since he couldn't say anything to them on the way out. The Detective quickly got up and made his way out the front entrance, his car was in plain sight since he'd found a spot right in front of the store, lucky him due to someone pulling out of that particular space as soon as he arrived.

In a matter of seconds he got into his car and drove off. Even taking a giant u-turn didn't slow things down due to a lesser amount of traffic at this particular time of day. Main Street wasn't exactly hopping at the moment with a lot of other drivers or foot traffic, not so much as one person walked passed him on the sidewalk. Not that Downtown Prime felt like a ghost town, but definitely quieter than usual. Things would pick up by about 5pm for sure.

Chauncey felt like he was merely going through the

motions heading towards the Woodward Hotel, which didn't make sense considering what he'd seen there the other night along with Triple B calling him to go out there for the same reason. Maybe because he'd been everywhere he could possibly go in Prime, nothing felt unusual about visiting any location in the city. That's part of being a Detective.

He arrived at the end of Main Street and turned onto Route 21. The Woodward Hotel was only about half the distance from Downtown Prime .Unlike the swamp, not that there was any reason to go out of your way to visit these places. Except for Chauncey where it's his job, but he wasn't keeping track of the time it took to get there. Before he knew it he got off at the exit which brought him onto Dow Avenue, taking a left under a bridge beneath Route 21 then stopping and taking a right onto Woodward Way appropriately enough. The hotel would be about a hundred yards up on the left.

The Detective saw Triple B and few other familiar faces at the edge of the front lawn of the hotel property. He parked his car directly across the street in either the parking or breakdown lane. There were no meters so it could more than likely be used for both of those reasons. He turned off the engine and got out then walked across the street to interact with the entourage of law enforcement, paramedics, and Morgue Men. At the most a dozen of them were there altogether.

As soon as Chauncey joined all of them no one at the scene including Triple B needed to clue him in on what happened. Whoever the corpse belonged to would be considered D.O.A. She had already been placed in a body bag but it hadn't been zipped up yet.

Naturally he wanted to take a closer look.

"Not yet!" ordered Triple B to the two gentlemen kneeling on the ground stuck with such an unpleasant task. At least they could keep her on the gurney.

Chauncey got down on his knees. The first glance at this woman's face clearly indicated that a whiter shade of pale was an understatement, even compared to an albino. However, something was different. An albino skin tone he could recognize right away, he had no idea how to describe this. He opened the sides of the body bag to get a better look at the entire front of the body. Despite the heavy amount of clothes on all he had to do was look at her neck, upper chest, arms and hands to determine if the skin color, or lack of, was consistent.

Affirmative, along with being the same person he saw on the way back from the crime scene at the Badlands from the previous night. But there was nothing glowing about it and he was positive the time of day, rain or shine, played no part as to the reason why. Yet one more thing came to mind.

"It's not there," said Triple B.

"Love Link?" asked Chauncey.

"No marks of any kind whatsoever."

"You sure?" asked Chauncey.

"Nothing," said Triple B. "No marks, cuts, bruises, scratches, tattoos, and definitely no Love Link!"

"Just glancing at the neck and chest area it's obvious there's no sign of strangulation."

"There's nothing suspicious," said Triple B.

"I still think it's a priority."

Chauncey looked up again at the two gentlemen, presumably paramedics, who were awaiting further instructions.

"Go ahead," he told them. "Take her, we're all set for now."

"Okay," said the one on his left. "You know where to find it."

"Yup," said Chauncey. "We'll be in touch."

It only took a few seconds for Chauncey to pick up on the dry sense of humor of this EMT. They'd crossed paths before. In their lines of work it's inevitable. This guy had to communicate with the Morgue Men far more than the Detective did, which practically qualified him to be one of them.

His name was Zack Larch, immediately Chauncey thought of Lurch from the Addams Family. He didn't resemble the character that much. Plenty of people have short light-colored hair, a stone cold look in their eyes, and a deep sounding voice. None quite like Lurch, though, but being around corpses regularly with a last name only differing with one letter made it easy to catch on to.

The Detective deliberately tried to keep the name Zack stuck in his head to the point where you have a song you can't get out of your head. He was hoping it would stick regardless of how long it might be before he sees the guy again who'd probably heard every single Lurch-related Addams Family joke imaginable. He quickly glanced at the other guy's nametag, Colin Mulligan to be precise, hoping the association might increase the memory. Still not as easy as name that tune, but helpful nonetheless. One note won't tell you much, two notes might. Three notes will ring a bell and are enough to make a chord out of it. Not as simple as connecting the dots or a paint-by-numbers approach, but something is better than nothing!

Chauncey stood up when Zack and Colin started zipping up the body bag again. He turned to face Triple B and say what he had to say.

"Tell Frosty to make this a priority," said Chauncey. "I know there's no indication of foul play, but this is important regardless!"

"You got it," said a voice behind him, which turned out to be Frosty.

Chauncey turned again to face the guy.

"How long do you think it will take?" he asked.

"I don't know," answered Frosty. "I'll put in a call right now and tell the guys to stop everything and move this to the top of the list."

"Thanks."

After saying that last word everyone at the scene cleared out simultaneously. Chauncey bet their rate of speed was probably a hundred times faster compared to their arrival. Then again, he had no idea how long they had all been there. He forgot to ask Triple B about that. It didn't matter, especially since there were no signs of foul play or any indication of physical injuries. Despite the unusual appearance of the corpse everything seemed pretty cut and dry. Of course that was far from the case. The Detective, Triple B, Frosty, the paramedics and everyone else present who so much as glanced at the body knew the story was nowhere close to reach the end, and wouldn't be for quite some time.

Chauncey knew this situation was a mixed blessing of sorts. No chance of being an open and shut case, who knew what the results would be after Frosty and the Morgue Men completed their examination? There had to be a connection to the recent murders, regardless of how this one died. A small amount of intuition and a large amount of logic determined that, practically dictating it. But the next step was inevitable: having to wait. Chauncey couldn't do anything until he heard directly from Frosty and got the okay from Triple B to move forward.

One step at a time, Chauncey thought to himself, something that suited him just fine. This meant he'd have no choice but to pace himself. Taking it slow made it easier to catch the tiny details and stay a lot more organized. He was just grateful to be in a state of mind compatible to the circumstances.

After getting back in his car Chauncey waited until everyone left the scene of the crime. The plan wasn't to search the property right away, but get a full view of the area that had been crowded for the past hour or so. The Detective knew he forgot to ask Triple B what the time frame had been, which he should have done when he arrived. But it couldn't have been too long considering the light amount of work that needed to be done. Just a quick examination by Frosty, Triple B finding no Love Link, and last but not least: Zack Larch (not Lurch!) and Colin Mulligan zipping up the body bag and whisking it away.

The moment after everyone had gone nothing visible to the human eye gave an indication that human activity of any sort had been there. The short length of the grass on the front lawn did catch Chauncey's interest, however. The Woodward Hotel had been out of commission for quite some time now. Occasionally the property got listed for some unreasonable and outlandish price even though realistically it could only be purchased as a fixer-upper, at least as far as Chauncey was concerned. Perhaps a realtor holding on to the property for an extended time period paid some local landscaping company to do a quick mowing job every couple of months as a half-assed attempt to keep up appearances. He also knew the place was located in a residential neighborhood. The City of Prime most likely had a Compliance Officer make sure it happened for one or both of those reasons, but without there being a mad rush either. It was rare in this day and age to worry about dealing with somebody like Dennis Rader a.k.a. the BTK Killer chasing people down over petty incidents like that. Granted, there would always be the small towns employing cops who had no problem being rude or pushing their power trips, but Prime was officially considered a city by anyone and everyone. Law enforcement had better things to do in highly populated urban cities like Prime and more so in Los Angeles, most of the time.

The time slowly passed from the middle to late afternoon. Not that there's a reason anything should feel different in just over an hour, it would still be a while before nighttime arrived. But for some reason it felt like it was dark out. As far as Chauncey was concerned there might as well have been a full moon out. Why he didn't have the slightest idea since an overcast sky was never an indication of the sun going down, even if you couldn't see it!

The Detective knew some of it was due to dealing with most of his cases at night. He also had to keep in mind that this "corpse" was definitely the same one he saw looking him straight in the eye on his way back from the Badlands the night before last. A fact he had to keep to himself for the time being, but not for long! For all he knows the thing glows in the dark!

No way, Chauncey thought to himself. Don't start coming up with crazy shit like that! It's just the stress and keeping your own hours, which are never normal! I don't want to tell everyone with the sunrise tomorrow a Headless Horseman will gallop in the wrong direction around a rotary!

A strong state of denial is where his head was at right now, who was he kidding? He knew what he saw, there's no doubt about it. He couldn't convince himself to call Triple B or Frosty, with the being the one especially having the right to know. He didn't want to start thinking about how this could unfold, but how could he not do that?

Impossible! No doubt about it! All he could do was hope the next couple of days would be relatively quiet. He already knew he had no other choice but to wait. If Frosty and the Morgue Men had their own show the next episode was bound to be interesting, and it wouldn't be long before they contacted Chauncey and gave him a detailed rundown of everything that happened and then some, not just your regular review! Thank God he wouldn't be able to tune in to the program until they called him.

One last quick glance was made while Chauncey started his car, nothing to be seen for sure and not the slightest hint of anyone renting a room at the Woodward Hotel. But with the autopsy of the corpse taken from here along with waiting for the results of Roy Cumberland and Stacy O'Connell who knew what to expect? Much less where else he would have to investigate? He might have to spend a few nights here himself, with the bright side being it wouldn't cost him anything.

"Time to head home," Chauncey said. "Waiting for results is equal to the thrill of watching grass grow, but if that's how it has to be for the next few days so be it."

He only wished Lady was lying in the passenger seat next to him. At least there would have been someone to talk to. Thankfully she'd be waiting for him back at the house.

CHAPTER 9

PAST TWILIGHT, that was the only way Chauncey could describe it. Or at least that's how it felt in his state of mind. The sun must be pretty much gone by now, even if it was impossible to see with the weather being the way it was for most of the day. It hadn't gotten dark yet, though it would be any time now. All he was doing at the moment was simply killing time, kind of appropriate with it being early in the evening and the movie he was watching. The 1982 cult classic Silent Rage starring Chuck Norris playing the usual tough cop trying to stop someone deemed an unstoppable killer thanks to an unfortunate breakthrough in medical science. In some ways this wasn't much different than Halloween II, which had been released less than a year before this. Getting shot or burned did nothing to stop this madman and good old Chuck's martial arts skills on top of that were no help either. In a way it didn't matter, you stop one murderer's rampage and before you know it another one surfaces and causes bloodshed all over again.

The Detective realized he was dwelling in a pessimistic state of mind, deep down he knew he made a difference in peoples lives. Part of him felt like he was in some kind of trance, still sensing the light of day the moment it got dark out, which happened right now. Something also made it seem like he was ahead of himself, when it feels like all day Thursday you keep thinking it's Friday. The only saving grace being when Friday rolls around you're back on track again. That's especially a good feeling if you're someone holding a nine to five job Monday through Friday. Not the case for Detective Chauncey Winfield. It never applies to any case he works on, and it doesn't matter if every aspect of a crime occurs during so-called normal hours that an average person lives by. At this point he knew he'd never encounter any criminals who only committed heinous acts during regular business hours, even if they were really organized and liked to keep a tight schedule. A killer doesn't think about time when their consumed with rage committing a murder.

With his mindset stuck somewhere between a light trance and concentrating on the movie he didn't hear his phone go off the first time. Even the second ring didn't sound very loud. But he quickly noticed the volume on it was up only halfway, and he didn't recall turning it down at any time during the last several hours. Naturally he turned it up again before he answered so he could hear whoever was trying to call him, but didn't take another split second to check the ID to see who it was.

"Hello?" he said very calmly, probably due to the trancelike state he was in.

"Detective Winfield?" asked the voice on the other end.

"Yes," he confirmed.

"This is Lurch."

Chauncey didn't recognize the voice, maybe someone

from a cold case or the beginning of a new case.

"Who?" asked Chauncey, with no clue who he was talking to.

"Lurch," the voice said again. "Remember you saw me and Colin put the corpse in the body bag at the Woodward Hotel earlier this afternoon.

"Zack Larch?" asked Chauncey.

"Yeah," he answered. "Most people don't remember that!"

"There's a first time for everything! I figured you'd already been called Lurch enough in your life."

"Thanks but it's not a big deal! I'm used to it and have a big enough sense of humor to deal with it!"

"So what can I do for you?" asked Chauncey.

"I'm at the morgue," he answered. "It's about the body found at the Woodward Hotel today."

"What about it?"

"I don't know what to say...when the lights are out I can see it perfectly."

"I'm not following you," said Chauncey.

"You should come down here," said Larch.

"How come Frosty didn't call me?"

"He's on his way. Your number is on speed dial here at the morgue, same with your boss but I couldn't get a hold of him."

"Triple B," said Chauncey.

"Right," answered Lurch.

"I'll be down shortly. I'm leaving right now."

"Okay."

Chauncey waited for Lurch to hang up, then immediately checked the caller ID to find out where the call came from. It was the main number from the morgue, not surprisingly.

"You should always pay close attention to detail," Chauncey told himself. "You're a Detective with a capital D!"

As soon as he stood up on both feet the dog looked up at him and gave him a wide-eyed stare, despite continuing to lie down. Not bad as long as little Lady didn't give him the sad look.

"Sorry," he said. "The powers you possess as a Jewish Viking could come in handy with or without Mel Brooks, but I'd hate it if anything happened to you. I don't even like to think about the fact that you'll be gone way before me!"

I can't believe I said that, he thought to himself, out loud and the only one present is the dog herself! What could be crueler than that? Come on, you mean well! Even little Lady Jane Spitz could understand that if she could talk.

Enough of the rambling and racing thoughts, maybe he could seek advice from other detectives to find out if they go through the same stuff he does. Psychiatrists have been known to get treatment from other psychiatrists, so it doesn't have to be viewed as being defeated. For all he knows that could be the case already. There are support groups for everything in this day and age, and if you can't find a magazine for it there's a website and an infinite number of accounts on Facebook. So much for privacy!

He briefly debated calling Ali to let her know he had to head out again. But she'd be coming over soon anyway, and he wasn't in the best state of mind to have to explain anything to her in great detail regardless if she asked him any questions. There wasn't a lot to talk about besides making sure the dog would be okay, the first priority living under his roof as far as he was concerned. She knew that already. He simply needed to concentrate on the task at hand, which meant getting his ass to the morgue.

Chauncey decided the best form of communication for the other special lady in his life would be the old-fashioned approach, simply leaving a note. A handwritten one believe it or not, using an actual pen and paper! The pen was easy to retrieve since he always carried a couple of them in his pocket, and a notepad, specifically defined as a post-it could be located at of all places on the kitchen table, what an incredible find! He could count his blessings being slightly organized considering where his head was at! A trancelike state and feeling a day ahead of the week didn't encourage a lot of multitasking or making mental notes of everything. An important lesson should be learned here: Do your homework! Just as much if you're a Detective! It might be alright for a student to hand theirs in late from time to time but in Chauncey's line of work lives are at stake more often than not!

This time, except for removing his jacket, Chauncey hadn't so much as taken off his shoes the entire time he was home. A bit unusual considering it was practically a ritual for him to change into a t-shirt and sweat pants if he knew he'd remain here for a couple of hours. More than a couple of hours had passed, and he certainly wasn't anticipating a phone call from someone at the city morgue, and especially not Lurch. A bit surprising the call wasn't made by Frosty. Then again, he didn't know the guy well enough, or have enough interaction either, to determine the methods being used for his specific field of practice, if any.

The Detective turned off the TV and quickly made his way over to the kitchen area. His jacket was hanging on a chair closest to the refrigerator. He put it on in a matter of seconds and pulled a pen out of his pocket. He leaned over and reached for the notepad a.k.a. post-its located smack dab in the middle of the kitchen table, which would be the most exercise he'd have to do in order to get ready to head to the morgue. Should he try to call Triple B on the way there? There's a good chance Frosty will arrive around the same time he does, obviously

Lurch will be there since that's who made the first call, maybe Colin Mulligan as well, but just because those two work together doesn't mean they're attached to the hip! Even Batman and Robin had separate bat poles! Actually he didn't know either of them well enough to compare them to the Dynamic Duo, but as far as he's concerned anybody working in their fields of expertise should be considered heroes in their own right!

Chauncey moved the pad of post-its closer to him, meaning the edge of the table he stood by. He didn't need to put any thought into what he'd write down, especially considering the fact that you don't need to write an entire chapter of a novel to explain to your significant other where you were going. Perhaps a sonnet or a bit of poetry might work, but not necessary this time around! It only took three words in large print to be specific: WENT 2 MORGUE. Simple as that, three words. Or two words and a number, or a four letter word, a number, and a six letter word with a small period at the end of it. However you want to describe it, or define it, is all good in Chauncey's book, and Ali could get in touch with him any time she wanted to if she felt the need to know anything else. She also had enough sense to realize he'd specify which morgue he'd be heading towards if it was out of town.

It felt good that little Lady didn't follow him over to the door when he opened it and headed outside. He could deal with the dog being attached to him but not overly attached, the last he needed to witness on the way out was a nasty display of separation anxiety. He much preferred to have her waiting at the door the moment he came home. As he made his way over to the car and got inside, he wondered if she got up and went into the kitchen after hearing the engine start.

"I'll never know," Chauncey said out loud.

The only reason for doing that was to help wake up

a bit. He didn't feel like making another cup of coffee before he left. Even Detective Chauncey Winfield has his limits. Just like the difference between a heavy smoker and chain smoker, not that either one of the two is very good for you. Maybe he should have had some tea before heading out, which felt appropriate considering the state of mind he was in. Perhaps he should stop at a convenience store on the way to the morgue.

Fuck it.

Backing out of the driveway, technically parking lot, became such a regular routine for Chauncey he barely put any thought into it. That might not be a good idea since he didn't recall looking in the rearview mirrors or turning his head around to see if anyone was coming. But he did make sure he didn't see any lights coming from either direction, so he could claim some type of precautionary method to his driving.

Not much but something is better than nothing, and it beats trying to get the last word in with everyone.

"Damn," he said. "Who do I really argue with? Just me and me alone! I get the last word in against myself which doesn't make sense, does it? I hope it's for the better, at least for focusing!"

At least in his own mind he tried to be rational, even though it felt like he had two minds about everything, or multiple minds for that matter. Could he have multiple personalities? That's a bit far fetched, but who knows? There has to be an underlying, or even undermining factor behind all of this.

"Stress," he told himself. "That's all, stress. I'm happy with my life but the mind and body can suffer from all kinds of negative effects if you're overworked, or overactive. Of course I've always had some minor form of depression despite not treating it, it's not that bad. Maybe its undiagnosed ADHD, anything's possible! I'll have to ask Triple B to find out if any type of treatment could put a black mark on my record. I should know by now considering how long I've been in this line of work! I guess you don't pay as much attention to formalities when you're a plain-clothes detective who operates independently."

When he finished talking to himself he barely noticed that he'd driven about a quarter of a mile down the road from his place. What really surprised him was not seeing another set of headlights from either direction so far. Not that he's complaining, at least some asshole wasn't tailgating him with high beams on! Coming from the opposite direction isn't so bad because they'll pass by you sooner instead of later. But considering it just got dark out and the rush hour may technically be over in Prime he still expected to see a good share of traffic. He couldn't complain, though, that meant it wouldn't take as long to get to the morgue.

Chauncey continued to feel a very strange sensation behind the wheel, nothing dangerous and definitely nowhere near feeling intoxicated. But he drove at a relatively high rate of speed yet it felt like the time was dragging. As he turned on to Main Street in Downtown Prime the sensation continued. Maybe two cars passed him going in the opposite direction and the only pedestrians he saw either got in or out of their parked vehicles. The most amazing part was hitting all green lights at every traffic stop he drove through, both in and past Downtown Prime. That should have picked up the momentum internally, as logic would dictate, but not tonight. To be fair it had turned into a slow day since interviewing Paul Raymond.

For some reason Chauncey tried to convince himself he was driving over a hundred miles per hour. Far from the truth since the odometer didn't come close to registering at half that speed, which is a good thing because even traveling at fifty miles an hour down Main Street looks like reckless driving. The visual of an excessive speed and a trancelike state, or even a dreamlike one kept him on his toes, but for those reasons it didn't feel very reassuring. It made him think he was feeling mild effects from psychedelic drugs that caused hallucinations, specifically mushrooms and LSD which he had very little exposure to. He did believe people who worked in law enforcement needed to set an example, kind of a practice what you preach or maintain a specific lifestyle to a certain extant, but many still needed to understand what it's like on the other side of the tracks, so to speak. In Chauncey's case he'd smoked more than his share of marijuana and had a handful of experiences with LSD and mushrooms, but the latter two were only on rare occasions as a young adult, long before he decided to pursue the career path that he did. While he wouldn't directly advocate smoking pot it didn't feel worthwhile most of the time to bust balls over a bowl or a few joints in this day and age. With Colorado benefiting as much as it had so quickly, who knew what could happen in the future?

Right before reaching the end of Main Street in Downtown Prime Chauncey started thinking about another classic b-movie called Death Race 2000. He couldn't remember very much about it except that it starred David Carradine and Sylvester Stallone right before having massive success with Rocky in 1976, and if memory served him right Roger Corman had some involvement with this picture, which made sense being a low-budget feature. Despite the title Chauncey hoped he'd survive long enough to arrive at the city morgue in one piece, and then some. He still felt optimistic enough to think that would be the case, now if only he could solve the case as soon as he got there.

Suddenly he remembered a specific scene from an early John Carpenter film Assault on Precinct 13 that had a speeding vehicle heading down a dark, narrow road. Not much different from Main Street in Downtown Prime at night except far more deserted. The driver, an inmate on death row, had to escape from a police station he'd been detained at due to a street gang keeping it under siege with the condition being he could head for the Mexican border as long as he contacted law enforcement beforehand.

He only made it so far.

Chauncey couldn't recall the actor's name playing that part but a lot of people would recognize him as the manager/trainer of Apollo Creed, played by Carl Weathers, in several of the Rocky movies. Despite a decent portrayal of a dangerous convict you felt a good vibe from this guy regardless, especially after explaining to his fellow inmate known as Napoleon Wilson that bad luck always followed him no matter what he did or where he went.

At least he admitted to being born under a bad sign.

Chauncey didn't believe in luck, or at least he didn't count on it for anything. You just do the best you can every day and get up and head out to do what you have to do. So this trancelike state he was in didn't help him very much, despite keeping him relatively calm. A lot of auto racers thrive on adrenaline and a need for speed but he wondered if any of them felt a sense of tranquility any time during the competition.

Who knows? Maybe he should try to find Death Race 2000 on DVD, it's probably pretty cheap and he didn't watch auto races enough to read into them successfully. Not that long ago online he read something about Roger Corman movies being available to Download or watch on YouTube for dirt cheap prices. He couldn't explain it but something felt more appealing about being able to hold a movie in your hands on disc or videotape if you still owned a VCR. He didn't like turning on a computer every time he wanted to watch something, unless it's random or obscure stuff you never saw on TV.

Man, to think that Roger Corman still knows how to make a quick buck after all his years in showbiz. Not bad for a guy who's at an age very close to the triple digits!

When Chauncey reached the end of Main Street all he needed to do was veer off to the right and go approximately half a mile down Loomis Road to reach his destination, which was also on the right. Soon he saw a brightly lit sign that read Montrose Morgue in the City of Prime. He didn't know much about the history of this place, except it had nothing to do with the late Ronnie Montrose or any of his songs like Rock Candy, Space Station #5, or Bad Motor Scooter. There was a Montrose family that existed for generations in Prime who were involved in it somehow, and the morgue itself was built on city property so the combination of the two went hand in hand. Besides that he didn't know anything and wasn't sure if anyone from the family still resided in the area, or were still alive for that matter.

At least they had somewhere to go when death knocked at their door, leaving Chauncey convinced that none of them needed to make reservations ahead of time.

As soon as Chauncey drove past the sign he took a right turn into the parking lot of the morgue. Within seconds he spotted Zack Larch, who he quickly remembered as being okay with being called Lurch, standing outside the front entrance of the main building with a wide-eyed stare even the Detective could spot from a distance. It wasn't creepy or unsettling from his point of view but a look from someone who just had a nerve-wracking experience. It surprised him he could sense that right away. He parked in a space closest to where Lurch was standing which was practically in front of the guy, probably reserved for employees only but very few cars were there and he wanted to know what was going on right away.

"How are you doing, Lurch?" asked Chauncey. "Something you wanted to show me?"

Lurch stood in the same spot under a dim fluorescent light by the front entrance, with a long pause before he'd say anything.

"Yeah," said Lurch, spoken softly somehow retaining a firm tone at the same time.

"Is Frosty here yet?" he asked, seconds afterward he heard a car behind him pulling into the parking lot. He looked back to see that it was none other than Frosty, who drove into the space next to Chauncey's car then got out and started to walk over to them. The Detective slowly walked up the steps to where Lurch was standing and Frosty followed.

"Am I parked in the wrong spot?" asked Chauncey.

"Don't worry about it," said Frosty. "That's not an issue right now, unless you're in a handicapped spot."

Point taken, he thought to himself, a split second after that he was surprised he even asked that question. He honestly didn't think he'd get as much of the answer that he received from Frosty when you considered Lurch had called them insisting they had to get down there. Using the speed dial to get in touch with Frosty, Triple B, and Chauncey was the closest thing to a 9-1-1 call, it seemed.

To be fair neither Chauncey nor Frosty knew what they were about to see, and Lurch hadn't said much in great detail about why they needed to be there other than it had something to do with the body found earlier today at the Woodward Hotel. Chauncey didn't take the guy seriously after saying something about seeing the corpse with the lights off, but he remembered the skin tone of it as being one he'd never seen before. He should have physically felt a part of the body, like the upper chest area or the palms of the hands, to get some kind of clue what he was dealing with, if possible. In his mind nothing glowed about the body upon the first glance, but curiosity grew wondering what he was about to see.

An awkward moment of silence took place while the three of them stood together under the fluorescent light in front of the main door. Definitely a bit more uncomfortable for Chauncey compared to when he first arrived and received what you wouldn't exactly consider a formal greeting from Lurch. They faced one another and stood approximately a four foot distance from each other creating a triangular shape.

Someone had to break the ice.

"So what's the deal?" asked Frosty.

"Don't know yet for sure," said Lurch.

"Is that the reason why you wanted us to get down here right away?" added Chauncey.

"Some kind of indoor UFO sighting?" asked Frosty.

"If you want to call it that," answered Lurch. "Let's go inside so you can see for yourselves."

Without saying another word, Lurch turned slightly to the left to open the door not paying attention to the small doorstop falling on the mat then headed inside. Frosty immediately followed with Chauncey being last, which made sense in his mind since he didn't work there. He considered himself a guest at the Montrose Morgue, so he had to follow rules dictated to him by Frosty and to a lesser extent Lurch. But Frosty couldn't make any decision much less give an opinion until a presentation was completed by Lurch.

Chauncey stood still for a second when he stepped inside. He waited for the door to shut all the way before catching up to Lurch and Frosty. At this time of night all of the entrances to the morgue could only be accessed by employees. This explained why Lurch used the doorstop to keep it open along with being oblivious to the thing dropping. Chauncey hadn't spent much time there but during regular business hours a lot of people who worked there naturally wanted to go out on their lunch break, most likely to an eatery on Main Street. Some of them might have been at Cameron's Coffee Café earlier today. Surprisingly he didn't know very many of them, in his line of work he figured he'd quickly recognize a lot of them right away. However, working in forensics the job requires you to spend most of your time indoors.

"At least you get to keep cool," Chauncey said, just talking to himself.

"What's that?" said Frosty.

"Nothing," answered Chauncey, raising his voice a bit.

"You sure?" he asked.

"Just thinking out loud," confirmed Chauncey.

He was surprised the guy could hear that well considering the distance was at least ten feet between the two of them with Lurch being further away. Chauncey caught up to Frosty and walked right behind him to display a 100% focus on the case, which he felt was very important at this moment.

The three of them walked to the end of the corridor toward the rear section of the building from the main entrance. When they arrived at the last door on the left side Lurch opened it and headed inside with Frosty and Chauncey directly behind him then walked over to a table, or slab as Chauncey liked to say, located roughly in the middle of the room. As expected a body was lying there with a sheet covering it. Lurch stood at the front section while Frosty and Chauncey stood beside him. He quickly removed part of the sheet covering the head and upper chest area and waited for a response.

"So what's the deal?" asked Frosty.

"Yeah," added Chauncey. "It's the same corpse you brought here from the Woodward Hotel, so what?"

"Tell me you're at least slightly disturbed by its appearance," said Lurch.

Chauncey and Frosty quickly glanced at one another causing internal jolts of nervousness. But what they saw they were already prepared for.

"We saw this already," said Frosty.

"We know it's something we've never seen before," added Chauncey.

"I made it clear that this would be a top priority."

"I know," said Lurch. "But I didn't think this could wait until tomorrow morning."

"What?"

Lurch covered the top part of the body with the sheet faster than he removed it then looked Frosty straight in the eye ready to give him important instructions.

"Turn off the lights," said Lurch, slightly shifting his eyes off of Frosty toward the light switch panel next to the door.

"Alright," said Frosty, not sounding too excited as he walked back over to the door to do so, slightly annoyed with Lurch putting the sheet over the body again, making him think the guy was trying to put on a magic act.

The lights went off. A few seconds would pass before Lurch removed the sheet again. But when he did there was no need to put the lights back on.

What the three of them set their eyes was something they had never seen before, especially true when Lurch pulled the sheet off the body entirely. The only clothing remaining on her was a tank top and a pair of shorts worn underneath what she'd had on earlier today. Lurch and Colin had removed the rest of it a few hours ago as ordered by Frosty, who originally planned to conduct a full examination the following morning.

Those plans were about to change.

The female corpse wasn't glowing, but that description might be used by an everyday person. With most of the body exposed it somehow lit the room in an eerily similar way to simply having the regular lights on.

The skin tone was only slightly brighter than the bulbs normally used, but that was the only difference.

Someone had to break the silence.

"What's happening here?" asked Frosty, in a mixture of tones no one could pinpoint, if that makes sense.

"If you can't answer that question," said Chauncey.

"Nobody can!" added Lurch.

Frosty, without hesitation, walked back over to where Lurch and Chauncey were and stood between them. He didn't think twice about turning the lights on again. It practically felt like they never went off to begin with. He was unable to come up with any kind of hypothesis much less theorize what the three of them were looking at. He checked for a pulse to make sure the visual condition of the corpse had nothing to do with it being alive or dead. He already did that hours ago but decided to do it again since he really had no idea where else to start the examination. He couldn't think of anyone to call that might help. Lurch, even Chauncey, could offer assistance but what would that accomplish?

"Maybe I should just call 9-1-1 and ask for someone who has expertise in God knows what!" stated Frosty.

"You're really stuck, aren't you?" asked Chauncey.

"I've never seen anything like this," said Lurch.

"No one has," said Frosty.

"Are you sure about that?"

"I don't know where to begin!"

"Do you need anything?" asked Chauncey. "You know this isn't my field of expertise, I wouldn't have the first clue what to do here."

"I know," said Frosty, with a surprisingly understanding tone. "That's why this is my job and you're the Detective."

"What are you going to do?"

"I've got a long night ahead of me."

"I'll stay and help if you want," offered Lurch.

"Come back first thing tomorrow morning," said

Frosty.

"Are you sure?"

"I'll need someone to help me with the paperwork."

"What time should I come in?"

"The earlier the better," confirmed Frosty.

"Gotcha," said Lurch.

"I'll get back you as soon as possible," Frosty told Chauncey. "Specifically when the exams are done, when that will be I have no idea!"

"The phone's always on," said Chauncey.

"Don't wait up."

"It'll be hard not to."

The Detective placed his hand on the corpse, specifically on the upper part of the chest a few inches below the neck. Despite the strange skin tone nothing felt unusual. For some reason he sensed the skin itself might be thicker than it's supposed to be, but there's was no way to explain that.

He decided to keep that opinion to himself. He wasn't sure if Frosty saw him touch the corpse to begin with.

"Where are you going to start?" asked Chauncey.

"With x-rays, I think," answered Frosty. "I'll just keep things simple, go step by step."

"Good idea."

"You want us to go?" asked Lurch.

"I think so," said Frosty. "Just do one more thing."

"What's that?"

"Turn the lights back on when you leave."

"You got it."

Chauncey started to walk out first. He looked back and saw Lurch directly behind him, flipping the lights on.

Let there be light, thought Chauncey, with or without power created by Thomas Edison.

CHAPTER 10

I'M BACK WHERE I STARTED, Chauncey thought.

That wasn't necessarily a bad thing it just meant he was back home again. He sat at the kitchen table doing nothing, not so much as waiting for a cup of coffee. Something he'd been so accustomed to brewing constantly whether he wanted to stay awake or not.

A lot weighed on his mind, naturally, which was keeping him up. His thought process was at a standstill, if that's even possible. He didn't feel restless or fatigued, or anywhere in between the two. The only way to describe where his head is at could be considered an emotional roadblock. He wanted to feel something yet somehow didn't feel able to. Perhaps Dr. Phil might see this as a territory requiring a massive amount of exploration. Unfortunately, despite what winds up in the press you can't just throw it all out there and tell the world everything while conducting a private investigation. In most homicide cases law enforcement hardly ever provide every single detail to the media, unless the case goes cold right away and they haven't uncovered a single clue.

At this point both ladies in his life were sound asleep. It was almost midnight. Ali had been in the upstairs bedroom for the past couple of hours. She'd finished her last aerobics class when he got called down to Montrose Morgue. She'd kept her regular schedule as usual, not that he needed to think twice about it, and hadn't put any thought into it when he left a note for her earlier.

Not that he needed to. They'd been together long enough that he pretty much always knew where to find her, and he didn't have to spend a lot of time looking for her. Detective work requires him to be anywhere and everywhere at any given time, and he tried the best he could to keep her posted in regards to where he'd be, even if it's just a note on a post-it stating something simple like: WENT 2 MORGUE.

Common courtesy, a lot better than dealing with controlling spouses!

The other "Lady" in his life was laying down a few feet from the TV by the bottom left hand side of the mattress kept there. She'd probably napped on that for a while and he hadn't noticed, partially expecting her to wander into the kitchen any time now. As long as she's content that's enough for him. Being a dog she has no choice but to rely on Chauncey all the time, but he often wondered who admired the other one more.

He started to reminisce about his childhood and recalled how content he was regardless of what went on around him. He kept himself entertained with stuff like model trains, comic books, and reruns of older television shows like Alfred Hitchcock Presents or The Outer Limits. For some reason, the suspense in those science fiction and mystery types of shows didn't get to him. Not bad for a seven year old, still scared by a lot of it but not resulting in endless nightmares throughout his upbringing, perhaps due to being part of a generation born after everything originally broadcast in black and white along with the MPAA creating ratings for colorized feature films allowing the so-called adult language, nudity, and increasing violence.

Chauncey first heard about horror movies that were far more dark and violent than anything he'd been used to around the age of nine or ten. The Friday the 13th series had made at least four or five pictures by then and the Halsey brothers Mitt and Geoff who lived a few houses up the road raved on and on about them. It was quite a bit to take in but Chauncey became intrigued by what he learned. Video stores were popping up everywhere, renting out movies on VHS videotapes to anyone who invested in a VCR. The ability to watch a movie when you wanted to instead of waiting to see it at a certain time on television or in the local theaters created a new type of freedom. In this day and age it might not seem like that big of a deal, especially if you didn't watch a lot of TV or movies to begin with, but this was the beginning of a new era.

Where to begin was almost impossible.

Laserdiscs came out first but not many people got into that, Chauncey never liked the fact they were as big as vinyl LPs and vaguely remembered two families owning them. Even now he can appreciate someone keeping their vinyl/record collection for music related stuff. After all they are considered collectors items so it's not that a big deal if you don't have a turntable ready for use, plus there's something still appealing about having certain albums you can show off to friends who are fans of various bands. Chauncey understood that feeling if you bought the first copies of Fleetwood Mac's early albums with Peter Green or MC5's Kick out the Jams, which he had floating around on CD somewhere. Plus the massive number of products put out by artists for release, or re-

release, exclusively on vinyl. A bit on the expensive side but there's got to be something to it, especially if a band like Pearl Jam gets into it and you considered the fact that their rise to fame came at a time when you could only buy new music on CDs or cassette tapes. He never took the time to research what their reasons might have been, but knowing enough about how the band did things after working against the largest ticket agency in the country at the time the logic behind it was simple: a matter of choice.

About a month ago Chauncey took the time to make a trip to some of his favorite collector's shops. The first place he stopped in he discovered an early Dr. Who soundtrack on vinyl. The reason he spotted it was simply from walking past that particular section in the store to check out the new DVDs. He wouldn't have made an effort to look for it either. By chance it just happened to be the first thing displayed at the very front of the brand new releases of electronic music. He honestly believed that several other customers had rummaged through it earlier and one of them randomly placed it in front when they were done. The asking price was a little over forty dollars, which isn't too bad for vinyl.

It's time to make a new investment. A turntable specifically, which will go nicely with the VCR which surprisingly still worked and DVD player, eventually he'd purchase another unit with a Blu-Ray combo, but not anything exclusively for just that. Videotapes he could let go of to an extent but he wanted to hold on to his DVD collection as long as possible. The two disc formats should remain a choice. If vinyl can make a huge comeback, why get rid of DVDs completely? Pearl Jam can appreciate that. Perhaps he should send a letter to the band, specifically to their singer Eddie Vedder, handwritten of course! There's one guy who'd dig communicating with someone not relying exclusively on emails!

No one likes to talk about it but people still enjoy finding Christmas cards in their mailboxes. That's probably the only thing making it worthwhile to step out into three feet of snow! It doesn't apply to anyone living in or near Prime, California, but in plenty of other parts of the country! Folks living on the opposite side of the continent like upstate New York or New England might agree that it gets pretty cold around here, but Chauncey would still bet on this area as being an easier climate to live in and you don't need to put together a polar bear swim team. Even now in Prime's coldest month of January he could walk knee deep into the swamps of the Badlands or swim in Prime River if he really wanted to, especially in the early evening with the sun shining bright all day, heating up the water significantly. That still makes Chauncey a bit of a wimp as far as he's concerned but could if he had to!

So what?! Chauncey thought. If he wanted to go for a swim a phone call to Prime State University and Sergeant Matheson could make arrangements to use the indoor pool in a second. In fact he'd be allowed to use it any time day or night as long as the Phys. Ed classes weren't in session. This thought convinced him he wasn't at that emotional roadblock anymore, but needed to focus big time and pool privileges wouldn't solve anything!

Maybe he could go on YouTube for a while and watch a few videos on there he'd seen countless times already. Something that would motivate him to go to sleep, it sounds contradictory, but it's effective for someone like Chauncey. The strange mind a Private Detective has. Then again, he never worked closely with any other detectives, so maybe it's just him. Perhaps he could ask Triple B to seek out retired detectives for consultation. It sounds like a perfect gig for his later years.

Chauncey Winfield, CPD, Consultant for Private

Detectives.

He liked the sound of that.

Right now he was grateful he didn't have to resort to playing Pokemon games on his phone as a hobby, or a distraction as far as he was concerned. Granted, when he was fifteen he did have that Nintendo handheld thing Game Boy. All he could remember about it was playing Tetris, but nothing else. It did seem like a pretty high-tech thing at the time, but he was fifteen. In this day and age men older than him were seeking fulfillment with Pokemon.

There's living proof that you can't blame everything on the current generation of kids. He didn't like hearing the adults putting all the blame on the kids when he was growing up and he didn't like hearing it now. Every generation, be it kids or adults, has their own set of problems, similar to a certain extent but cropping up in different ways. A lot of people would tell him he didn't understand because he never had kids.

He didn't care.

"Game Boy," he said. "Is it one word or two?"

"Detectives need their sleep," a voice said softly.

Chauncey felt two hands placed softly on his shoulders. Ali stood behind him yet he hadn't heard her enter the kitchen, he looked down and saw Lady sitting by his right foot staring up at him.

"Do you know?" he asked.

"Put it to rest," she said.

"You're right."

That was the last thing Chauncey said before getting up and went upstairs with her to the bedroom.

Lady followed.

CHAPTER 11

I<small>T WAS EXACTLY</small> 8:30 A<small>M</small> the moment Chauncey woke up. He'd shifted his eyes to the left for a split second to look at the alarm clock on the table next to him which verified that. He hadn't set it last night to be up at a certain time, he didn't need to.

Ali had already left, and he vaguely remembered something about her having a class early this morning. He never kept tabs on this stuff, meaning he never wrote it down. He was a bit surprised he didn't hear her wake up, though. She always made enough food for the two of them. He hadn't so much as heard the alarm on her phone go off, either. Then again it wasn't unusual for her to wake up beforehand, but he wouldn't have objected to an early morning breakfast.

He had a pretty good idea why she didn't wake him up.

Detectives need their sleep.

She's right about that.

Chauncey glanced over to the right to see Lady resting

on the right side of the bed, close to the bottom end. He remembered her following them up here, but had no recollection of her hopping up there to join them. She probably slept on the floor for a while first, most likely in the hallway at the top of the stairs. That's a favorite spot for her, and for all he knew she didn't attempt to get up here until after Ali left. Depending on her mood she may not have been interested in treats or leftovers, influencing her decision to remain upstairs.

"I must have fallen asleep the instant I hit the pillow," Chauncey said, not to anyone in particular despite keeping half an eye on the dog.

He was somewhat relieved he'd slept the whole night without interruption. Not even feeling the need to get up for a trip to the bathroom. He'd cherish more nights like that. It's the little things in life that make a difference!

The ring on the cell phone went off. Chauncey reached for it on the nightstand beside him. The first glance reminded him he forgot to plug it into the charger overnight. A little annoying since he was usually pretty good about remembering to do that. When he reached for the phone he turned it slightly sideways to see if he'd recognize the number on the caller ID. Not paying attention to the fact that it was at the very edge of the nightstand and accidentally let it fall to the floor.

"Fuck!" he shouted.

Now all he cared about was reaching down as fast as possible to grab hold of it. At this point he didn't care who it was. Triple B, Sergeant Matheson, or Frosty, the girlfriend, the dog somehow being able to find a way to play a prank, or some random census bureau or telemarketers selling something he wouldn't give a shit about.

The goal was to answer the phone.

"Hello?" he said, in a surprisingly calm tone.

"Is this Detective Chauncey Winfield?" asked a female voice on the other end of the line, a bit dryly.

"Yes."

"This is Jane Newton returning your call."

"Oh, hi," he said. "I've been trying to get in touch with you."

"I know," she said. "Professor Horace and Paul Raymond both told me I should call you."

"I can't remember," he responded. "Did I leave a message for you at your office extension?"

"I don't know. I'm at my desk right now. I received plenty of calls the whole time I was gone. I haven't started looking through any of the messages yet. I got your cell number from Professor Horace."

"I see. That makes sense. Did you know Roy Cumberland or Stacy O'Connell?"

"Yes," she said, then paused for a moment. "I knew both of them, very sad."

"You met up with Mr. Cumberland the night he died," said Chauncey. "Can you shed some light on that?"

"Not much to tell. We had dinner together, not a date, he was very interested in what was going on here at Widen Laboratories."

"Did he say anything about Widen Laboratories or Prime State University for that matter?"

"How so?" she asked.

"Derogatory," he answered.

Chauncey wasn't sure if he worded that appropriately. Being derogatory, at least in his way of thinking, had little to do with going against the establishment.

He didn't have the first clue what he was asking her. Too early for this question and answer session, coffee needs to be had first.

"I don't know about that," she said. "He had a way about him I found interesting. He seemed to want to understand all sides to things."

"Three sides to the story," said Chauncey. "And then some. Am I on the right track?"

"That sounds about right."

"Can we meet later?"

"Of course," she said. "Do you like coffee?"

"You're a mind reader!" he answered.

"Let me get back to you," said Jane. "I'll see what time I can meet with you here at my office later today."

"At Widen Labs?"

"Sure."

"Will that require special clearances?"

"With me," she said. "Not exactly, I'll call you back as soon as I can, okay?"

"Great!" he said. "I'll talk to you later."

He hung up his phone, if you will. Usually he waited for the person on the other end to do that. This time his sudden good mood got him to do it first. It's nice when someone who's connected to a case takes the incentive to track you down. Most times you have to expect it to be the other way around.

Chauncey immediately sat up, pulled the blanket off, turned to the left and placed his feet on the floor. He had a gut feeling that things might go smoothly today. Plans were being put into motion by Jane Newton with the first call, and he could take his sweet time getting his shit together since she most likely wouldn't get back to him for hours.

He stood up then made his way to the bedroom door, which had either been left open all night or Ali had left it open when she got up for work. Perhaps Lady followed her downstairs when she made breakfast hoping for some leftovers then after that came back upstairs and pushed the door open again to get back on the bed and keep her master company.

Chauncey honestly had no clue why he was contemplating all of these possible scenarios, except maybe because he had quickly realized that he couldn't get into some deep in-depth conversation or question and answer session with Jane Newton. He had to give himself more credit, what he was trying to do was get the gears in motion inside his head so he could concentrate better when he met up with this Jane Newton. Not bad considering he woke up at 8:30 in the morning and hadn't made his first cup of coffee yet!

After passing through the open doorway he turned right and down the hall he went. Not much to tell after that besides walking downstairs and turning left into the kitchen, which was great since he didn't have to put any thought into it much less use turn signals. They'd be useful in a Crowded House and heavy traffic, but Don't Dream It's Over. Your day is just starting, Chauncey.

His cup had already been placed in the Keurig with the usual flavor ready to go at this time of the morning, the Breakfast Blend specifically. Chauncey was pretty sure Ali had set this up before leaving for work, convinced she wanted to have breakfast with him this morning but remained adamant he needed his sleep yet didn't want to say anything more about it.

He pushed the device down to start the coffee brewing, a split second after that he realized he forgot to check if enough water had been added.

Big deal, he'll find out in seconds if that's the case.

It wasn't.

His significant other was usually pretty good about this stuff.

As he waited Chauncey turned around to place his cell phone on the kitchen table. In another minute or two the Green Mountain Breakfast Blend flavored coffee would be ready. Strange, if he had some type of celebrity status he wouldn't mind being a spokesman for Green Mountain coffee, even if it made him seem like a sellout and got paid a huge amount of money.

On the left was the refrigerator, when he turned back around he opened it to get the half & half he always needed to have with every cup of coffee he made. Enough time had passed for his cup, or much technically, to be filled. He grasped the handle and pulled it towards him and poured a small amount of the half & half in. He placed the half & half on the counter, not sure if he'd be having a second cup, much less finish this first one.

He knew the answer to that.

So did everyone remotely acquainted with him personally or professionally throughout the years.

After feeling the first taste, barely the first sip, the cell phone went off again. Chauncey turned back around so he could face the kitchen table again. He leaned down slightly and reached forward attempting to use his right hand to grab it while holding the coffee with his left. Being in a rushed mode he used too much of his strength when the tips of his fingers touched the phone he pushed it across the kitchen table causing it to fall to the kitchen floor.

"Again," said Chauncey. "I ought to take up air hockey! Who knows if that's a score but it's worth a shot!"

He placed his coffee on the kitchen table and rushed over to the other side to grab his phone. He kneeled down and got back up in a matter of seconds then pressed the answer button to take the call and placed it against his ear.

Again he forgot to check the caller ID.

"Hello?" he said.

"Hey," said the voice on the other end.

"Who is this?" he asked.

"Frosty," answered Frosty, naturally.

"What's up?"

"Have I got some stories to tell you," stated Frosty.

"Yeah?" asked Chauncey. "Is it about the Jane Doe?"

"Sort of," said Frosty. "Come in later and we'll discuss

that one. Like I said I worked all night on that and the x-rays alone tell a story."

"What else you got?"

"I got some of the autopsy results back, the other two victims specifically."

"Roy Cumberland and Stacy O'Connell?" asked Chauncey.

"Those are the ones," answered Frosty, in a lighter tone.

"Are they interesting?"

"I think so. I have never found this in anyone in all the years I've done this."

"Found what exactly?"

"What was in their digestive systems, the food that I found in each of them is nothing unusual. Probably matches up to whatever meals they had before their deaths, if anyone ate with them."

"I can find out for sure with one of them," said Chauncey. "I just received a call from someone who I'm pretty sure was the last person to see Roy Cumberland alive, I know they had dinner together."

"Good to know," added Frosty.

"Will you get to the point?!"

"Sorry."

"What else did you find?"

"It's a little bizarre."

"What's bizarre?" asked Chauncey, calming down a bit.

"It just doesn't make sense," answered Frosty. "Snake venom was detected in both of their digestive systems."

Chauncey kept quiet for a minute. He'd never heard anything like this either, ever. He tried to stay positive.

"We got a lead," he said, sounding optimistic.

"I don't know about that," said Frosty. "Like I said you can't make sense of it."

"Why not?" asked Chauncey.

"Swallowing snake venom is not fatal!"

"Really?" asked Chauncey.

"When's the last time you heard about someone dying from drinking snake venom?" asked Frosty, sounding more intense.

"You're right about that," said Chauncey. "I've watched a lot of stuff on the Discovery Channel about reptiles, venomous ones in particular and it never got brought up once."

"Exactly!" exclaimed Frosty. "So why would this stuff be in their systems? It's injected into the bloodstream, the result of being bitten! There were no bite wounds on either of the victims!"

"Not as far as I knew, no."

"Did you look into their backgrounds at all?"

"I found out quite a bit about that Roy Cumberland guy, but Stacy O'Connell not so much."

"And?" asked Frosty, sounding a bit demanding.

"I doubt either one of them belonged to cults requiring them to drink snake venom, animal blood, or anything else that doesn't belong in a shot glass."

"Can you get down here anytime soon?"

"Sure."

"We've got a lot to talk about."

"Okay."

Chauncey waited for Frosty to hang up the phone.

He started thinking, should he call Professor Horace about this? No, it's best to wait until after he meets with Frosty.

He hasn't found out everything yet, much less seen anything.

Jane Newton will get back to him when she gets back to him.

It's time to shower and get dressed and make a return trip to the Montrose Morgue. He heard the sound of tiny footsteps, or paws, enter the kitchen.

Naturally it was little Lady, he looked down at her feeling the need to say something to somebody.

"Back to the morgue I go," he said.

CHAPTER 12

WHEN CHAUNCEY RETURNED to the Montrose Morgue for the second time it felt like he never left. The traffic he encountered on Main Street on the way over hadn't deterred him. Naturally more cars were on the road since it was midmorning. The majority of the working class in Prime operated on the traditional 9 to 5 schedule, as expected. Surprisingly he found a decent parking space rather quickly and not far from the one he had the night before, the most reassuring part being a legitimate spot for visitors and he wouldn't have to worry about being ticketed or towed. He was just grateful he didn't have to put money in a meter.

After locking up the car he walked over to the same entrance he went through the first time. An employee, probably an RN, stood outside the door using her left foot to keep it propped open while finishing a cigarette. She probably left her badge inside.

"You hear to see Frosty?" she asked.

"Yeah," he answered. "He's been at it all night. Did he

come up for air?"

"Briefly," she said. "He poked his head out the door a couple of minutes ago and told me he was expecting someone, Detective Chauncey, right?"

"You got it."

"I thought so. He just picked me at random since I was going outside for a cigarette."

"Random courtesies are just as good as common courtesies."

"They can be."

"Thanks especially for waiting at the door," said Chauncey. "And you are?"

"Danielle Locke," she said, pointing at her nametag. "I work on the first floor, too, right down the hall from Frosty."

"I should have noticed that right away."

"Nobody's perfect."

"Not enough coffee in me, either."

Chauncey took another step forward and reached for the door handle. After grabbing it and pulling it forward he entered and RN Danielle Locke followed. A handful of others employed here were present in the corridor, very easy to determine by the proper dress code for their positions. Not like it was, but formalities still played a key role in the medical profession, at least to a certain extent.

Despite observing all of this Chauncey didn't read into it any further, barely making a mental note of it. Still he felt a little more alert after the brief interaction with that last person, the RN named Danielle Locke, he reminded himself. Try to remember who she is, at least while you're here. In case you see her again after talking to Frosty, she's smart enough to catch you looking at her nametag!

He didn't need to be directed or escorted to his destination. It was very easy remembering to head toward the last door on the left side. It may have seemed like a bit of a walk since it was at the rear section of the building, but with the foot traffic only being a handful of employees it was nothing compared to the road traffic on Main Street.

Montrose Morgue is technically the name of the facility and considerably large for a morgue itself, but with Prime being an urban setting it does high-volume business for the city. They're the only game in town for the dead. Prime's Assisted Living Center for the Elderly is also located in the building, which makes perfect sense if the residents are close to death, anyway. That's Chauncey's take on it. He wondered how far in advance you could sign up for these services even though he was nowhere close to the retirement age.

Remembering that RN's name and briefly contemplating his retirement had taken up enough time between entering the facility and arriving at the door where he'd find Frosty. Upon entering one last thing came to mind: Danielle Locke, that's the name.

The Detective arrived at the last door on the left, wasting no time entering the room to see Frosty turn his head and stand up straight without blinking an eye. Chauncey was the only person the coroner expected to see so there was no need for a grand entrance. The conversation would begin after taking a couple of steps down a small staircase and walking towards where the guy was standing.

"Right after you left last night it didn't take long to figure out we had something never seen before," said Frosty. "Just taking a few x-rays proved that."

"Do x-rays have any real significance in autopsies in this day and age?" asked Chauncey.

"Not as far as I'm concerned," answered Frosty. "But a first glance at this shit and it's all you need!"

"Seriously?" asked Chauncey.

"You think seeing this corpse glow in the dark last

night was nuts? That's only the beginning!"

Frosty shifted his head for a second so he could look at the corpse again then shifted it back to look Chauncey right in the eye.

"I'm not going to begin to go over everything I found last night," said Frosty. "I'll keep it plain and simple."

"You put a lot of time into this," said Chauncey. "You did an overnighter to find out everything you needed to, primarily to help me out. I'll bet you need to get some shuteye. Detectives certainly do."

'You're right about that, but I won't get a good night's sleep for a long time much less during the day. Not after all of this!"

"This corpse glows in the dark!" declared Chauncey, pointing at the woman's body on the slab as he liked to call it, also grateful that Frosty didn't ask to turn off the lights again. "Did you actually think I expected the findings to be normal?"

"You're right," said Frosty, cooling down a bit. "I mean who would? Sorry about that."

"Don't sweat it. Nobody could've expected this. That Lurch guy was the one who called us in here, did you guys talk about it?"

"Yeah, I even had him sign a confidentiality agreement."

"What's in it?

"He can't discuss the case with anyone until, at the very least, the autopsy is officially completed."

"Good idea."

A moment of silence began. Not because of patriotism, their minds needed to rest for a second before exploring this subject any further.

It would be like no other.

"Out with it," Chauncey stated firmly, he had a smile on his face to show that he was just expressing humor by busting balls.

"No problem," said Frosty, holding up a manila folder

with some sheets of paper inside.

"What's this?" he asked.

"Just hold on to it," said Frosty. "Keep it hidden somewhere safe, don't tell anyone about it. Not even your girlfriend, not even your dog!"

"Is an explanation about to begin?"

"Of course, I'll start off by saying it's a blessing that Xerox machines are still widely in use."

"I take it this is required reading?" asked Chauncey, raising the folder in the air for a split second to show what he was talking about.

"Sight reading," said Frosty. "But it's not sheet music by any stretch of the imagination. Call it Autopsy 101."

"I'm all ears. I'll be all eyes later on when I sit down to take a look at this."

"You'll need to be, I'll tell you that much."

"Are you beating around the bush or do you plan to begin the explanation needed here?"

"Of course," said Frosty. "I just don't know where explaining all of this really begins. Montrose Morgue is the only place in the city where all the dead corpses are legally allowed to be, but that's only the human corpses. There's more to it with this one."

"More human than human?" asked Chauncey with the sense of humor showing itself again, but only slightly.

"If that was the case it would probably still be alive… and I'd be very optimistic!"

"Is there less to explain somehow?"

"There's more here but I can't explain what I found! Simple x-rays were proof of something else altogether! All we're equipped to deal with at the morgue are human beings but that was only part of what I found!"

"Only part of what you found?"

"I did a lot of research online last night," said Frosty. "That's what I spent most of my time doing. I had to check the anatomies of other living species to figure out what I was dealing with, and I still don't have a lot of answers."

"So there's another animal inside this one?" asked Chauncey.

"You could say that, partially. Chauncey I found reptile DNA here! But that's not the worst of it! I can't figure out what kind of reptile it is! She is, or was, human with reptile DNA factored in as well, but the rest of it is... unknown."

"Unknown?"

"Yeah," said Frosty, in a quieter tone.

Chauncey had to think for a minute, and an idea came to him very quickly. He didn't want to jump to any conclusions, but had a pretty good idea about where to start.

"Reptiles," said Chauncey. "Start with snakes, go back online and look up everything you can. Compare all the information you find with what you found starting with the x-rays, step by step in a coroner's method of course."

"Just snakes?" asked Frosty.

"Yes," answered Chauncey. "Unless you think it's a good idea to process the findings at random for comparison."

"I didn't process anything. I researched everything online here. That's why I just poked my head outside real quick to tell someone to keep an eye out for you."

"Good idea. Keep a lid on all of it until we know what were dealing with."

"If I researched and processed everything using the Morgue's central computer everything would go on record right away. They can find everything I look up on the computer in here but it's not considered as anything official. Unless I look up what the best way is to poison someone to death and a body arrives the next day and that's how it happened."

"It buys us time."

"What's next on your agenda?" asked Frosty.

"Going to meet up with someone I've been waiting to talk to for a while," said Chauncey. "A person of interest since this whole investigation started."

"Who is it?"

"Her name's Jane Newton. She works at Widen Laboratories and Prime State University, the latter just occasionally according to Sergeant Matheson. She's on the payroll, I know that much."

"It took this long to get in touch with her?"

"She left town the night Roy Cumberland died, I don't know where she went but I plan to find out when we get together."

"Is that where you're going right now?"

"No, she called me this morning. I'm supposed to see her at Widen Labs sometime today. I need to wait for her next phone call to confirm the exact time."

Chauncey and Frosty paused for a moment neither of them sure who'd speak up next.

Frosty broke the ice, so to speak.

"They have tight security there," he said.

"I've heard that," added Chauncey. "Hopefully my first trip will help me determine fact vs. fiction, depending on what I get to see."

"I hope you don't have to put on a radiation suit or anything resembling that."

"Same here if that happens I won't have the slightest idea as to what's fact vs. fiction."

"That's what they're hoping for!"

"Corporations, conspiracies, and fascism," said Frosty. "The list it goes on and on, does it ever end?"

The two of them laughed together for a second until Frosty spoke up again.

"Of course not!" he stated.

"I'll talk to you sooner instead of later," said Chauncey.

The Detective quickly turned around and headed

towards the door. Back up the small staircase he went and exited he did. Down the corridor he went and headed outside. This time no employees were present anywhere. At least a handful of them he passed on his way in, now it felt just as quiet as the night before. Danielle Locke was nowhere to be seen either, not that he expected to.

He was just grateful for total recall, despite only a brief visit.

CHAPTER 13

CHAUNCEY HAD NOTHING ELSE TO DO after meeting up with Frosty. The only thing that came to mind was to go back to Cameron's Coffee Café again. He had to wait for a call from Jane Newton, when that would happen he had no idea. He hoped she'd be the type to keep her word on something like that. Of course pulling double duty at Widen Labs and Prime State University most likely meant she had some sense of responsibility. Sergeant Matheson claimed she was on the payroll at the school, obviously not in a high position, but being full time at Widen Labs and working closely with Professor Horace emphasized some importance.

Suddenly his phone went off. A quick glance would show that someone left a text message. He checked the message section and it simply read: 1pm OK?

Jane Newton, obviously, prompting him to text back with one simple word: Absolutely!

Hopefully she interpreted that as a positive attitude combined with great enthusiasm. Not really the case, but he definitely wanted this get together to occur as soon as possible. The last piece of the text conversation came from her saying: C U then!

That works for Chauncey, despite her being very informal for someone he talked to for the first time early this morning. A quick check of the time read it was shortly past 12pm, meaning he didn't have to wait long. He got up and walked over to the register to pay for everything, not much except for a cup of coffee with free refills and a tip, the full amount he spent equaled the price of two coffees. It was the least he could do, the least he wanted to do.

He was a bit surprised to see only one other person in there, a guy sitting at a table on the opposite side of the restaurant eating a Danish and reading a newspaper. That would change after he left, in a little while people who worked in many different places on Main Street in Downtown Prime would arrive in droves. He'd been a regular here long enough to know the pattern.

However, he had no desire to wait around and witness the masses pile in. Something he had seen enough of already. A place like that didn't need to let many people in there to justify labeling it as a mob scene. Cameron's Coffee Café was considered by everyone to be small business compared to all the other eateries in Prime, be it a fancy restaurant or fast food joints. Chauncey hoped it would remain in business for many more years, maybe until he became eligible for retirement. That may sound idealistic, but you never know.

Upon exiting Chauncey headed towards his car parked in the space located directly in front of Cameron's Coffee Café. He was grateful he'd arrived there early enough to get it since every space was now occupied in both the front and rear of his vehicle, and it wouldn't be long before someone took that spot. Immediately after starting the engine and inching out someone stopped and put their directional on anticipating his departure. For some reason he didn't mind knowing he'd put enough money in the meter for this person about to pull in, who could probably enjoy their entire lunch break without having to worry about getting a citation.

Random courtesies can be as good as common courtesies, if not better. He got reminded about that this morning at a morgue, of all places.

Now to make the trek to Widen Laboratories, feeling strange he already knew how to get there despite never setting foot on the property before. First he had to get out of Downtown Prime and on to Route 21, head in the direction of the Badlands but get off at the exit before. Not much had been there prior to the company buying all the land there, practically deserted except for a few dilapidated houses. If anyone had still lived in one of them or retained any ownership, the bank would have bought them all off long before a purchase had been made. Chauncey had never known anyone who resided down there.

The area had been considered as nothing more than forgotten housing projects until Widen Laboratories came along, worthless land of no interest to anyone. Decades ago Montrose Morgue may have sent people down there to knock on doors randomly and ask if anyone had died recently and offered to take the corpses off their hands. Back then most of the residents were very poor and unable to afford a telephone, cell phones and voice mails were unheard of. Chauncey found it disturbing enough that the Woodward Hotel had been empty so long in an area still populated and active regardless of the Jane Doe, or whatever it was, discovered there.

Processing all of these thoughts on the way there would keep Chauncey from getting riled up over the hectic midday traffic on Main Street in Downtown Prime. He had to admit he was looking forward to his visit at Widen Laboratories, a place he'd never been before, a rarity working in law enforcement in Prime as long as he had. Of course he'd worked on several cases throughout the years where he told himself he'd seen everything.

This morning's trip to the morgue may have convinced him to stop saying that, permanently.

Chauncey didn't want to talk to anybody about it, either. Part of him didn't want to look in the manila folder Frosty gave to him, despite whatever determination brewed inside of him to solve this case.

Now he wanted more coffee, but Jane Newton had asked him if he liked it. Of course he did, so naturally he assumed there'd be some waiting for him when he got there.

He'd manage until then.

He was already outside of Downtown Prime and getting onto Route 21. A few exits up and he'd be close to Widen Laboratories. A sign at the exit clearly stated that's where you get off at, which Chauncey knew but never thought about it before, neither the sign nor the exit number.

By now Chauncey knew he drove past the Woodward Hotel. Not because of driving past the exit to get there or being able to see the place, he just sensed it. Frequenting certain areas as often as he had meant he knew it by the back of his hand. In another minute or two he'd reach the exit he needed to take, exit five to be precise. A mental note taken on that one, but forgot to take a close look at the sign stating Widen Laboratories was in that direction. The color of it was important to him to increase memories of this trek to a new place.

For a Detective it's the tiny details that matter, not all the time but you never know when they'll come in handy. Something simple and in comparison to most things irrelevant might trigger an association giving you leads. For Chauncey something as trivial as the color of a road sign might jog his memory. Of course he had to keep in mind that he'd never visited Widen Laboratories before so there might not be any meaning behind it, but that doesn't mean he should rule it out.

Predictably, the name of the road at the end of the exit ramp was called Widen Road. He vaguely recalled seeing tractor-trailer trucks coming down here, but never thought much about it. Logic dictated they'd all be coming and going from Widen Laboratories. Perhaps the city should consider changing the name to Wide Load Road. Then again, Chauncey only saw the big rigs every now and then. He could imagine a CEO only two pounds overweight getting pissed off at that proposal.

Someone who thinks too much of himself as a CEO ought to be named Lard Ass and should be encouraged to gain more weight to have enough room to shove his head up his own ass.

Wishful thinking, Chauncey thought. For a guy like that it would do a world of good, someone who can't get enough of the smell of their own shit.

He should learn to eat shit, too.

The Detective needed to remind himself that he was looking forward to visiting Widen Laboratories, even if the only reason is for curiosity's sake. The brief interaction he'd had so far with Jane Newton was an indication everything would go smoothly after this morning's phone conversation and informal text messaging a little while ago.

Regardless, he still felt slight jitters.

Pre-conceived notions should never be the deciding factor in how things will go. Chauncey knew that, but had no idea what he was getting himself into. The murders of Roy Cumberland and Stacy O'Connell weighed heavily on his mind, as both of them had connections to Widen

Laboratories, and he couldn't say anything about Jane Doe. He didn't know what to say about that.

A brown colored sign with white lettering spelling out Widen Laboratories with an arrow below it pointing right told him where to go. The trip down Widen Road gave sight to spread out deserted land, strong hints to swamps and forests with trees and bushes here and there. The housing projects from years back had been long gone, yet the views of nature surrounding the place was something Chauncey found unsettling.

"Something strange about this," he said. "You'd think letting nature take over after what this place had been would be a smart move."

While absorbing the views surrounding him he didn't realize how slow he was driving.

"It's been decades since anybody lived here," he said. "And I can't imagine anyone hiking or camping out here, either. I kind of doubt anyone would get lost out here, unlike the Badlands. I'll bet the company has fancy electronic surveillance equipment that can detect everything imaginable. They're probably tracking me right now, best to go the speed limit and look straight ahead and pretend to be oblivious to all of this."

"They can probably hear me too."

Chauncey's famous last words, for the next few minutes at least, even if he's the only one listening.

He continued down Widen Road for another mile or so, at this point he half-expected to see either a gas station or convenience store. In an area like this tailor-made for a small town atmosphere the locals could get away with the combination of both and call it a general store, a concept not completely lost to everyone in this day and age. Not that it ever went away.

Most likely there had been something resembling that a long time ago, long before Chauncey Winfield enrolled as a student at Prime State University, long before he'd even heard of the city of Prime itself. He wasn't caught up on current events as much as he thought, either. Sergeant Matheson told him the college was owned by Widen Laboratories, and had been for quite some time now. It didn't surprise him completely, lots of people still don't know about the Rothschild family.

Chauncey had no room for superstition in his line of work, but couldn't shake the eerie vibe he felt. Nothing remained of what used to be here, yet a strong presence was detected, possibly the wildlife unseen by the naked eye, and then some.

"It's a ghost town," said Chauncey. "The Woodward Hotel is a spring break in Daytona compared to this."

Could a corporation make it possible for nature and fascism to coexist? The two aren't meant to exchange hands as far as he's concerned. It doesn't matter what the suits decide to sponsor they can't make money by fixing the world's problems. At the end of the day it's the same story over and over again: power does what it wants, and they want it all.

"I'm just glad I don't have debates with anyone revolving around phony idealism," he said. "Not even with the dog."

See it for what it is instead of what it ought to be.

Reality inspires fantasy, how can anyone know what they don't want out of life without a little hardship? Or at least know a person who needs someone to lean on, and that someone is you?

Paul Raymond seemed like he could use a mentor, someone to act as that big brother he should have had. Chauncey wouldn't mind doing that to a certain extent, as long as it didn't lead to blind hero worship and the kid could think for himself instead of being a yes man.

Chauncey slowed down to take a look at a large sign posted on the left side of the road. It simply spelled out: Welcome to Widen Laboratories. He couldn't decide if it made him feel like he was about to head into a military base or a federal prison, probably both.

He put on the directional to turn left, despite the fact that no one was around to do that for. Working in law enforcement always made him think about setting an example along with the better safe than sorry speech, here it just didn't apply. However, it wouldn't surprise him if somehow someway the corporation had their eyes on him. Upon entering the first thing he looked for were speed limit signs. Places like this, meaning military bases and federal prisons, always had strict policies with speeding on the property. If he got a ticket here he wouldn't be able to get out of it despite his credentials, it wouldn't jeopardize his job but Triple B would have to bring it to his attention.

Chauncey drove about a hundreds yards in and was soon surrounded by trees. So many different types he couldn't fathom and didn't know where to begin. He was not an expert in forestry but he knew some by sight and it felt like a combination of the Redwood Forest and the Amazon Jungle, was that possible?

"There's a first time for everything," said Chauncey. "This is definitely a first in a city I thought I knew for years, and this is no city!"

So far not a single speed limit sign in sight, but that didn't convince him to push his foot down harder on the gas pedal. His rate of speed remained at approximately twenty miles per hour, fair enough in his estimation for being a stranger in a strange land. Up ahead he could barely see a gate with a guard standing outside, still quite a distance away, however, at least a quarter of a mile. He was just grateful he still had the ability to make out what it was.

He kept his eyes focused on what lied ahead, despite feeling affected by the nature around him. He didn't want to start thinking about what kind of exotic wildlife might have taken up some kind of residency in the trees surrounding him. No one really knew what kind of wildlife existed out in the Badlands, so he wouldn't have a clue as to what he'd find here.

All of a sudden Chauncey felt what he could only describe as a flaming sensation. You'd think he'd say it's a burning sensation, but there was no fire or feeling of heat increasing, even with the window on the driver's side door only being halfway down. The heat and the air conditioning were completely off, and despite no real winters of any kind in Prime it never gets blazing hot in the month of January. But that wasn't the issue, Chauncey sensed that the trees surrounding him had gone up in flames, even though there was no visual evidence to support that claim.

As he got closer to the gate what he still could only describe as a flaming sensation began to fade away, feeling less and less of it until the feeling vanished completely. The smell of a fire had been non-existent the entire time, so there was nothing to report to the guard up ahead. Unless he wanted the guy to think he was on drugs. He estimated the distance between them to be thirty feet which prompted him to take out his wallet and have his ID ready for inspection, assuming tight security was the norm at a place like Widen Laboratories, nothing better to do out in the middle of nowhere.

Chauncey rolled his window all the way down and extended his left hand out with both his driver's license and law enforcement credentials in it. The guard remained standing still approximately ten to fifteen feet away.

"I'm here to see Jane Newton," said Chauncey.

The guard nodded, just barely, leaving him unsure whether or not he should go ahead. He waited another couple of seconds to be sure then drove forward. Not exactly a welcoming committee.

Luckily he didn't have much farther to go to reach the main building. Moments after the nearly non-existent exchange between him and the guard he could see it up ahead, thankfully not needing to travel down another long and winding road. Pretty cut and dry description of where he was: Widen Laboratories: Main Facility. A mostly white-colored building with visitors parking near their front entrance, more convenient than his last two trips to the Montrose Morgue. Shortly after pulling into one of many available spots, he sensed the surroundings were easier to take in. The spooky nature of Widen Road and the entrance leading up to the guard at the gate were long gone. The water fountains and beautiful flowers would catch anyone's eye. The company must have its own gardening crew, and well paid on top of it. Even Chauncey was surprised by how much he got taken in by all of it. Homogenized constructions like these were no match to endless mountain tops rarely touched by humans or the widespread land in the Midwest, but for now he was happy to be rid of that flaming sensation. Although he didn't expect Fantasy Island, he could use a laugh by having a little guy like Tattoo come out to greet him.

"Whatever," he said, smiling a bit.

It wouldn't require a lot of effort on his part to get out of the car and walk to the main entrance and go in the front door. Maybe the entire company had been expecting him with hopes of granting every wish he desired.

Yeah right.

After heading up the walkway from his car and turning right he came to a set of large double-glass doors. He opened the one on the right and went inside. A woman sitting at a desk about twenty feet away from him, presumably a secretary, stood up straight and stared him in the eye without moving a muscle.

"I'm here to see Jane Newton," said Chauncey.

The secretary remained quiet, stood completely still for a few more seconds before her eyes shifted to the right, her right specifically, prompting Chauncey to look to his left.

A woman, small in stature with a very light-colored skin tone and long, straight black hair appeared walking down the hallway on his side and proceeded to walk up to him and extend her right hand to greet him.

He knew exactly who it was.

"Jane Newton," she said, as they shook hands.

"Of course," he responded. "Finally someone gets a word in edgewise around here."

"When we know who's expected the only ones who will say anything are whoever you're meeting with."

"An odd procedure," added Chauncey.

"To say the least," she replied.

Despite the bizarre formalities, this introduction did not feel unpleasant. The guard could have been a store mannequin as far as he was concerned, and it would have been perfectly alright had that secretary not been at the front desk. But this Jane Newton clearly indicated the way things were done around here coincided with how the old saying goes: it is what it is.

Chauncey was glad he picked up on that. Hopefully the two of them wouldn't go into a detailed discussion about everything he went through to get to this point.

Not likely, and that suited him fine.

"Follow me," she said, in a pleasant tone.

Without hesitation, Jane Newton turned around and headed back down the hallway. Chauncey immediately followed. A short distance they traveled before taking a right then an immediate left into what he assumed was her office. Upon entering he realized how dimly lit the reception area and hallway had been, completely surrounded by white walls. It didn't make him feel like he entered a psychiatric unit but it was a strange contrast, and the bright lights in her office felt like a bright, sunny morning. True he might not be much of an early riser but it was okay by him. Coffee was waiting in the form of two white ceramic mugs, one for her she grabbed a hold of and one at her desk. The chair in front of it most would assume is for guests and visitors prompted him to have a seat. Jane Newton naturally went behind her desk and sat down.

"I just made it a few minutes ago," she said, using her eyes to focus briefly on the coffee mug in front of him.

"Thanks," he responded, picking it up by the handle with his right hand and bringing it towards him.

"I'm anxious to know how it turned out."

"Okay."

Chauncey drank approximately a quarter of it on the first try.

"Good by me," he said. "What kind is this?"

"Kind of an original thing," she answered. "A mix of stuff we grow here at the company."

"With the beautiful gardening that's outside?" he asked.

"Would you like to see it?"

"Some other time, what we need to talk about can't wait any longer."

"Of course not," she said. "I'm sorry I didn't find out about Roy Cumberland until after I left and Stacy O' Connell on top of that. The timing on my part couldn't have been worse."

"How could you have known otherwise?" asked Chauncey.

"I guess I couldn't have."

Asking that question made it sound like he wasn't accusing anybody of anything, he knew that approach was the best way to start the conversation. It also helped that he very much enjoyed the coffee, putting himself at ease too.

"Roy Cumberland," he started. "What can you tell me about him?"

"As much as possible I hope," she answered.

"Did you know him well?"

"Well enough," she said. "Going back to the start of the fall semester, he was a graduate student at Prime State. I think his main courses were Environmental Science and Psychology."

"Professor Horace said something about Roy being in one of his classes, he assumed it was just for obtaining additional credits to finish school sooner."

"In most cases you'd think so. Roy became very interested in what went on behind the scenes at the university, especially since Widen owns Prime State. He also wanted to learn more about the kind of research conducted at Widen itself."

"Herpetology is a big thing here obviously. Professor Horace conducts a lot of independent studies at the school. It doesn't take a genius to figure that out. Then again, I didn't know Widen Labs owned Prime State until the night of the murder."

At that moment Chauncey finished his first cup of coffee, the second he placed the mug back on her desk she snatched it up and poured some more. Before he knew it a second cup was ready for consumption.

"Weren't you a student there yourself?" asked Jane Newton.

"A long time ago," he answered, smiling and holding back a laugh.

"Of course," she said. "The buyout took place in recent years. It's still news to many people living in the city."

"The more I think about it," said Chauncey. "It had to be a long process as these things take time. I'm starting to recall when new construction was being done at Prime State there were lots of posts stating Widen Laboratories was involved. I guess I assumed your company was merely financing it, but I didn't know anything about a merger or a complete buyout. It makes sense, though."

"A long process and a constant work in progress," she said.

"Naturally," he said. "You said Roy Cumberland wanted to know what went on behind the scenes both here and at Prime State was he hoping to gain employment at either place after finishing his studies?"

"Possibly," she answered. "I'm not quite sure what his main goal was in that respect. His background would have been useful at Widen Laboratories in some shape or form. Everyone around here familiar with us knows about one thing."

"Herpetology," said Chauncey. "It beats discussing herpes, or getting it."

"A venomous snakebite could change your mind."

"Let's NOT find out!"

He started drinking his second cup of coffee. He didn't think he pushed any buttons with that last remark. She seemed to be on the level and rolled with it. He wasn't sure about her sense of humor, but Widen Labs was an odd place. As she expressed when she introduced herself the odd procedure conducted for arriving visitors, expected visitors mind you.

"Have you ever been bitten?" asked Chauncey.

"No thank God," she answered.

"Come close?"

"Once or twice," she said. "In my line of work you do need hands-on experience with reptiles. Fortunately, I don't need to use my hands as much as used to. One reason I won't complain about spending more time at my desk in an office."

"So you don't like to roll up your sleeves and get your hands dirty?"

"I wouldn't say I don't like to, it's what I went to school for, and part of the job. But I like having space,

Professor Horace stays on top of things at the university and I'm able to get statistics and updates any time of the day or night. It's interesting being able to step back and see results and observe everything from a distance."

Chauncey racked his brain for a minute. Trying to remember what Paul Raymond said that had something to do with her official title at Widen Laboratories. He was surprised not to see anything on her desk indicating what it might be, and he didn't recall seeing her name posted on the door outside the office. The strangest part for him was realizing that the entire room was just white walls. Not a single picture or anything else you might see hung up and framed inside places like these. He figured she'd have put up one of her fancy degrees directly behind her or other random achievements, at the very least some kind of certification from the board of health or something.

Now it came to him.

"I talked to Paul Raymond," said Chauncey.

"I know him quite well," she responded.

"He said something about your official title here having to do with independent studies."

"Head of Independent Research for the Corporate Division," she stated.

"Does Widen Laboratories have an official title for Professor Horace?"

"Head of Independent Studies for the Academic Division," she answered.

Pretty cut and dry, Chauncey thought. She's making it sound like they both have the same position, but in their line of work you can't put it in the same shit different day category.

"Is there any difference between Research and Studies?" he asked.

"Not really," she said. "The only reason for that is because his main focus is at Prime State University."

"And your main focus is here, right?"

"To an extent, yes," she answered. "I'm sure you know I help out Professor Horace in the school lab quite a bit and teach classes occasionally."

"Are you the only ones from Widen Labs who do that?"

"For now, yes," she replied. "But that could change at some point down the road."

"When?" asked Chauncey.

"Don't get too anxious," said Jane Newton. "That won't be for quite a while. It's only projections being made by the company and it depends on who we hire along with what Prime State wants to do when more of their long time professors retire."

"How involved is Widen Laboratories with Prime State with the university's hiring process?"

"It depends on the department."

"Can you break it down for me?"

"Athletics, Maintenance, and Food Service are departments we have no involvement with but that could change. Right now the focus is on Academics and Administration."

Chauncey already knew Professor Horace and Jane Newton were the only ones who had their hands in the academic stuff, but he needed to find out more about the business side to things.

"I know Widen Laboratories technically owns Prime State," said Chauncey. "But can you give me an idea how the ownership part is handled?"

"Naturally Widen brought in its own people," answered Jane Newton. "A lot of red tape and shuffling papers back and forth, it's still being treated as a 50/50 deal."

"But it's not."

"The dust is still settling keeping everything quiet."

"It makes sense," said Chauncey. "Most people around

here still don't know about this, I was one of them until recently."

"It helps to stay informed," she added.

"Is there any chance that Prime State will be rechristened as Widen University?"

"I don't think so," she answered. "We want to retain a school spirit."

"Who's we?" he asked.

"The company mostly, like I said it's been in the works for a long time, before I came aboard even. I'm involved in some of the meetings and considered a consultant, but my input on this matter is minimal."

Chauncey felt Jane Newton had been answering the questions with a broad overview, but didn't think she was being too vague or evasive in any way. Not yet. Let's see how much she knows about the second victim.

"What can you tell me about Stacy O' Connell?" he asked.

"Irish girl," said Jane Newton.

"Born and raised?"

"As far as I know, she worked here at Widen Laboratories until recently."

"What prompted her to leave?"

"Nothing prompted her to I guess I should rephrase that. Technically she wasn't employed by us. She was under contract for the past year. She worked for a government facility on the East Coast."

"Exactly who?" he asked. "What branch of government?"

"She was involved in scientific research," she answered. "But that's all I can tell you. I'd have to get clearance from the top brass here to elaborate more."

"Alright," he said, keeping a calm demeanor, finishing his second cup of coffee already. "Just so you know, you'll most likely have to do that, this is a murder investigation. I'm not making any allegations towards you or Widen

Laboratories it's just part of the deal."

"I know," she responded. "I understand that. You won't be met with any resistance, not on my part."

"Is there anything else you can tell me about her?"

"Despite Ms. O' Connell's contract ending with the company she was supposed to accompany myself and several others on what you would call a "Research Mission" for Widen Laboratories but backed out at the last minute."

"A research mission," said Chauncey. "I've never heard that one before."

"We were sent to Africa for reptilian studies, but that's all I can say about it."

"I understand. I must say Ms. Newton that I believe you're trying to tell me as much as you're permitted to, but we'll definitely have to meet up again."

"That won't be a problem," she said. "There's a little bit of coffee left would you like it?"

"Sure," he said, showing a smile.

Jane Newton took the cup and poured the last of the coffee in it. At least half-full in Chauncey's estimation, but he wasn't about to complain. Consumption on his part took less than a minute.

"Would you like me to accompany you on the way out?" she asked.

"That would be very kind of you."

The two of them stood up simultaneously. Chauncey waited for Jane Newton to come out from behind her desk and followed her out of the office. They headed down the same hallway leading back to the main lobby. The secretary who gave him the cold stare on the way in was sitting at the desk and didn't so much as glance at either one of them. He couldn't decide which experience was worse: locking eyes when he first arrived or acting like he didn't exist on the way out. Probably some bizarre company formality pushed by top executives at

Widen Laboratories. As far as he's concerned, however, personality, or lack of it, can limit things immensely.

"I'm sure we'll meet again soon," said Chauncey.

"I'm looking forward to it," said Jane Newton.

Despite the pleasant meeting and accommodations, Chauncey was taken aback by how smoothly everything had gone. They were discussing the murders of two people she obviously knew well. He wouldn't accuse her of being uncaring. Perhaps she was trying to be professional and act neutral. He concluded Widen Laboratories was definitely run in an unorthodox manner. It made everyone who worked at Montrose Morgue look like Bugs Bunny or Daffy Duck with supreme intelligence and rational states of mind. It was easy to picture Danielle Locke, even Frosty for that matter, expressing compassion for random people on the street, and these folks have to see dead bodies every day!

Nonetheless, Chauncey turned his head toward Jane Newton and looked her in the eye, nodded then opened the double-glass doors and headed outside. In no time he walked back to his car and got in and started it. He expected to get the same treatment from the guard at the gate he got from the secretary on his way out. As soon as he arrived back at the gate his speculation was confirmed. The guard was still standing in the same spot and staring straight ahead, leaving him to wonder if the guard was remotely fazed by his presence to begin with. When Chauncey was twelve he got to see the hourly Changing of the Guard routine in Washington D.C. At least enough life existed in that soldier to march back and forth, leaving a positive impression on him as a boy and at least slightly raised his level of respect toward the military, despite having no desire to join up ever. But this guard shouldn't so much as have a pulse in his opinion.

As he started heading back to Widen Road the senses went up again, this time to the point of overload. Not in the same way it was the first time, which he labeled as a flaming sensation. He felt the spirit of the wildlife surrounding him, if that's understandable. Perhaps a number of animals made their homes in the exotic nature combining the Redwood Forest and the Amazon Jungle. Chauncey couldn't begin to imagine what might be out there like boas, bears, or a species unknown to most of the world's population, or one created by Widen Laboratories itself. That's too far-fetched in his mind regardless of Frosty finding an unknown element in that Jane Doe's corpse, an explanation will surface eventually.

He arrived at Widen Road, slowly pulling out and making a right turn but stopped completely. His eyes focused on something out in the swamp lands ahead of him, something that shouldn't be there, something you're not supposed to see.

The residents from long ago started to appear out of the grass and marshes, rising up and walking towards Chauncey, or at least trying to. It felt like they were getting closer and closer despite not being able to step onto the pavement itself on Widen Road. None of them looked particularly grotesque, not like anything you'd see on the Walking Dead. Yet their ghostlike appearance still revealed a slight amount of decay, difficult to describe unless you witnessed it firsthand. They weren't actually speaking but Chauncey felt what they were trying to tell him. Their lives, their land, everything that stood here long ago had been taken from them. The population had dwindled throughout the years but the happiness shared between them kept the community closely connected. Something in the air undetected by the eyes, ears, sound, and smell of humans began to make everyone ill, and that was just the start of it.

A handful of the residents discussed amongst each other a slight, sour taste felt on the tips of their tongues that went away in a short period of time. They assumed it was nothing and didn't talk about it ever again. Yet within a few months one at a time someone would develop sudden flu systems which quickly vanished but the person would die in their sleep in a few days, and not necessarily overnight in bed, quite often they'd have dozed off on their front porch or in a recliner watching television (those who could afford it) in the middle of the day. One death occurred right at the general store. Old Rudy Morgan had gone in to for the regular midday shift at 10am, business as usual happened and the place would empty out around 1pm after the busy lunch hour. Shortly afterwards nine year old Wes Matthews, who lived with his mother a few houses down the road went in to buy a candy bar for himself and the local newspaper for his mother. He went up to the counter to pay for the merchandise and saw Mr. Morgan's head faced down next to the register. Assuming his mom's good friend fell asleep on the job he shook him slightly and told Mr. Morgan it was him. No response. A second and third time did nothing either, so he ran outside and saw Mrs. Gordon, who arrived in her car and the moment she got out young Wes ran up to her in a panic.

"What is it, Wes?" she asked.

"It's Mr. Morgan!" he said.

"What about him?"

"He won't wake up!"

Mrs. Gordon immediately went inside with Wes right behind her. She went up to the counter and saw Mr. Morgan lying face down with his head turned sideways. She knew CPR and checked his vital signs on his neck and wrist. No pulse and it only took a few seconds to figure out he wasn't breathing. She knew the right thing to do was call 911 but she decided to call Montrose Morgue instead, they'd have to take care of everything anyway.

As much as she didn't want to make it look hopeless

for little Wes, much less tell the poor kid Mr. Morgan was dead, there was nothing else she could do. She comforted the boy as best she could and called his mother on the payphone outside the front door to tell her what was going on. Within minutes Ms. Matthews showed up, shortly after that an ambulance from Montrose Morgue arrived. A small crowd of people from the neighborhood slowly gathered at the store parking lot, maybe a dozen of them. It didn't take long for everyone to find out what happened. Old Rudy Morgan was a good friend to a lot of people there and hadn't shown any sign of illness except for a brief bout of the flu. The worst part was that everyone knew Old Rudy Morgan wasn't that old. He was fifty-five. But he was an old soul with a kind heart who made time for anyone who needed a helping hand.

Chauncey couldn't understand how he suddenly knew all this had happened. This was way before his time, possibly before his birth even. So what significance would this have? He dismissed it as a modern day myth or folklore he made up in his head, perhaps a movie he saw recently supposedly inspired by a true friendship triggered the idea for a good story. Mr. Church it was called, with Eddie Murphy playing the title character. A departure for the actor, very straight-forward with little of the comic edge audiences were used to yet still retaining plenty of charisma. It may have not been a masterpiece, but much better than critics said it was.

However, Chauncey felt drawn to what was approaching him. Most of these so-called people were rising up out of a tiny creek he could see off in the distance heading directly toward him. He pressed his foot on the gas and traveled a short distance down Widen Road. After about half a mile something inside of him felt the need to stop. Upon doing so he turned off the engine and got out of the car. Without giving it any thought he walked out onto the grassy swamplands where the spirits of the old neighborhood were dwelling. For some reason they were unable to, or at least resisted, crossing onto the pavement of Widen Road. The airborne illness was the start of it all. The construction of Widen Road along with Widen Laboratories must've been the icing on the cake, even if the residents had been long gone before it began.

After a short distance, maybe twenty feet in, Chauncey's legs started sinking into the ground. The first thought that came to mind was quicksand, but it felt like he was stuck in cement. He looked down and realized he sank in up to his kneecaps, but that wasn't the worst of it. Something prompted him to raise his arms up and look at his hands, what started happening was beyond belief. From his palms then slowly up his arms, soon sensing it throughout his entire body, he was decaying, turning into a corpse and it looked like this would be his final resting place all while he kept slowly sinking into the ground, and not being able to do anything to stop it.

While sinking into the ground and decaying simultaneously the process seemed really slow at first. But before he knew it he was up to his eyeballs, moments later he was completely gone. For a few seconds everything was completely black then somehow he felt able to climb up through the dirt and mud he was buried under and get back onto the land. This time he was rising out of a grave, his own. He didn't need to look at the tombstone directly behind him, he just knew. While all this happened his body returned to its living state, the skin returning to normal, his eyes regaining their vision, and his hair growing back again. It felt great returning to human form again but it was just as unpleasant as the decaying process.

As soon as he climbed completely out of the grave and got back on his feet he stared straight ahead to see Jane Doe standing in front of him. She somehow rose from the dead and escaped from Montrose Morgue. She put her hands around his neck and started strangling him. Soon he fell back down on the dirt he just crawled out of. Her massive strength kept him from defending himself in any way. Then she began to shout his name out.

"Chauncey!" she yelled, repeatedly.

He recognized the voice, and it was Ali's.

"Chauncey!" she yelled out again.

He woke up in his bed to find Ali standing over him trying to wake him.

He couldn't believe where he was.

"What time is it?" asked Chauncey.

"It's four," she answered.

"Am or pm?" he asked.

"Look outside!"

The curtains on his bedroom window were open and the sun was shining bright. He didn't need to look to know the answer, but after what just happened...how did he get here?

"It was dark out when I got up," said Chauncey.

"What do you mean?" asked Ali. "You just got up now! The sun is practically shining on your face!"

"I was at my grave," he said. "That Jane Doe tried to strangle me so I'd die again!"

"Do you have any idea what you're saying?!"

"Yeah," he answered. "I went to interview Jane Newton at Widen Labs. How I got back here.......I don't understand!"

"There's another Jane in all of this?" she asked.

"Sorry," he said, hoping he could somehow explain all of this. "Jane Doe's the body they discovered at the Woodward Hotel, Jane Newton knew the other two people who got murdered. I just met with her at Widen Labs a few hours ago."

"Obviously she's Jane Doe because you don't know who she is."

"Yeah she's at Montrose Morgue."

"Let me get this straight," said Ali. "You were at your grave while it was dark out and this Jane Doe was there trying to kill you.......again?"

"I had just crawled out of it."

"You rose from the grave? It doesn't look like you've died yet!"

Chauncey didn't know how to respond to that. If he told Ali his body began decaying when he sank into the ground on Widen Road then became fully resurrected after rising up out of his own grave to stand face to face with Jane Doe who started strangling him so he'd die again is something most people can't fathom on the first attempt, best to write it off for now.

"This whole thing is crazy," said Chauncey, despite not really feeling that way. "I don't know what I'm saying."

"An intense dream, for sure!" said Ali. "I've never seen you like this...ever!"

She's right about that. Best thing now is to add a bit of humor into the situation.

"Thundermutt!" he called out. "A Jewish Viking could come in handy right now."

Seconds later Lady wandered into the bedroom. Most likely she'd been chilling out in the hallway by the top of the stairs.

"Are you sure you're alright?" asked Ali.

"Yeah," he answered. "I've got to write this stuff down, never had dreams like this before."

"Good thing it was just a dream. I'm going to start dinner in about an hour. Do you want some coffee made in the meantime?"

"Sure. You do that and I'll be downstairs in a minute."

"Alright," she said, then turned around and walked out of the bedroom. Lady immediately followed. At least someone has the right idea. All he wanted to do right now was just try to snap out of this.

"That part where you stand up and stretch is easy," he said. "But the way they shake themselves is something I've never been able to figure out. But I don't think anyone has."

Chauncey was talking about dogs, naturally. Talking out loud about stuff this added more humor to the situation, motivating him to get out of bed. As soon as he got on his feet he stretched out his arms and opened his mouth and did it in such a way to mimic other dogs, not that there was any point in doing this since no one else could enjoy the entertainment.

But there's nothing wrong with doing something for your own personal amusement. Now if he could only figure out how to shake his whole body the same way dogs did, a lot of people might pay big money to see that.

"Only a dream, huh?" he asked himself.

No, it's not.

CHAPTER 14

CHAUNCEY WENT DOWNSTAIRS and headed into what was best called the living area. He made himself comfortable sitting in the recliner and turning on the television. By the looks of it a rerun of Snapped was on. It would only be another few minutes until Ali had coffee ready for him. He reached down to the right to pick his laptop up off the floor then simultaneously elevated the chair back as far as he could and placed it on his lap. He opened it up and turned it on to find he had full internet access at his service which meant he wouldn't have to wait to get online.

He immediately went to Google and searched for Montrose Morgue's main website. If he remembered correctly they kept all of their clients' obituaries on file ever since the place was founded. Hopefully he could find whatever information he needed online, at least if it went as far back as 1967. Lucky for him a link appeared on their main page specifically titled Obituaries. He clicked on that and got exactly what he expected to find, the most recent deaths in the past few days, one of which was Roy Cumberland. Curiosity tempted him to see if one had been written up for Stacy O'Connell yet, but that wasn't important right now. The Detective needed to go way back, exploring history more or less.

A search option was available for deaths by name or year. Chauncey's hunch told him to start the search by the year, so he typed in 1967. In a matter of seconds all the names of the deceased popped up from that time although not listing them from January to December but in alphabetical order. A similar setup compared to his search for Jane Newton's extension at Widen Laboratories. He hoped the process wouldn't take half as long as before. Without the aid of coffee in the next couple of minutes he could easily picture himself falling asleep.

Luckily that wouldn't be the case.

He had the option to scroll down on the first letters of the last names starting from A to Z. M was at the halfway mark and a few clicks on the down arrow key got him there in just a few seconds. It didn't take long to find what he was looking for when he came across the listing of an R. Morgan, the best part being that was the only what with that last name, which was nice since it's a common name. When he clicked on R. Morgan and the obituary popped up the first thing he saw was the man's name spelled out as Old Rudy Morgan with no quotes or parentheses surrounding the Old part. However, without so much as starting to read it, he had a feeling that wasn't the actual birth name.

The obituary contained the standard information:

1) Rudy Morgan, but no mention of a middle initial.

2) The birth and death dates, May 4, 1912 – August 18, 1967.

3) The cause of death listed as a brief illness.

4) No living relatives in the immediate area.

Nothing surprising to Chauncey, except no middle initial, and Rudy is usually a nickname, but not always. One thing did grab his attention right away, as it would most people. A piece of writing or poetry from Mr. Morgan himself, most likely requested to be printed in the obituary per order of the deceased's will.

"When the time comes for me to pass away
I hope it occurs on a warm, summer day
I do not wish for this until I am old
But to speak of it now makes me somewhat bold
When my eyes close I will truly see
And understand what it truly means to be free."

R. Morgan

In sounded like he got his wish, Chauncey thought, he died in August and was known to everyone as Old Rudy Morgan, though he probably didn't anticipate anything on that particular day.

"Caffeine fix at your service!" declared Ali, standing beside him on the right with his coffee ready.

"Huh?" said Chauncey.

He paused for another second before looking to the right.

"I thought you'd smell it all the way from the kitchen," said Ali. "I figured you'd be as jumpy as the dog when we feed her beef jerky or pepperoni!"

"Sorry to disappoint you," he said, but in a light-hearted tone.

"You're really a lot more preoccupied with this particular case, more than most. When all's said and done you'll probably be able to use all the information you're gathering as a thesis for a graduate school program!"

"You might be on to something."

Chauncey took the coffee from her and placed it on the tray on the left side of the recliner. He'd found everything he needed to know so far. He exited out of

Montrose Morgue's website and got off the internet all together then turned off the computer and closed the laptop and put it back on the floor right in front of Ali's feet.

"You think you'll be able to sleep better tonight?" she asked.

"I hope so," he answered. "There's more to that dream than I thought."

"Is that Jane Doe now a part of the cast in The Walking Dead?"

"If only it was that simple," he said, still speaking in a calm tone knowing Ali understood him but was trying to add some light humor to the situation.

She had the right idea.

"Anything you can shed some light on?" she asked.

"Not yet," he said.

That wasn't true by any means. But he didn't know what to tell her. It still felt far-fetched, and he didn't want her to suggest consulting a psychic.

"Steak tips?" she asked.

"For dinner I assume," he said.

"Or macaroni," she added.

"Whatever works for you," he answered. "Just cook what you want, one or both."

Leave it up to her, he thought. She's the one making dinner for both of us. He didn't want to treat her like a short order cook at Denny's or something. Not that he ever would, but this particular case was starting to consume him and that wasn't about to change anytime soon.

CHAPTER 15

It was bright and early the next morning, for Detective Chauncey, anyway. Just a little after 8am, so yeah that's especially the case for him. He'd actually woken up shortly before the alarm clock had gone off, which had been set for Ali, and she was definitely taken by surprise. He'd had a good night's sleep despite what happened yesterday afternoon, and nothing would deter him from finding out everything he needed to know.

Chauncey was back at Montrose Morgue, specifically where all of their files and storage were kept. He'd arrived nearly half an hour ago, pulling in at the same time Frosty had who immediately told him that no new information was available in regards to Jane Doe along with anything else connected to the case. That was fine since he was there to explore a new angle that literally came to him in a dream, but he wasn't going to reveal that last part to anyone.

Frosty understood what Chauncey meant by all of this since he was the one who wanted to keep information searches under the radar with Jane Doe. He didn't expect to find reptile and unknown DNA in her much less discover snake venom in Roy Cumberland or Stacy O' Connell's digestive systems, the latter being especially strange since it can't cause fatalities. He had no reservations about providing the Detective with an all access pass and the keys to the office where all the old files were kept. He didn't ask Chauncey for any kind of explanation either, especially with how mysterious the results had been so far on his end. He really didn't think the guy would believe any of it.

Chauncey would be able to provide a story to cover up what he was doing if he aroused suspicion with the other employees at Montrose Morgue. The Prime Police Department needed to update information on a retired officer who passed away last October. He called Triple B the night before and the two of them concocted this scheme to give him an excuse to poke through Montrose Morgue's files legitimately. Anyone who had authority over Frosty who had questions could contact Chauncey's boss or provide the name of the retired officer, Owen Orwell, to whoever answered the phone at the station. Chauncey's actions would be explained as necessary formalities, something a morgue would know plenty about!

The Detective discovered the information he was looking for. Despite the fact that Mr. Morgan's obituary had been posted on Montrose Morgue's website, everything else he needed to find out about had to be searched for manually. A coroner's findings of any kind: be it autopsies or toxicology reports are usually not available to the public, at least not in their entirety, especially ones dating as far back as Old Rudy Morgan.

Then again, most people aren't looking for information like this either. Not when it's someone who's been dead for almost half a century. Most of their friends and relatives passed on a long time ago, and if Wes Matthews was still alive Chauncey would bet he'd moved out of the area completely and by now probably had plenty of children and grandchildren to look after.

Chauncey's pulled out the file on Mr. Morgan and began to read through it. The cause of death was a mild heart attack, and the deceased was probably unaware of the symptoms indicating having one since there had been no history of heart problems of any kind with himself or his immediate relatives, none of whom resided in or around Prime. However, it had been noted he'd been treated for the flu a short time before his death, but no connection was found between that and the heart attack.

There was also a brief mention about the possibility of resin in the lungs. Chauncey had no idea what that meant but the reports said nothing about Mr. Morgan being a smoker and there were no additional findings. However, a group of numbers and letters were listed below it: U44R21. What did that mean?

Whatever it meant, Chauncey knew it was important. He'd never seen anything like this in these reports and would bet that it wasn't a license plate number. He took his cell phone out of his pocket and went to text messaging so he could type in U44R21 which he would send to Frosty, but not right away. He just wanted to have it on record for the time being.

Six pages of reports were in Mr. Morgan's files. The majority of it was just standard information from a coroner's report along with the obituary printed on page one. This is usually the case with this stuff, at least in Chauncey's experience. He found the same thing when he opened Officer Orwell's folder and he only needed the last two pages from Mr. Morgan's files, which he put in Officer Orwell's folder then put Mr. Morgan's back in the cabinet and shut it and locked it. He didn't expect anyone would be going in there anytime soon, but to be on the safe side he signed his name on the clipboard at the front desk indicating he'd taken Officer Orwell's folder to deliver to the Prime Police Department. Even though he was pretty sure no one would miss it this made sure no one would question his actions.

After supplying his signature along verifying which folder he took as well as his times in and out Chauncey headed for the door. On the way out he turned off the lights, he saw no point in wasting electricity if no one else was in there. As soon as he was out in the hallway he shut the door and locked it, when he turned his head he saw the RN Danielle Locke walking towards him. As expected she stopped to say hi.

"So we meet again," she said in a pleasant tone with a smile.

"How are you?" asked Chauncey.

"Okay," she answered. "What brings you back here?"

"Formalities I suppose."

"Oh?"

"I had to get some information for the police department."

"Is it connected to the recent murders?" she asked.

"No," said Chauncey. "They need to update their records in regards to a retired officer who passed away last October, Officer Owen Orwell, Triple O to many of them. Just like the supervisor I answer to Boss Bobby Burrell who most people call Triple B."

The conversation was a bit of a smokescreen. He had no idea if anyone called Officer Orwell that. It probably wasn't true, worse came to worse if she found out anything he could tell her that's just his sense of humor.

"Triple O, huh?" she said. "It sounds like he'd pal around with 007!"

"You never know," he responded. "Triple O had his place in American Law Enforcement and James Bond thrived in the British Secret Service!"

"If you're licensed to kill you might do okay for yourself!"

They both shared a quick laugh. He didn't have a lot to worry about if he blew his cover.

"Have you talked to Frosty?" she asked.

"I saw him when I came in," said Chauncey. "Maybe you can help me."

"How?" she asked.

"Let me call him."

Chauncey got his cell phone out of his pocket to call Frosty. He went to his list of contacts for the name and pressed a button on the left to call. There was an answer after the first ring.

"Hello?" said Frosty.

"It's me," said Chauncey.

"What's up?"

"Can I hand over the pass and keys to the RN I'm talking to named Danielle Locke?"

"Sure," answered Frosty. "Were you able to find everything you needed?"

"Yeah," said Chauncey. "I have something I need to send to you."

"Can't you just come see me?"

"It's stored in my phone. I can text it to you right now."

"Okay," said Frosty. "What is it?"

"I don't know," said Chauncey. "At first glance you'd think of a license plate number, but I don't think that's what it is."

"Just send it to me and I'll look into it."

"Awesome! I'll talk to you later!"

Chauncey hung up and went to the message section where he stored the information he wanted to send. He opened it and quickly reread what he'd typed in it a short while ago: U44R21. He hit the send button for it to go directly to Frosty.

Mission accomplished.

"Parking tickets?" asked Danielle Locke, in a light-hearted tone.

"Maybe," answered Chauncey. "It might have something to do with insurance, I'm not sure."

"Did Frosty do an autopsy on Triple O?"

"Probably, someone in his family forgot to cancel his policy, or they kept the car in his name."

He just made it up as he went along.

As he spoke he knew he didn't sound consistent, especially considering he'd said to Frosty it most likely had nothing to do with a license plate number.

Maybe it's not so bad to just roll with it.

What's the harm if she doesn't catch on?

"Great seeing you again," said Danielle.

"You too," said Chauncey.

"Will you be back here again anytime soon?" she asked.

"You never know," he answered. "But the way it's going I'd say most likely."

Chauncey and Danielle headed towards the front entrance. As soon as they reached the doors a bunch of cars began piling into the parking lot.

"If you leave now you'll miss most of the mob coming in," she said.

"Them?" he asked.

"That's right."

"Your coworkers are really that bad, huh?'

"No," she stated. "There's just too many of them coming in first thing in the morning for my taste. That's why I get here early, to avoid the mad rush."

"I hate the 9 to 5 grind," said Chauncey.

"Same here," she responded.

"Until the next time," he said, opening the door.

Off he went.

CHAPTER 16

CHAUNCEY FOUND HIMSELF back at Cameron's Coffee Café, no that he'd made any plans after leaving Montrose Morgue. No crime in killing time, one type of death you can contribute to without facing repercussions. Perhaps wasting time is worse than killing it. If he'd planned to come here he could've referred to this place as Triple C while conversing with Danielle Locke about Triple B and Triple O.

At some point it would've gotten stale.

He was right, until next time.

The phone rang. He picked it up off the table and checked the ID. It was Frosty. There'd been no news so far. He'd just left there an hour ago, a break in the case this quick? Not likely.

"What's up?" he said.

"You found something alright," said Frosty. "That U44R21 thing is not a license number. "

"What do you mean?" he asked.

"It dates back to lung resin research nearly fifty years

ago."

"It makes sense, can you expand on that?"

"Yeah," answered Frosty. "The U refers to an unknown resin found in peoples systems upon death with the 44th type discovered. The R stands for the resin found in Mr. Morgan's lungs and the 21st case of a death deemed unsuspicious."

The Detective took all of the information in rather quickly. The explanation sounded simple, but it was only the beginning of the epic about to unfold. He did not have any hands-on experience or expertise in the medical field. He knew this had to do with lung cancer with Frosty referring to research and terminology from half a century ago, but that wouldn't make it any easier in the long run. All he could do was let this particular guy, an experienced coroner, discuss this until it reached a point where he couldn't understand what was being said.

"All I know is resin is connected to lung cancer," he said.

"That's right," said Frosty. "The research was in the early stages back then, or at the very least slow moving."

"So what have you got?"

"I can't confirm anything yet, that will take time. But I found something interesting in Mr. Morgan's records. His findings match what's in Jane Doe's body."

"I don't think he had reptile DNA!" exclaimed Chauncey.

"No," said Frosty. "I'm talking about traces of resin I found in Jane Doe. I don't have a sample available from Mr. Morgan, but U44R21's description matches the results in what I have here."

Chauncey paused for a minute, then thought of a response to that.

"A textbook result?" he asked.

"You won't find this in textbooks," explained Frosty.

"Not how I'm describing it. The U. R. codes were used specifically for research here in Prime more than fifty years ago."

"Is it possible everything is outdated and changed?"

"It's possible, but I don't think so. I'm going to compare the findings to terminology used today. With any luck I will find a sample stored away somewhere, specifically Mr. Morgan's."

"After fifty years," said Chauncey. "You really think so?"

"It's a long shot," said Frosty. "The research was important enough by the city's standards so it's bound to be somewhere. You were able to find all the information on this guy rather quickly."

"That's true, so I guess anything's possible."

Both of them stayed quiet for a minute. Obviously this was a big step forward in the investigation, but that didn't mean the next step would come as quickly.

"Let me do some poking around," said Frosty. "We need to keep this quiet. I don't think anyone has gone looking for this stuff in years!"

"You're probably right," said Chauncey. "And if you find the sample you won't be able to match the physical results right away. I got into law enforcement long before the CSI syndrome entered the picture!"

"Don't get me started on that CSI shit!" chuckled Frosty.

"Talk to you later."

Chauncey placed his cell phone back on the table as soon as Frosty hung up. He couldn't understand why he didn't feel a sense of urgency over this case, especially with three bodies turning up over a short period of time along with what happened to him after leaving Jane Newton's office. The "Love Link" found on the first two victims proved the killer wanted the cops to know there was a connection. The snake venom found in the digestive systems made no sense, the exception being the killer intentionally taunting law enforcement. He still had to keep in mind the physical similarities of Stacy O'Connell, Jane Doe, and.......Jane Newton!

It just dawned on him. Maybe Ali was onto something when she called him out on both Jane's after walking him up. There were definitely resemblances between the three women, he saw it right away with the first two, but Jane Newton wasn't a corpse! But not enough where you'd think they'd be relatives or test subjects in a cloning experiment, something the government has probably been doing for decades.

It wouldn't surprise Detective Chauncey Winfield.

A few years back Chauncey had a hobby, more of a phase he went through, where he'd compare head shots of different actors to find resemblances between them. Film studios always tried to find a specific look, especially back in the golden age of television. He recalled pictures printed off the internet he used as bookmarks for whatever he was reading. The first ones that came to mind were Van Williams, who played The Green Hornet in the mid-1960s, and Jeffrey Hunter, known for his portrayal of Captain Pike in the pilot episode of Star Trek's The Original Series "The Cage." Right away you'd think the two actors were brothers, possibly twins, yet still able to tell the difference between them. Chauncey felt bad for Hunter passing away accidentally, only slightly over forty. If he'd been the age he's at now back in the 1970s and working in Hollywood maybe he'd have suggested doing a television movie or two using the original cast of the Star Trek pilot episode with Van Williams taking over the role of Captain Pike. But whether or not Mr. Williams would've been interested in doing something like that, he couldn't say. The Green Hornet only lasted one full season, yet quite an accomplishment back then considering an Asian actor got second billing as the sidekick Kato, played by the one and only Bruce Lee.

Another example of physical similarities between two actors Chauncey couldn't ignore: William Hartnell, the first Dr. Who, and Jonathan Harris, Dr. Smith on Lost in Space. Keep in mind that Dr. Who had been developed by the British Broadcasting Corporation and filmed exclusively in England while Lost in Space was filmed on the other side of the world in a studio in Hollywood, California. Chauncey wasn't sure which show came out first, but chances are the casting agents kept close tabs on each other back then........ and now most likely.

The last one he could think of he loved pointing out to both diehard science fiction and comedy buffs. Patrick Troughton, the second Dr. Who, with a hairstyle and short stature to match, bared strong resemblance to Moe of The Three Stooges. He hadn't really noticed until he finished college and started getting back into Dr. Who again when VHS tapes were still being sold. One particular store he frequented an employee who recommended videotapes of the second Dr. Who pointed it out. Something he never forgot, and never would.

Now, if he only possessed a working T.A.R.D.I.S.

CHAPTER 17

CHAUNCEY PULLED INTO THE PARKING LOT at the complex. He parked in his usual spot, not that he felt entitled to it. Whatever was available suited him. Ali's car was parked on the left. Another car he didn't recognize was in the space after hers, colored black with four doors but couldn't see it clear enough to determine the make and model, which he could do occasionally. Mrs. Watson's car was in the usual spot on the right. He turned off the engine and turned his head to see Ali standing in the walkway looking at him. He got out of his car and walked over to her.

"How's things on the inside?" he asked.

"I don't know yet," she answered. "Not in your place."

"Did you just get here?"

"Yeah, sort of, I was visiting with Mrs. Watson."

She must have come outside a couple of seconds ago, which explained why he didn't see her when he first arrived.

"How is our favorite landlord?" he asked.

"Alright," said Ali. "She introduced me to someone named Oliver, an electrician."

"What needs to be worked on?"

"Nothing yet," she answered. "I think he might be a friend as well."

"Someone she's dating?"

"I don't know about that, he's an older gentleman."

Chauncey and Ali heard some noise, specifically a front door opening. Mrs. Watson's, whose entrance the two of them were standing in front of in the walkway at the bottom of the stairs. She stepped outside with another individual following her, presumably Oliver.

"How are you, Chauncey?" asked his favorite landlord.

"I'm quite well, Mrs. Watson," answered Chauncey. "Who's your friend?"

Mrs. Watson and her friend, a man with a stocky build, dark hair and a trimmed beard, maybe sixty years old, made their way down the steps. When they approached him Chauncey extended his right hand to introduce himself.

"Chauncey Winfield," he said.

"Oliver Wood," said the older gentleman.

"All of her wood?" he asked.

"That's right."

"Are you sure?"

"Why wouldn't I be?"

Ali started to smile noticeably, trying not to laugh. Chauncey was having one of those days, the kind that caused his unusual sense of humor to emerge. It was probably a good thing she was the only one to notice.

"Good point," said Chauncey. "Don't mind me."

"He's not on his regular schedule," said Ali. "So he's a little slow today."

"Gotcha," said Oliver.

Mrs. Watson handed business cards of Oliver Wood's to both Chauncey and Ali.

"He gave me a bunch of them." she said.

"Is he officially the new electrician for the complex?" asked Chauncey.

"We'll see when I have to call him to repair something," she answered.

"Fair enough," he responded.

"Unless you know how to fix something that's not broke," said Oliver.

"Good point," added Ali. "I'm glad the four of us were able to have this introduction.

"Me too," said Chauncey.

"Alright then," said Mrs. Watson.

The four of them shook hands and Chauncey and Ali headed toward the Detective's place while Mrs. Watson and Oliver Wood headed toward the parking lot, presumably to go out somewhere. The Detective and Ali walked up the front steps of his place, when they reached the front door he took out a set of keys and unlocked it. As soon as he opened it his eyes focused on something he hadn't seen before. The dog was waiting for them, which wasn't unusual, but she just stood there with a wide-eyed stare and shaking.

"What's the matter, Lady?" he asked. "Are you cold?"

Both Chauncey and Ali kneeled down to stroke her fur a bit. She wasn't cold, she was scared.

Lady slowly began to back away, then slowly turned around and walked out of the kitchen. She stopped at the staircase leading upstairs then turned around again to look at Chauncey and Ali. She turned her head every few seconds to look upstairs then looked back at the two of them while still visibly shaking.

"I've never seen her like this before," said Ali.

"It's like she's trying to tell us something," added Chauncey.

The Detective paused for a moment, the only logical thing to do was go upstairs and check things out. He decided to go upstairs by himself to see how the dog would react.

"Stay with her," said Chauncey.

"Are you sure?" asked Ali.

"I think so."

"What if she decides to follow you up there?"

"That's fine, let her."

Chauncey placed his right foot on the first step while looking over at Lady. She didn't budge, as soon as he took another step she backed away considerably, even more so compared to when she greeted the two of them at the door.

"Something's up there," said Chauncey.

"Or something bad happened up there," added Ali. "Do you think somebody broke in?"

"Anything's possible."

That question convinced him to take his gun out. He held it in his right hand but kept it down since he didn't anticipate having to shoot anyone, but with Lady being as scared as she was he had no way of knowing what he was up against. He couldn't afford to take any chances. Not with everything he'd been going through lately, he wasn't sure if any of it had sunk in yet with everything that happened after leaving Widen Laboratories, knowing about Old Rudy Morgan, crawling out of his grave with that Jane Doe trying to choke him back into it, then waking up in his own bedroom.

He had to be ready for anything, because he couldn't make sense of it so far!

Chauncey slowly crept forward, step by step. As he reached the top of the stairs, he sensed vibrations throughout his body with a slow, humming sound occurring simultaneously. He didn't know if this was caused by something he was about to discover or if it resonated within himself.

Whatever it was kept him at a crossroads, despite

continuing to press forward.

As he crept down the hallway, he looked to the right to get a good look inside the bathroom. The door was wide open, with no indication of any recent activity. Truth being told he didn't use it much except for showering in the morning, and not on a daily basis since he could use the downstairs bathroom for the same purpose. Both had full bathtubs as well so he wasn't very finicky, unless he felt he needed more space then he'd stick to the one upstairs.

Up next was the spare room, which was also easy to check out with the door left wide open and most of the stuff inside having little interest to anyone but Chauncey. Not even, he thought, since he honestly couldn't remember the last time he looked through any of the half-dozen or so boxes in there. Some were kept inside the closet with a handful more against the wall by the left side of the window. On the right was a small couch equipped for two people at the most, Lady could snuggle her way in between them but that would be pushing it, not that he could remember the last time he'd sat on the thing. As he made his way inside he looked outside the large window more suited for a downstairs living room area. The sun wasn't shining but it was very bright outside, also contributing to that were the thin, light blue colored curtains he left open all the time. It hadn't been used as a guest room in ages, and he reminded himself that everything he kept in there would be of little interest to anybody...including him!

He took one quick look around the entire room. Nothing but a few boxes and wide open space. Of course there's the television sitting on a table next to the door and a small desk to the right of it with a computer he rarely used. His laptop suited him fine except for the days he crawled out of bed and didn't want to get off his ass, at all! That only happened about once a month, and to be fair of all things the swiveling chair included with it is very comfortable. Nothing to see here, and most likely whatever scared poor Lady wasn't hiding in one of the desk drawers and wouldn't jump out of one of the boxes, either.

Then again, stranger things have happened. Chauncey knew that better than anybody, and still hadn't admitted it to himself.

Not entirely.

One thing still eating away at him was the vibrations he kept sensing. He stopped right before the doorway leading back out into the hallway and looked down at the television placed on the table beside him. He took notice of a tiny red light on directly below the screen meaning the television was turned off. If he turned the television on that it would go off and a green light located about a millimeter to the right would go on. Just thinking about that made Chauncey think he could direct traffic with a remote control. With technology advancing as quickly as it does it could be happening already. It might be a little tough without a yellow light at certain intersections but nothing's perfect! He ran through plenty of them throughout the years. He bent down to reach to pull the plug out of the wall behind the television. Upon doing so he immediately realized this was not the cause for these vibrations he sensed. He decided not to do the same with the computer, not that any lights indicated if it was on or off.

Technology was not the culprit in this particular case.

The only place left for Chauncey to check was the bedroom. He went back out into the hallway and turned right. Immediately to the left was his bedroom with the door closed tight. He couldn't recall if he'd closed it all the way when he got up this morning, but preferred to think he'd done so! At this point, however, he didn't want to assume anything. He didn't have the first clue what these vibrations were all about, much less where they were coming from. On top of that he swore he could hear a faint buzzing sound, which would have made sense if the TV was still plugged in! Now it's time to move on to the last place left unexplored.

The Detective wasn't about to take any chances, so he raised his right hand up holding the gun with his finger on the trigger. He didn't know if it was loaded or not. Truthfully, he did, but couldn't recall the last time he fired the thing. Hopefully, it wouldn't jam on him when he needed it the most. He quickly glanced down to make sure the safety device was off, affirmative. He placed his left hand on the doorknob and slowly turned it, then pushed the door open as slowly as possible. If the carpet on the inside had been any thinner a light touch might have done the trick. Then again, he hoped he'd never have to break the door down to get into his bedroom either.

Chauncey used his left hand to push the door open and kept it near his waist level with his right hand several inches above it holding the gun. Directly in front of him was his bed. Nothing was out of the ordinary, even stuff that was out of place. A pair of pants and socks left on the floor from the other day (not surprising!) with sweats and t-shirt at the foot of the bed (definitely not surprising!) which he wore around the house the majority of the time. The bed had been made nicely, could he have been responsible? Maybe Ali did the chore earlier, but not likely. This was something he actually did frequently enough where he didn't have to think about it, even if it wasn't a daily routine. Kudos for the (somewhat) single guy!

Instinctively he looked to the left with nothing to be seen so far, but he knew he wasn't alone. The vibrations he sensed kept on rising and felt it on the floor he stood on. That faint buzzing sound grew rapidly in his ears, yet he couldn't think of what it might be. He looked to the right and turned his head further to look behind the door with nothing to be seen there either. The vibrations and buzzing sounds grew louder, closer, and more nerve wracking as each moment passed. Chauncey turned his head back slightly and stared at the wall to see a shadow rising close to his height. What it could be he had no idea, without hesitating he just turned around and fired several shots on whatever crept up behind him.

This was the one time if he hadn't shot first he wouldn't have believed his own eyes and been eaten alive. To describe this thing by starting from the beginning was nearly impossible. All he knew was this creature had its mouth open making a hissing or buzzing sound when he fired his gun. It collapsed almost instantly, and he knew right away it didn't swallow the bullets. Those went through the back of the head and the blood splattered on the wall behind it. He took notice of that before he even remotely considered looking down at the floor as time seems to stop in these situations.

Even Chauncey needed time to grasp this.

Granted, the first thing he had to tell himself was he might never know what he was grasping. Looking down at the floor told him this was the tip of an iceberg. Everything he'd gone through in the past several days couldn't come close to what he's set his eyes upon. It was some kind of snake. He knew that when he stared this thing in the eyes only seconds ago but that hadn't registered until after he shot it. Somehow he came to the conclusion judging by the size it was part python or boa constrictor. The look on the face and in the eyes made him think of a cobra. The skin colors were black and white, some thick-striped but not as cut and dry as zebras are. Too much blood flowing all over it and on the floor soaking into the carpet made it difficult to describe the outer features.

While taking this in emotionally Chauncey hadn't noticed Ali standing directly behind him. She took a tiny breath and he turned around instantly. He knew it was her but an ever growing, cautious instinct fed the need to be ready for anything. The dog stood at the doorway but wouldn't come in eventually running off and heading back downstairs. Chauncey heard that perfectly, which he couldn't do before.

"What is that thing?" asked Ali.

"Some kind of snake," said Chauncey. "And something else, what I don't know!"

"The carpet will have to be removed!"

"That's fine! I never liked the lame, light blue color, and it's too thin!"

"Yeah," she said. "The blood will soak right through it."

"I know," he responded. "It's gone to shit!"

"What do you want to do?"

"Nothing yet, there's only one guy I can think of to talk to about this. Do I still have a bunch of large trash bags in the cabinet above the sink?"

"I think so, but the blood will soak right through them!"

"I know," said Chauncey. "We'll just use those to start with! We'll need to get a bit creative with this one!"

"I don't want to use any of the duffle bags from the fitness center!" exclaimed Ali.

"Don't worry about it! There's a giant suitcase in the closet in the other room I've had no use for...until now!"

This particular cleaning task took at least forty-five minutes with details neither Chauncey nor Ali wanted to describe to anyone, much less have to do again.

CHAPTER 18

PROFESSOR HORACE HURRIED to the main entrance at his lab when he heard knocking which occurred repeatedly, persistently and loud. Whoever it was must have really needed to talk with him. He could've sworn he left the double doors unlocked when he returned with take out food he got from a Chinese restaurant in Downtown Prime. Up until now he didn't think it was possible for someone to pound on the doors that loud, especially to the point where the sound echoed as far back to the area he'd been working in.

Learn something new every day.

The moment he opened the right hand door he recognized the man he'd met not long ago: Detective Chauncey Winfield, who stared him straight in the eye holding the largest suitcase he'd ever seen in his life.

"You're not a light packer, I take it?" he asked.

Without hesitating, Chauncey entered the room immediately. Professor Horace moved slightly to the right to accommodate the Detective's actions. He didn't want to be plowed down by someone else's baggage, or his own for that matter. This incident played out where he followed the visitor into the lab instead of the other way around.

"This should be interesting," he said.

"You damn right!" stated Chauncey.

The Detective marched over to a lab table with a couple of notebooks on it which Professor Horace used earlier in the day for research purposes. Some people still need to write stuff down even in this modern day and age, especially if you're doing everything yourself, which was often the case in with this particular Scientist. Chauncey stood on one side of the table making Professor Horace instinctively stand on the other. Chauncey leaned over slightly to unzip the suitcase he'd placed beside him.

"Clear it off!" he demanded.

"Alright," responded Professor Horace, remaining calm. The task wasn't difficult only having to remove a few notebooks.

Chauncey was still bent over slightly with the suitcase open, rummaging through it causing the unmistakable sound of a plastic trash bag being untied. Professor Horace had no clue what this guy was about to show him.

"I know what you're thinking," said Chauncey. "I'm not here to dump my personal garbage on you!"

"I was pretty sure from the moment you walked through the door you weren't lugging in trailer trash!" said Professor Horace.

Chauncey paused for a second then bent down further to grab the suitcase from the bottom. He didn't think about what he was doing except for making sure his hands were placed far enough underneath in order to lift it up and dump everything out in one try. He didn't think a single word could describe specifically what was contained inside. As soon as he spilled the reptilian abomination out onto the table, anyone who laid eyes on the thing would've felt the same way.

You had to see it to believe it, yet even Professor Horace was taken aback in a matter of seconds.

"What can you tell me about this?" asked Chauncey, in a bit of a demanding tone.

Professor Horace couldn't say anything. The blood flowed out of the creature's body and slowly oozed all over the table. If he hadn't been in such shock, he would've grabbed a mop or leftover newspaper so it wouldn't spill down onto the floor. Thank God no one else was around to witness this mess while still trying to let this sink in. He knew this was some kind of snake, beyond that he had no idea.

"From the reptile family, obviously!" snapped Chauncey.

"I gathered that much," responded Professor Horace.

"What do you make of it?" asked Chauncey.

Less than a minute had passed since the Detective dumped the contents out of the suitcase. The Professor already knew there was more to this than simply being a snake.

"I can't put into words," said Professor Horace, pausing for a moment. "It's some kind of snake, some kind of mutation..."

"You got anything like this in the lab?" asked Chauncey.

"I do now."

The first glance proved there was nothing like it. Otherwise Professor Horace would have had a definite answer for Chauncey right away.

It's no secret that Widen Labs has conducted unusual reptile experiments over the years," he said. "But I've never seen anything like this. Not from a birth or the result of an experiment."

"Do you visit the Widen facilities often?" asked Chauncey.

"Not really, no. The one who goes back and forth all the time from the university to the company is Jane Newton."

"Why am I not surprised?"

"What's that?"

"Nothing, so this goes over your head?"

"From a scientific perspective, absolutely!" said Professor Horace.

Both of them just stood and stared at whatever this reptilian abomination was for another minute or so. It is usually considered Detective Chauncey Winfield's job to get someone else to talk, this time he was the first one to crack.

"You think there's some nasty venom in it?" he asked.

"I don't know," said Professor Horace. "Whatever's in it I'm sure it's nothing I've ever......."

"The other samples you detected from the other bodies were standard venom, right?"

"That's one way to describe it."

"Does that make it sound less lethal?"

"For the moment, yeah!" stated Professor Horace.

The Detective had to give himself a little credit. He wasn't intentionally trying to soften the impact of having to view this mutated snake-like creature lying dead before their eyes, anything to balance the level of sanity.

"What now?" he asked.

"This is it," said Professor Horace.

"What do you mean?"

"This is my work for tonight, and tomorrow! And as long as it takes after that!"

"Okay," said Chauncey.

"Yeah," said Professor Horace. "Everything stops as of now, I don't know how long it will take to get some definite answers but I want to know what this thing is even more than you do!"

"You may be right about that."

Detective Chauncey Winfield wouldn't argue with Professor Horace on this one. The man's a renowned Herpetologist with a capital H necessary in this case. He was just grateful things would move forward immediately, making his job in Law Enforcement a whole lot easier.

However, he needed a breather in the worst way.

"Is your nephew around?" he asked.

"I think so," said Professor Horace. "Why do you ask?"

"You'll be busy for a while, right? We had a good talk last time. I'll pop in and say hi again. Do you think you'll need his help up here?"

"No, this will go way over his head! Hell, it's over my head! I wouldn't know what to say! Don't tell him about this, okay?"

"No problem," said Chauncey, a bit shaken.

"Don't tell him you were here, either. I don't want anyone to know what's going on. Not even you until you hear from me!"

"You got it."

A part of Chauncey wanted to stick around and figure out what the deal was with this thing. But he knew with the state of mind he was in he'd probably crack. There's something to be said for knowing your limits. Certain circumstances call for that, and this is one of them. It didn't mean he was limited when it came to his actual abilities, but in his mind he'd reached a breaking point.

Professor Horace lifted up his lab coat to get his cell phone out of his pants pocket He pushed maybe two or three buttons then put it up to his right ear. None of this caught Chauncey's attention until the Professor spoke.

"The Detective's here again," he said. "He wants to pop in and see you again……..okay."

"What's up?" asked Chauncey.

"Paul said you can stop by."

"You'll need to call Sergeant Matheson or whoever's in the C.P. office."

"Huh?"

"You know, to grant access to get into that basement apartment of his!"

"Right, why don't I just take a walk with you and use my I.D. badge to get you down there?"

"Are you sure that'll be alright?"

"Yeah, don't worry about it. You're not going to do another interview, are you?"

"Nothing of the sort," said Chauncey.

"They'll think it's just me letting one of his friends in to see him," said Professor Horace. "He said you guys hit it off during the first visit."

"Interview technically," said Chauncey.

"Then I stand corrected," said Professor Horace. "You took it pretty well walking in on him while......."

"Don't worry about it."

They shared a quick laugh together. Professor Horace put his cell phone into the right bottom pocket of his lab coat then turned his head toward the direction to exit.

"I'll trust you to lead the way," he said, smiling.

"Yeah," said Chauncey. "That won't be too hard."

Chauncey was amazed at the Professor's clarity considering what he just dumped on the guy. It made him realize that everyone should take a deep breath when a crisis like this falls into their lap. A smart scientist should possess enough common sense to come up for air periodically. Perhaps some of these traits had an influence on the nephew.

Anything's possible.

CHAPTER 19

AFTER A BRIEF WALK AND SOME SMALL TALK with Professor Horace, who accompanied Chauncey to grant him access to visit with Paul Raymond again, he began his second venture into the basement of the Widen Science Building. He had to admit he wasn't as taken in by its surroundings this time around. He didn't notice anything different or out of place as he headed downstairs again, it was just as immaculate as before and the white walls still looked as if they'd never been touched by human fingerprints much less crawled on by a single insect. Of course many of Horace's reptilian specimens could be found only one floor above here along with the present he dropped off a little while ago. So that could change at any time.

As he got off the last step of the light blue carpeted staircase onto the tan colored tile floor he immediately looked to the right to observe another white wall along with the windows located at the very top by the ceiling. He didn't expect to see anything different and he hadn't, but he quickly figured out why his excitement was non-existent with what he saw. The sun shining in through those windows during the daytime created a breathtaking sensation, more than he'd realized. He could see fine with the lights on down there but it didn't provide the same feeling. Amazing how night and day can make all the difference to the environment you're in. He'd have to ask Paul if he felt the same way about it.

The Detective heard some noise behind him. It was easy to figure out what it was even before he started to turn around. It was the sound of a door opening. As soon as he turned his head he saw who he expected to see: Paul Raymond.

"Hey," said Paul, standing at a halfway open door originally designed as a storage closet converted into a bedroom.

"How are you?" asked Chauncey.

"Not bad."

"A little different when you're expecting someone, huh?"

"Believe it or not I haven't smoked at all since the last time you were here."

"Seriously?" asked Chauncey.

"After you walked in on me that time I figured I should be a little more cautious," he said, shifting his eyes toward the windows at Chauncey had been focused on. "Not the same as being here in the daytime."

"I was going to ask you about that. It's not just me."

"Far from it," said Paul, opening the door all the way giving Chauncey the cue to enter.

Chauncey walked towards Paul, who turned around when he reached the entrance then followed the young man inside. This time a small, swiveling office chair had been placed only a few feet from the bed with a folding wooden tray to the right of it. He immediately took the initiative to sit down.

"You a coffee guy?" asked Paul, as he started to sit

down on the bed.

"Damn straight," answered Chauncey.

"I can make some if you want, won't take long."

'Sure, but don't feel you need to right away."

"Alright," said Paul, as both Chauncey and himself shifting their eyes toward the folding tray he'd left his bowl on. "I'm sorry about that. Do you want me to put it away?"

"Don't worry about it," said Chauncey. "You can even spark it up if you want to."

"Seriously?" he asked.

"Sure," said Chauncey, smirking slightly.

"What about you?"

"With all the shit I've dealt with the past couple of days it might do me some good!"

Paul hesitated for a moment then chuckled.

"That's a first!" he said.

"What?"

"Approval," answered Paul.

"From someone in Law Enforcement?" asked Chauncey.

"Yeah!" he said.

"There's a first time for everything I suppose!"

They both laughed out loud simultaneously. The Detective felt like he was starting to smoke already. He barely paid attention to Paul picking up the bowl off the tray then sitting down on the bed. Within seconds the young man took a lighter out with had The Walking Dead featured on it and sparked up.

"Do you follow the show?" asked Chauncey.

"What show?" responded Paul.

"The Walking Dead," he said, pointing at the lighter.

"Not really. I do like it, though."

"Yeah, I hate how it feels like a major task to keep updated with a series week after week."

"I know what you mean," said Paul. "Doesn't it feel like

with the invention of DVDs which have entire seasons on them it gives you less incentive to follow everything?"

"Absolutely," said Chauncey. "Same with all of those web series shows out there. As much as I love the concept I'm just not motivated enough to keep up with them. Everything I've heard so far about Daredevil sounds intriguing it's just not where my head's at. Who knows? Maybe someday, hopefully sooner than later, I'll be able to absorb all of this."

"The more you have, the less you want."

"You may have a point there, Paul."

Unlike Clinton, Paul inhaled as much as possible. As soon as he took the bowl out of his mouth he offered it to Chauncey, who leaned slightly forward to grab hold of it. He honestly had no clue if the guy was serious about how it might help, until now.

Chauncey put the bowl up to his lips with his left hand and lit Paul's The Walking Dead lighter with his right. Seconds later he sparked up and inhaled, lightly. He honestly couldn't remember the last time he got high but he recalled his dislike of the burning sensation in his throat, which he felt instantly after taking the first hit. It didn't change his mood. Not for the worse. That was the only part he didn't like. The moment he took the thing out of his mouth the conversation began.

"How long has it been?" asked Paul.

"What?"

"Since you got high," he said.

"I have no idea," answered Chauncey. "When you're in my line of work you're not associated with a lot of people who are into this, not heavily."

"Do you think they'd tell you?"

"Probably not," he said, shaking his head while handing the bowl and lighter back. "A lot of cops don't even like to talk about drinking."

"Really?" asked Paul.

"Yup, doesn't matter if they're straight as an arrow or if they hit the bottle morning, noon, and night."

"Almost sounds like a reflex."

"That's one way of putting it."

"Do you think it'd be different if they switched from being boozers to stoners?"

"I've asked myself that question a number of times," answered Chauncey. "I'm a Detective so I should know what I'm talking about. I don't have the first clue. Like everyone else in the world our problems will still exist no matter what, all the drinking in the world's not going to change that. Would smoking weed be a better choice? I don't know, but I will say this: at least you won't get a hangover!"

"That is true!"

"The only other problem, however, is you do have your share of paranoid cops. I'm not talking about hard asses who like to bust balls. It's just their nature. For these guys getting high could make that trait worse."

Chauncey and Paul passed the bowl back and forth again and each of them took another hit. Chauncey already started thinking he might be rambling too much already, and he wasn't convinced he was feeling the effects of the weed coming on, not yet. He was already thinking too much, something he was doing to himself so he couldn't blame it on getting high. Thinking too much is just part of being a Detective, in his case at least.

"How long until this stuff hits you?" he asked.

"You'll know when it does," answered Paul.

"Can you give me any time frame at all?"

"That's all I can tell you."

How often does this kid smoke? A lot as far as Chauncey knew, and he didn't doubt the kid's honesty about not having any since the last time he was here. But he figured Paul would at least have a vague idea, especially if you have the same stuff repeatedly.

"I don't check my watch every time I take a hit," said Paul.

"That's a good point," said Chauncey, preventing him from becoming annoyed with the kid not having an answer.

"Any other cult films come to mind?" asked Paul.

"Sure," said Chauncey, sparking his interest, so to speak.

"Like what?"

"Ever seen any of the Phantasm movies?"

"Hell yeah!" said Paul, with enthusiasm in his voice rising.

"You have to love The Tall Man!" stated Chauncey.

"I think that character had the potential to be a superhero villain."

"I always thought so, too."

Chauncey and Paul passed the bowl back and forth to one another and took hits again. Chauncey made sure he inhaled more this time, which was strange since he knew he didn't care for the burning sensation he felt in his throat. But he hoped to feel stoned sooner instead of later, so this rationalized doing so. As soon as he took the bowl out of his mouth and handed it back to Paul again he had more to add to the discussion.

"It makes me think of Swamp Thing," said Chauncey. "Don't get me wrong I love that French actor who played Dr. Arcane but The Tall Man could've done an equally good job."

"Angus Scrimm," said Paul.

"That's right. Didn't you also find it funny that the two main characters Mike and Reggie were played by actors named Michael Baldwin and Reggie Bannister?"

"Actually Mike eventually changed his professional name to A. Michael Baldwin."

"This is true. Yet I seriously doubt there's any connection to Alec Baldwin or any of the other brothers!"

"Not likely."

"I wonder," said Chauncey. "Maybe the director used their real names to make things easier or if he had them in mind when he wrote the script?"

"Who knows?" asked Paul. "Remember someone else played Mike in Phantasm II. I think his name was James Le Gros. I know he popped up in a lot of stuff for quite a few years after that. I'm pretty sure he got on that show about the lawyer. You know the one who's with Harrison Ford now."

"I remember. I'm surprised different actors weren't used in every film, especially if you consider the amount of time between all the sequels."

"Yeah, it's amazing the same guy played The Tall Man in all five films."

"All the different actors who portrayed Leatherface," said Chauncey. "Or Michael Myers, I think Rob Zombie's movies were the only ones to use the same guy twice in a row."

"I think the Texas Chainsaw Massacre remakes with R. Lee Ermey used the same guy," added Paul. "But you're right, it's not often. Kane Hodder played Jason four times in a row but there are a dozen Friday the 13th movies so it only counts for a third of them."

"I have to admit I was a bit surprised he wasn't brought back for Freddy vs. Jason, especially since Robert Englund came back as Freddy. Audiences wouldn't have accepted anyone else."

"Maybe because one guy played Freddy all along whereas Friday the 13th and Jason were established long before Kane got involved. The studios probably thought there wasn't as much of a risk involved since the character had been played at least a half dozen times before him."

"That makes sense and you can't keep it up forever. You had Bela Lugosi and Boris Karloff as Dracula and Frankenstein in the black and white Universal movies in the 1930s but when Hammer Films created colorized versions of these characters they brought in Christopher Lee for both of them! What a lucky break for that guy! I can understand the fear of typecasting but to be embraced by the public the way he was!"

"Don't forget The Mummy!"

"How could I?" said Chauncey. "Lightning struck three times in his case."

"You're right about that," added Paul. "I just wish a guy like Kane got the same respect and appreciation."

"There's a lot more now than ever. Both the internet and the increasing number of horror conventions have helped considerably, don't you think?"

"That's a good point."

Chauncey could feel something coming on. A jolt perhaps but not one to give him the shakes or feel jittery for that matter, a strange sensation for sure. He felt a bit more relaxed and far more aware, not so much of his surroundings but where his head was at the moment.

Hopefully that's a good thing.

"I don't know about you," said Chauncey. "But I don't mind if horror stuff keeps a certain cult status. It's not for everybody and I kind of like the fact that to a point I can still call it my own."

"True," said Paul. "Retaining a certain novelty does make it a bit more special. You're right it's not for everybody, even if it was and they still don't dig it more for us!"

Time to get back to the subject of horror movies, Chauncey thought.

"Did you ever see the Hatchet series?" he asked.

"All three," answered Paul. "Good old Kane shined in those, too."

"He could've easily played Bane in a Batman movie, as good as Tom Hardy even."

"I wouldn't mind seeing him as The Punisher or Batman

for that matter!"

"Why not?" asked Chauncey. "But if he played Batman he'd have to be clean shaven."

"Not all the time," said Paul. "As Bruce Wayne he can keep the facial hair just not as Batman."

"He could be credited as The Dark Knight and The Bearded Bruce Wayne."

"Keep the capital T in there!"

They both burst out laughing. Whether or not they would've found this funny a short while ago who could say. Discussing stuff like this just for fun was a warm welcome to Chauncey. The best part being it kept the gears in his head moving.

"Who played Jason in the so-called Friday the 13th remake?" asked Chauncey.

"Derek Mears," replied Paul. "I think he appeared in one of the Hatchet movies, too."

"That's right! Who played him in Freddy vs. Jason?"

"I'm not sure. I remember seeing an interview with he did on that DVD made for the thirtieth anniversary of the series. He looks like he could play a really good Frankenstein."

"Agreed!" exclaimed Chauncey. "I saw that too and thought the same thing."

"They could keep the Monster's look similar to what's his name from the 1930s films," added Paul.

"I wouldn't mind if he looked like the actor in Mel Brooks' Young Frankenstein, who played him?"

"Peter.......Boyle?"

"I think so," said Chauncey. "Gene Wilder was great in that, same with Marty Feldman, I didn't mind the fact it was filmed in black and white."

"Me neither," said Paul. "But I'd rather it be made in color at this point. Obviously try to keep a bit of the tone and style from the early films but not an exact copy."

MICHAEL JAMESON

"Not like the Psycho remake where it was done shot-for shot. I appreciate the fact it had never been done before, there's a first time for everything. But that's about it."

"Agreed," said Paul.

Chauncey heard the door slam shut from behind, giving him a bit of a jolt. He thought it closed the moment he walked in. Then again, he had to admit he wasn't paying attention. At the same time Paul turned the radio on to play a favorite CD, Link Wray with the first song heard by their ears being Rumble, at a very low volume.

"I thought the door was shut already," observed Chauncey, quickly glancing behind him.

"Same here," said Paul.

"To be honest, I wasn't really paying attention. Not smart for a Detective."

"Neither was I, but I know who did it."

"What do you mean?" asked Chauncey. "It didn't shut on its own?"

"Nope," answered Chauncey. "I'll have to introduce you to the other tenant residing down here."

"Huh?"

"You heard me, hold on a second."

Paul handed the bowl to Chauncey then stood up and walked over to the door to open it, but only a few inches. Of all things a black cat wandered in and slowly made its way over to Chauncey, greeting him with a wide-eyed stare then turning around to take a few more steps and jumping onto Paul's bed.

"This is Mr. Smith," said Paul. "Also a resident of the Widen Science Building, basement level like me."

"Is he yours?" asked Chauncey.

"More or less, Uncle Stan lets him stay here with me most of the time."

"You're telling me he shut the door?"

"That's right. We've caught it on camera before. He

205

stands up slightly and pushes it shut with his front paws."

"Like a dog!"

"Exactly!" stated Paul.

"I'd love to see that," said Chauncey, smiling.

"I've got it on my computer, I can find it if you want."

"That's okay, some other time."

Chauncey placed the bowl back on his lips and took another hit. He removed it and handed it back to Paul while inhaling. This time he didn't feel much of a burning sensation.

"So the cat shuts the door on his own," said Chauncey.

"That's right," said Paul.

"Do you think he could find his way to Washington, too?"

"It's funny you say that, he's a rescue from Washington."

"D.C. or the state?" asked Chauncey.

"The state I think," answered Paul. "Like me."

"Did you ever see the movie?"

"Mr. Smith Goes To Washington?"

"Yeah, that's in black and white too, I think."

"A really long time ago and I don't remember anything about it, you?"

"I don't think so," said Chauncey. "It's one of those movies a lot of people have heard of but never actually seen it."

"Kind of like Gone With The Wind," added Paul. "Everybody knows about it but for the most part a lot of people haven't seen it, not from our generations."

"Someday I hope to, supposedly George Reeves had a small part in it as a gravedigger or something, years before Superman."

"I heard that, too. I'll have to look online. I bet you saw The Wizard Of Oz a bunch of times growing up!"

"You got it," said Chauncey. "I know L. Frank Baum wrote the thing, the books anyway. Never read any of them."

"Me neither," said Paul. "Supposedly in the original story Dorothy wore crystal slippers instead of ruby ones, I wonder why they changed it?"

"It's Hollywood, so who knows? You made me of think of something else."

"What?"

"The Frankenstein movies from the 1930s," said Chauncey. "I read Mary Shelley's novel in High School. I originally saw the movies when I was a little kid and decided I'd watch the first one again. In the book Dr. Frankenstein's first name is Victor and his best friend's name is Henry but got switched in the movie."

"Perhaps Henry was a more popular name back then," said Paul.

"Possibly, I wouldn't be surprised if an error was made in the script and by the time someone noticed most of the filming had been completed and the director figured fuck it.......too late!"

"Could be, with James Whale directing it you never know."

"That's right," said Chauncey. "You know more about this stuff than I do."

"I also have a lot more free time on my hands," said Paul.

"At least you're not out causing trouble."

"I guess I could be a real dick if I wanted to!"

"That's my job," said Chauncey, chuckling a little.

"A Private Dick, right?" added Paul, joining in on the laugh.

"At least it's guaranteed I'll never expose myself...not in this line of work!"

They both burst out laughing hysterically. It felt great sharing the same sense of humor. Chauncey didn't want to say anything, but the effects of the weed probably had something to do with it as well. More and more he was letting his guard down, so to speak.

"The same thing happened with The Incredible Hulk," said Paul. "Remember?"

"What?" he asked.

"David Banner, remember?"

"Oh yeah on the TV show, I forgot about that."

"I honestly think it sounded better."

"Same here, Stan Lee always gave his superheroes identities the most ridiculously simple names: Peter Parker, Matt Murdock, or Bruce Banner for that matter."

"It sounded like a name you'd hear with Daffy Duck's lisp," said Paul, before attempting to do a half-assed impression of the character. "Bruce Banner!"

"That sounded pretty good!" said Chauncey. "Do you do a lot of voices?"

"First time ever," he said.

"Your first attempt?" asked Chauncey. "As a Private Dick I'm dumbfounded!"

"First time doing that one," he answered. "There are others I can do but it's been a while since I've practiced. The only audience I have is a black cat."

"Bad luck there?"

"I don't know about that. I'm not big on luck."

"Remember Sylvester couldn't catch a fucking mouse if his life depended on it!"

"Shut up!"

The two of them laughed out loud simultaneously for the second time, it would be another minute or so before the conversation started again.

"Hold on," said Paul. "Sylvester wasn't all black, was he?"

"No," said Chauncey.

"He was black and white, just like that skunk."

"Funny thing is that skunk could easily send off a distant early warning, and still stood a better chance at catching a mouse before Sylvester."

"I'll bet Mr. Smith here has more social skills than

either one of those characters."

"You just reminded me of something," added Chauncey.

"What?"

"Another old black and white horror movie The Black Cat with Bela Lugosi," he answered.

"I've seen that, been a long time, though."

"Same here," said Chauncey. "I've got to dig that one out of my closet most likely. I think I still own it on VHS. It's interesting when you think about it."

"How so?" asked Paul.

"Both the combination of the title: The Black Cat and starring an actor who'd soon be down on his luck."

"Luck may have played a part in it," said Paul. "But I think self-destructive habits and living beyond his means played a part as well."

"Who knows?" added Chauncey. "He's been embraced by multiple generations as Dracula for nearly a century now. What he left behind for audiences to enjoy should be remembered over the bad times ALWAYS."

"I'll smoke to that!"

Paul took another hit off the bowl. After taking the first hit a cell phone started ringing. Chauncey's to be exact, who pulled it out of his pocket and pressed the answer button and placed it up to his left ear.

"Hello?" he said.

"I can send someone out tomorrow if you want," said a voice on the other end, it was Professor Horace.

"For what?" he asked.

"There's a bit of a mess where you found this I'd imagine."

"Right...I won't be sleeping in my own bed for a while and I don't need nightmares on top of it. I have no idea how to get that stuff, whatever it left, out of the carpet!"

"I hear you. I'll call in the morning and give you a time."

"Okay," he said, then hung up the phone.

"What's up?" asked Paul.

"That was your Uncle," answered Chauncey. "I've got to go, let's talk more soon!"

"I'm always up for it!"

Chauncey quickly stood up. Before he could so much as begin to contemplate heading towards the door Mr. Smith took the liberty of shutting the door behind him and Paul he had to ask himself: Did I tell Professor Horace I found the present I dropped off for him in my house?

He honestly couldn't remember.

Should he take Paul's offer of coffee before leaving? Nah, forget it!

Chauncey turning down coffee, there's a first time for everything.

CHAPTER 20

It was 10 am the next morning back at Chauncey's place. He and Professor Horace were in the kitchen having coffee. He was glad he had enough sense not to have any wake-up juice last night while visiting Paul considering what they were smoking. He certainly wasn't going to tell his present company about it. Thank God plans were made today for damage control instead of last night, actually an inspection. The real damage done was what Chauncey brought to the Professor's lab at the Widen Science Building, justifiably in many ways. But an indescribable mess remained in Chauncey's bedroom upstairs, which he hadn't set foot in since he and Ali gathered all the remains of the snakelike abomination into garbage bags. She insisted on bringing the dog back to her place overnight, which he agreed to and joined them there after leaving Paul's place. Luckily she had two late evening classes to teach meaning she wouldn't be there when he arrived. He really didn't want her to smell the weed on him, not that she would've gotten angry about it, but it would've been unexpected. What they don't need are more surprises, good or bad.

Chauncey met up with Professor Horace out front earlier this morning followed by three people he didn't recognize. Not that he would've since they were a team of experts brought in to check out the disaster in his bedroom upstairs. He hoped they'd clean up the mess as well, less work for him to do! But right now he wasn't in the position to ask for any favors, much less ask a lot of questions. He wouldn't know where to begin since he had no idea what he'd gotten himself into. All he knew was these guys got the call last night from Professor Horace to fly out directly from the Pentagon in Washington D.C. He half expected them to be from the Widen Labs facility despite his unusual visit there with Jane Newton along with the long, strange trip he'd had after departing, which he hadn't told anyone about.

Professor Horace mainly worked for Prime State University yet still answered to Widen Laboratories, but Chauncey believed that task had been left to Jane Newton since she obviously spent the most time traveling back and forth from both places. After their meeting he wondered how often she went away on Safari on such short notice with Professor Horace knowing little to nothing about it.

Whoever was in the bedroom upstairs Professor Horace said had been flown in directly from D.C. and you think he'd bring someone in from Widen Labs. Had he not contacted anyone from the company and simply gone over their heads? Chauncey figured he would've notified them first out of loyalty. Perhaps he didn't want to attract more negative attention to Prime State University after the murder of Roy Cumberland or maybe he's starting to get suspicious of who he's been answering to.

The Detective became intrigued by these theories,

to say the least. But he needed to keep in mind that's all they were, and ones he had thought of on his own, all he could do was wait for those people from the Pentagon Professor Horace called upon to finish what needed to be done, in his bedroom of all places. Quite odd considering most bedroom activities will take place in the White House or by people who reside in the White House. But in the Pentagon it's unheard of, even for a simple inspection. Chauncey honestly had no idea if there were any bedrooms in the Pentagon. Perhaps that will be a good question to break the ice with these Pentagon people. He might get an answer any moment now, even if he preferred continuing small talk with the present company.

"Are they good friends of yours?" asked Chauncey.

"Not really," answered Professor Horace. "Dale I've known for quite some time now."

"Dale?"

"Dale Shusterman."

"Go on."

"A very interesting background, he studied Herpetology quite extensively."

"Like you," said Chauncey.

"That's not all," he added. "He started out earning a degree in Neural Science do you know what that is?"

"Has to do with the brain, I think," answered Chauncey.

"Exactly, along with that and the Herpetology there's a bit of Zoology in there and a brief stint in the military which is classified, he's not allowed to say what branch he was in much less when or what he did."

"Herpetology, Neurology, Zoology, and the military. Anything else?" asked Chauncey.

"Actually, yes," confirmed Professor Horace. "He grew up in the extermination business."

"Exterminating what?"

"Mostly bugs."

"Gotcha, my Uncle did that for a long time."

"If I remember right that was the same story with him, he worked directly with his Uncle from a very young age. All through high school and college, took over the business for a while when the poor guy passed away suddenly, I guess they were pretty close. Did you ever learn anything about the business yourself?"

"No, my Uncle was living in Florida all the years he did that stuff. I think he'd have preferred it as a part-time hobby. It sounds like Dale has quite the diverse background almost to the point of contradiction, starting out killing insects to studying the brain and reptiles and the military and on and on and on."

"I guess he's worked both sides of the fence when it comes to nature and animals."

"Tell me if you're studying neurological stuff in college is it strictly human brain activity or all forms of life?"

"I don't know," said Professor Horace.

"You of all people don't know?" asked Chauncey.

"I imagine it's primarily human, but I'm not the right guy to ask."

"I figured you could answer that easily."

"You can't know everything about everything."

"That's a good point."

Chauncey realized how strange it felt not having the dog with him. Little Lady was always nearby except for now, the first time ever since taking her in many years ago. Hopefully this particular situation wouldn't last long and everything will revert back to the way it was. She could do okay staying one night at someone else's place, especially Ali's, but that's as far as it goes. Too bad he can't bring her to Paul's place. She wouldn't harm the resident cat Mr. Smith. However, her intense, overly friendly greeting would scare the piss out of it. She'd be super-excited to make an introduction but charging towards any cat with a tail spinning at warp speed along with barking in its face would be like expecting an insect to be okay with being crushed by a giant foot. Perhaps someone like Dale Shusterman could appreciate the comparison after spending a childhood in the extermination business.

"Do you think it'll be alright spend the night here when Dale and his friends finish what they're doing?" asked Chauncey.

"I have no idea," answered Professor Horace. "Believe it or not this is a first for me too."

"First ever?" asked Chauncey. "But you said you've known Dale for a long time, there must've been something..."

"I mean a situation like this one. I'm used to dealing with stuff at the school lab or at the company's main facility. Most of the time Jane Newton keeps tabs on that since I hardly spend any time over there."

"Is that why you called these guys in from the Pentagon?"

"You're right on the money," said Professor Horace. "I've never known about anything like this occurring outside of Widen Labs. I've never heard of anything this extreme happening at the facility either, despite a lot of bizarre experiments taking place there that the public would never find out about."

"Seriously?" asked Chauncey.

"I've never taken in anything at Prime State University which remotely resembles what you brought in last night! Widen Labs would never let something like that get out...or would they?"

"You're not sure, are you?"

"Not anymore!"

Chauncey could tell Professor Horace was agitated just by his tone of voice, if only slightly. He was obviously stepping into unfamiliar territory despite such an extensive background working with reptiles. At this point neither of them knew what to expect from these so-called inspectors from the Pentagon. Chauncey still had no idea what official title Dale and company held. Is this a cause for alarm? Of course, but everything that's occurred recently is!

The Detective didn't have a clue how to explain to Professor Horace what happened after meeting with Jane Newton. Chauncey wasn't sure how the poor guy would take it having such a close working relationship with her. On the surface it's best to keep the impression she's a longtime trusted colleague until he says otherwise. If he's bringing in people from the outside to investigate he might not have a lot of faith in whatever's going on at Widen Laboratories. Being suspicious of Jane Newton is another matter altogether, but he needed to know about the incident eventually.

Over three hours had passed since Chauncey started his day. He'd set the alarm for 6:30am but woke up several minutes before it went off. Anticipating the kind of day he would have was next to impossible. Be it Professor Horace, these folks from the Pentagon or anyone else involved in this morning's activities, whatever they told him he would have to take their word for it. Not the best thing to rely on, no matter how good his instincts are.

Chauncey knew Professor Horace was in over his head too so there wouldn't be any deception on his part. It didn't take a genius to figure out he'd probably be upstairs assisting these people if he knew what to do. The Detective honestly believed both him and his nephew could be trusted.

The Detective found it a bit odd he didn't hear much activity occurring upstairs. He just realized this. However, he had to keep in mind when Ali vacuumed up there he couldn't hear it very well in the kitchen or anywhere else downstairs for that matter. As soon as he finished thinking about it he could barely hear a door close, presumably the one to his bedroom. The faint sound of footsteps came next which got slightly louder once they reached the staircase. Chauncey could easily tell it was more than one person, perhaps it was a blessing this didn't create much noise otherwise it might have sounded like a herd of elephants! A few seconds later they reached the bottom floor and a trio, two guys and a girl to be precise, walked in to the kitchen and stood a very short distance between Chauncey and Professor Horace. All three wore white coveralls and sunglasses. The one in the middle stepped forward and made eye contact with Professor Horace before shaking hands.

"How's it going, Dale?" asked Professor Horace.

"Doing alright, Stan," answered Dale.

"I know you didn't have much of an introduction earlier, this is Chauncey."

Dale turned his head to shake hands with Detective Chauncey Winfield.

"I'm happy to say you won't need to get an expensive carpet cleaning job done anytime soon," he said.

"That sounds like a good thing," said Chauncey.

"It most certainly is."

"I appreciate it, a lot less work for me to do."

"Don't mention it."

"Who's your team?" asked Professor Horace.

"Where are my manners?" Dale asked himself. "To my left is Hank Roswell and to my right is Kelly Price."

Hank Roswell took the time to make eye contact with both Chauncey and Professor Horace and nod.

"How are you?" asked Kelly Price, in a quiet tone glancing at Professor Horace before turning her head to look at Chauncey and nodding as well. Very polite for such a strange looking group of people making them come off a little less mysterious, but not much.

"The two of you go put all our stuff back in the vehicle," said Dale. "We'll meet up outside in a little while."

Without hesitation, Hank Roswell and Kelly Price headed to the door and went outside. Chauncey noticed the black backpacks they wore, prompting him to ask Dale about them.

"You guys are able to carry all the equipment necessary in those backpacks?" asked Chauncey.

"You'd be surprised," answered Dale. "A lot of the latest and best technology available to us has become quite portable, if you get what I'm saying."

"Good things come in small packages?"

"You got it."

"What can you tell me?" asked Chauncey, being as straight-forward as he could.

"I think it's safe for you to stay here again," said Dale.

"Alright," said Chauncey. "I need to know more than that."

"I'll meet up with Stan at the Prime lab in a little while and give him all the info I have so far and samples of everything we've collected."

"You're very well-informed, Chauncey," stated Professor Horace. "And not just because you're a Private Detective. But a lot of this stuff will go over your head if you don't have any expertise in the fields Dale and I specialize in. There's a much better chance of me being able to explain everything he and his team did up there in plain English after we're done chatting."

"I hear you."

"Are you sure?"

"Yeah," said Chauncey. "I know you'll do whatever it takes to make this as easy as possible."

"Really?" asked Professor Horace, sounding a bit skeptical.

"I was a student at Prime State University, long before you or Widen Labs came into the picture, and graduated for that matter."

"What was your major?"

"Sergeant Matheson will be able to find all that info in the computer system if you want to know. Make it as easy as possible for you and explain everything in plain English."

Chauncey couldn't help but smile and laugh a little, moments later so did Professor Horace, even Dale smirked slightly.

"I'll call you later," said Professor Horace, leaning forward to shake Chauncey's hand and headed for the door. Dale did the same and followed.

CHAPTER 21

A FEW HOURS HAD PASSED since Professor Horace, Dale, Hank and Kelly departed Chauncey's place. The Detective saw this as an opportunity to enjoy the quiet time he always cherished. But he had to admit it didn't feel right without Lady around, regardless if the dog was sitting by his side or completely out of sight. All of that would soon change. Ali was going to stop by a little later on and bring the dog home. He had no idea if she'd just be dropping the pooch off or if the two of them were having dinner together. He called her right after everyone left to tell her the property was now confirmed as safe quarters again. She had two thirty minute classes to teach back to back and would stop by after that. She hadn't said anything about what her plans were later in the evening. The more he thought about it he started to realize that he should know her schedule by now. It also occurred to him he hadn't gone upstairs to check out the condition of his bedroom. He honestly believed he could take this Dale character's word that everything was okay, but being a Detective meant he should always see for himself. Yet he remained hesitant. Perhaps still feeling disbelief at what he saw up there, despite shooting the snakelike thing and collecting what was left of it for Professor Horace along with confirmation from a so-called expert that the coast was clear.

Chauncey hadn't set foot on the staircase. The more he thought about it he realized he'd barely stepped out of the kitchen, except for using the bathroom. Everything that happened so far slowly sank in. Processing all of it took time, for him at least. That might be why he hadn't checked the bedroom. Perhaps he was too scared to do that by himself. Even having the dog nearby made him feel less isolated. He wouldn't let Ali venture upstairs for any reason without knowing what to expect.

"I'll be afraid of my own shadow when this case is over," he told himself.

Chauncey was almost convinced this case would never really be over, despite what he just said out loud, to no one in particular. At least having the dog around would make him feel like he wasn't talking to the kitchen floor. He began to count the tiles, which he'd just noticed were square and measured the same length on all four sides. Maybe he could estimate the exact number of inches without having to lean over or get down on his knees, definitely less than a foot for sure.

The Detective needed something better to do, so he retrieved his gun from his jacket, which was hanging on the chair nearest to him at the kitchen table. He'd put the weapon in the right bottom pocket earlier that morning just moments before meeting up with Professor Horace and Dale's entourage of reptile experts from the Pentagon. He'd rather think of them as a Triumphant Trio, which he decided to find out if that was the case by taking a trip upstairs.

Chauncey took one step at a time. He kept the gun

down but his finger stayed on the trigger. This second trip upstairs felt like an eternity, even compared to the first time. When he reached the top and stared down the hall he sensed the eerie sound of silence, whatever that meant.

In his mind there's only one way to describe it: dead silence.

A clock ticking, a fan blowing, even breathing would be something. Right now he couldn't so much as hear himself breathe through his nostrils, which he didn't feel the need to question, that he was sure of. At least this time he wasn't crawling out of a grave. There's something to be thankful for! The trek down the hall to the bedroom door went rather quickly. Then again, the distance was a bit shorter than the staircase. Not by much, though.

Or is it?

Like the kitchen tiles, Chauncey hadn't thought about it until now. It shouldn't matter at a time like this when you don't know what you're up against.

"I'm not supposed to be up against anything," he muttered to himself.

He's facing the fear in his mind. What happened yesterday is long gone. At least it's supposed to be. He'd rather face the music anything by Sandy Denny would be nice right about now, wishful thinking.

Chauncey stood in front of the bedroom door. He used his left hand to turn the knob and kept the gun aimed at the floor with his right hand but didn't consider anything to be a target, hopefully he wouldn't have to. He slowly pushed the door open and stepped inside focusing his eyes on what he should have been expecting the whole time: NOTHING.

"Good vibrations...meaning none," he said, referring to what he heard when the snakelike thing was in here before he shot it.

He stared at the floor. The light blue carpet didn't

look so bad this time around considering how bad it looked before. If he hadn't lived here he would've believed nothing happened.

Mrs. Watson doesn't need to know.

Instantly something triggered in Chauncey's mind, prompting him to turn around and fire a bullet. He shot the same snakelike abomination he'd faced before, or did he? Suddenly it vanished and everything went back to normal, but how? No trace of blood or whatever had splattered all over the place the last time, how is that possible? His gun was down, he immediately checked to see it was fully loaded with the safety on, he never opened fire?

Chauncey heard a little commotion downstairs, coming from the kitchen specifically. It was Ali and Lady, obvious with the faint sound of door opening and a single bark. He wanted to get down there before either of them settled in and wasn't sure if the upstairs part of the house should stay off limits.

"Are you in here?" called Ali.

"Yeah," he said.

He'd reached the top of the stairs by the time she called out to him again.

"What's happening?" she asked.

"Groundhog Day," he answered.

"What'd you say?"

"Nothing," he said, by that time he was downstairs.

"Did you say Groundhog Day?" she asked as Chauncey made his way into the kitchen.

"Forget it."

"I don't think were there yet, still a while until Valentine's Day."

"I know, we were talking about that Bill Murray movie this morning."

A total lie, he thought, but what else could he tell her?

"Really?" she asked, laughing. "You and.......?"

"Me and Professor Horace along with some friends of his," he said.

"What brought that up?"

"I have no idea."

"How does the bedroom look?"

"Fine," he stated, half-heartedly. "It looks like nothing ever happened but we need to stay out of the upstairs area for a while, they sprayed some stuff that takes a few days to set in completely, and for the sake of being extra-cautious."

More lies but better safe than sorry, a weak excuse to think up at the last second. Are good intentions better than the truth? He had no idea. Luckily a very lovely distraction presented itself: the one and only Lady Jane Spitz.

"How'd she do after I left this morning?"

"Fine," said Ali. "I brought her with me to class she chilled in the office the whole time."

"That's my girl!"

Before another word was said the lights went out, along with the digital clock on the microwave. Once in a while this happened, so Chauncey expected everything would come back on in a couple of minutes. Even Ali didn't seem surprised, yet he couldn't recall the last time she'd been here the last time it occurred. Truthfully, he didn't remember either.

"The fun never stops here," said Ali, staying rather upbeat.

"I'll call Mrs. Watson and make sure she's okay," added Chauncey.

He pulled the cell phone out of his pocket and pushed the top right button to go to contacts and pressed 9 which brought up W for Watson and hit call. After the first ring she picked up, a first for her.

There's a first time for everything, he thought.

"Hello?" said Mrs. Watson.

"It's Chauncey," he said. "How are you?"

"I'm alright."

"Is the power working in your place?"

"I'm watching TV with the lamp on next to me, why?"

"Everything just went out over here we'll wait a little while and see what happens."

"Call me in an hour if nothing changes," she said. "I'll have my friend Oliver come over and check things out."

"Perfect," he responded. "I'll talk to you later."

Chauncey had forgotten all about his brief introduction with Oliver Wood, he was amazed he remembered the guy's full name right away, at least Ali didn't need to remind him.

"She'll get that Oliver guy to come over if the power doesn't come back on," he confirmed.

"How long should we wait?" Ali asked.

"About an hour," he said. "Hopefully the electricity will be back on before that."

"Let's hope so!"

Chauncey glanced down at Lady, who sat still like a statue, staring straight ahead at nothing. He didn't know if it had anything to do with the power going out or if she still felt nervous because of what happened last night. He couldn't sense if she felt anything. Then again, he wasn't quite sure where his head was at either, so how could he expect her, a dog of all things, to be on solid ground?

He couldn't, not emotionally.

"Your gun's out," said Ali.

"What?" he asked.

"Why is your gun out?"

Chauncey forgot he had his weapon out throughout the entire conversation, pointed at the floor with the safety on. That's a good thing, but it's the only good thing. He really didn't want Ali to deal with the paranoia growing inside him.

"It fell out when I put the jacket down," he said, pointing at the chair where he placed it. "Luckily the safety was on."

Yeah right.

"For some reason I just threw it on the table when everybody was here earlier," he added. "It didn't occur to me."

Dead silence.

"Not until a few minutes ago, right before you showed up. You can understand that, can't you?"

"Of course," said Ali.

"It's been so crazy around here, not the normal kind of case I usually get. I did decide to take it upstairs with me because I didn't want to take any chances, a little spontaneous on my part but you have to improvise sometimes, especially in my line of work."

"I know."

Chauncey could feel the tension in his body decreasing, little by little. He had no reason to be defensive towards Ali, who's been handling this great considering what happened.

"This is all new to me," he said.

"It is for both of us," she added, reassuringly.

"You're right. I'm trying to keep that in mind."

"I know you are."

A quiet moment occurred just then, perfect to embrace one another. Not that they needed to, nor did they. Out of nowhere the dog stood up, placing her front paws on Chauncey above his knees. Talk about a tension breaker! He had half of a broken biscuit in his right pocket, but before he gave it to her he made a point of putting the gun back in the jacket pocket. After doing so he reached in his pants pocket and grabbed the half-broken biscuit, and Lady popped up again to take it from the tips of his fingers. He wondered if she liked the ritual more than anything else, she's never had a massive appetite.

Good things come in small packages.

CHAPTER 22

CHAUNCEY WAITED OUTSIDE in the backyard by the basement door for Oliver Wood to come out. He didn't consider the basement to be much of anything, not even a storage area since neither he nor Mrs. Watson ever used it. Hopefully Mr. Wood wouldn't stumble onto anything out of the ordinary. It just occurred to him many reptilian creatures might attempt to make a home for themselves down there being so damp, cool and isolated. But he couldn't be too sure about that since he couldn't remember the last time he set foot in there, if ever. On this occasion it would've made sense to have his gun out and escort the gentleman inside, probably more so after the fiasco in his upstairs bedroom. He should've told Ali to place something, anything in front of the staircase to keep Lady from wandering up there. Then again, she was the one who sensed what was going on first. The animal instinct kicked in right away, meaning she would be the least likely to venture up there anytime soon.

"She's the smartest one out of all of us," he told

himself.

"What's that?" asked Oliver Wood.

The electrician seemed to pop out suddenly, interrupting the conversation Chauncey was having with himself, not necessarily a bad thing.

"Nothing," he answered. "I was just waiting for you."

"I don't think you'll be living in the dark anytime in the near future, unless you need new bulbs for any of the lamps."

"What'd you find?"

"Nothing," said Oliver.

"What do you mean nothing?" asked Chauncey.

"I meant nothing wrong, not really."

"So you did find something?"

"Nothing out of the ordinary, are you sure nobody's been down there?"

"Recently?" asked Chauncey.

"Very recently," answered Oliver. "Like today."

"I don't think it's possible. Mrs. Watson gave you the key, right?"

"Yes she did," said Oliver, holding it up in front of Chauncey with his right hand.

"Because I don't have one," said Chauncey.

"You can hold on to it, I think she was getting ready to go out when I talked to her."

Chauncey took the key and clenched it in his right hand, not very tight, but enough to remind him it was there.

"So what's the story?"

"Just a couple of switches in the fuse box that needed to be switched from off to on, simple as that."

"What are you saying? Somebody came down here and shut my power off?"

"Unless the lights aren't back on right now as we speak, that's what it is."

Chauncey glanced up to look at the window near

where his TV was, a light went on and he saw Ali for a split second and she waved to them. Seconds later she turned the TV on. The volume was up a lot louder than he remembered. Isn't that always the case? Same with car radios, too! If only the investigations went beyond simple noise complaints, perhaps he should take up paranormal research while he's at it.

"Do you think there could be a bad connection? Some faulty wiring, perhaps?" asked Chauncey.

"Anything's possible but I doubt it," said Oliver. "You don't have a fuse box in your unit, do you?"

"No and neither does Mrs. Watson, what's down there's all you'll see."

"Keep your eyes open, okay? If anything happens call me, here's another business card this has my cell number on it."

"Like what?" he asked taking yet another business card with his left hand.

"Anything unusual," said Oliver. "Like the lights going out again all of a sudden. I don't think there's anything to worry about but you never know."

"Thanks."

Anything unusual this guy says, he thought, maybe it's time to add paranormal research to his job description. He took the card and glanced at it quickly, nothing fancy and simply stating Oliver Wood — Licensed Independent Electrician with two phone numbers listed on the bottom, then put it in his pocket.

"Can you wait here for a second?" asked Chauncey.

"What's up?" asked Oliver.

"I just want to take a quick look in there myself."

"Okay, the light's still on in there, the switch is on the left."

"That much I do remember," recalled Chauncey, with a quick smirk.

Chauncey nodded then headed to the basement

door. He had to duck slightly to enter but didn't need to once he got inside. He still felt the desire to because the ceiling had only two, maybe three inches clearance above his head. Mrs. Watson should not convert this into a studio apartment anytime in the near future. Paul's place is a palace compared to this, and it's not meant to be anything more than a storage unit! Some stuff you can work with and some stuff you can't. Maybe he just didn't want to because of his own lack of ambition, and his skills as a handyman were nil to none.

The basement still felt dark inside despite Oliver leaving the light on. Of course he had to consider the possibility of a low watt bulb. He turned to look but quickly realized he was already too far away to be sure. No big deal, as it was the only light for the entire basement so there wouldn't be a huge difference.

Then again, when was the last time anyone was down here?

As he got closer to the fuse box a strange but very familiar sensation came over him, the feeling that something else, a living creature, was in the room with him. Impossible! He knew that yet looked around the entire room just to be sure. As he stood in front of the fuse box and checked several of the switches he realized the small door used to open it had been removed completely. He didn't think Oliver Wood was responsible, what would be the point? He didn't see the electrician carrying anything after reemerging from here as both hands were free to give him back the key and another business card, one with a private cell number on it. He hadn't taken the time to make sure and Mrs. Watson most likely had the number as well so he could get it from her anytime.

Chauncey stared directly at all of the switches in the fuse box concentrating intensely. He got slightly dizzy just standing there staring, nothing too see down in the basement. He felt a presence from behind but he turned around and saw nothing. There was a shadow, he didn't see it but he sensed it, does that make sense? Of course not and that's why he wouldn't say anything about it, not even to Ali. Some thoughts you should keep to yourself, especially if you're a Detective. Some things can't be explained until you've got the answers. Why he didn't have his gun right now he couldn't say. There was nothing to shoot at, but everything that happened so far he had to keep reminding himself to expect the unexpected. A snakelike abomination in his bedroom, the field trip to Widen Labs before that, who knew? The shadow he sensed was dark and on the floor, could he be at risk? He didn't take pride in killing but saw no other option at this point.

Shooting at shadows, don't put that in the report! Some stuff you should keep to yourself, especially if you're a Detective.

Chauncey wasted no time heading to the door and exiting the basement altogether. He wasn't remotely fazed seeing Mr. Wood standing there waiting for him.

"Did you turn off the lights?" asked Oliver.

"Oh...right!" said Chauncey, taking a step back to lean inside and reached for the switch to turn the light off. He leaned back out and by forgetting to duck slightly let his hair brush the top of the door, at least he didn't scrape his head. He immediately shut and locked the door, clenching the key in his right hand again for a split second before putting it in his pocket.

"Everything okay?" asked Oliver.

"Yeah," answered Chauncey, slowly, quietly, and reluctantly, but truthfully.

"You look like you saw a ghost."

"It's too dark down there, even with the lights on."

"Perhaps someone could wear a glowing white bed sheet over their head."

Chauncey knew the guy was only trying to keep a sense of humor about it, no matter how mild-mannered or dry sounding he might be.

"That'd be fun," said Chauncey. "It makes me think about the old Scooby-Doo cartoons."

"Right," said Oliver. "Don't forget ghosts weren't real!"

"Or monsters, witches, goblins, or vampires, and a person could never convince anyone of being a venomous reptile!"

"Reptiles?" asked Oliver. "What brought that up?"

"Nothing," he answered.

"Are you sure?"

"Yeah, I'll talk to you later. Say hi to Mrs. Watson for me if you see her before I do."

Any snake would love to take up residency in that basement considering how cool and isolated it is down there, he thought.

CHAPTER 23

TWO DAYS HAD PASSED since the never-ending excitement occurred at Chauncey's place, which was interesting with the whole point of his job being to look for action and adventure elsewhere. Home is meant to be a place of solitude, at least in his mind. Instead all of the mystery and horror happened under The Detective's own roof right before his eyes.

He was back at Prime State University in the Widen Science Building seeing Professor Horace in the lab where the two of them first met. Also present was Dale Shusterman, perhaps best-described as the Prodigy from the Pentagon. Actually Chauncey didn't want to put the guy on a pedestal just yet, much less anyone else.

Blind Hero Worship: The Detective's definition of the worst way to look up to someone no matter how great you think they are. Somewhere down the line you'll be disappointed. It's not fair to them and an unrealistic expectation coming from within. Unfortunately, by the time you figure that out it's a long time after you've lived and learned such a hard lesson.

"Any chance you want to look at the snake?" asked Professor Horace.

"What?" responded Chauncey, interrupted from his train of thought.

"What's left of it anyway," said the Professor. "It looks really nasty with the bullet you fired into its mouth but I'll bet you didn't find it attractive to begin with."

"Not if I don't have to!"

"I didn't think so."

"We've got all of the data analysis we need," said Dale.

"For now," added the Professor. "We only know what we're dealing with to a certain extent despite our expertise."

"Something beats nothing," said Chauncey. "You can't solve all your problems instantly and simultaneously."

"Sounds like you've got the patience needed for the process," said Dale.

"One step at a time," said Chauncey. "I don't think I could wait as long as you guys for results, I'm surprised to be here it's only been a couple of days."

"Me too," said Professor Horace.

"Why's that?"

"It's what we don't know that baffles us. Generally we know what to expect with just about any type of reptilian species brought in. Like most scientists you wait for a confirmation of any analysis by going through all the routine steps no matter how long it takes, regardless of what you know right off the top of your head."

"Go on."

"The uninvited houseguest you discovered in the bedroom of all places......."

"I'll stick with Ali, and if I did cheat it would be with another human, I'm sure she feels the same way!"

"I would never question that," said Professor Horace, smiling slightly. "When I started an analysis of a small blood sample it raised red flags instantly. A huge portion did not match anything in the system."

"Did you notice anything unusual right off the bat?" asked Chauncey.

"That's just it! There was nothing unusual at all! I've worked with so many reptiles over the years I know what to expect like a doctor who routinely draws blood from a human patient. Actually it's a little more complicated than that but you get what I mean."

"I do."

"Almost like a seismograph detecting the largest earthquake occurring right under your feet," added Dale. "You might not feel anything but I'd rather use that as a comparison instead of an alien invasion."

"You might not be too far off," said Professor Horace.

"That's another subject altogether, Stan! Don't get me started or you'll wish all we had to worry about were little green men!"

"If they're midgets we can kick them," added Chauncey. "If they're the size of action figures we can step on them and if they're green AND edible they might do miracles for a vegan diet!"

The three of them enjoyed the humor, proving so by laughing together. Not out loud, light chuckling and quick smiles. Chauncey honestly didn't know how or why certain things he said just rolled off his tongue, but if the mood improves and it creates a more optimistic atmosphere there was no reason to complain.

"The truth is out there...or up there," said Dale, pointing up with his right hand.

"Not the ceiling I hope," said Chauncey.

"Way up there...where the stars align from time to time."

"So you think eating alien flesh might be healthy for us?"

"You never know being carnivorous by nature,"

answered Dale. "What we lack in our diet may not exist on Earth so it's not far-fetched to think what we need could be found on another planet in a galaxy far, far away."

"Unless the planet got destroyed long ago," added Professor Horace.

"I'll bet if it's an all desert planet you won't find much," said Dale.

"How did we go from talking about snakes to little green men to Star Wars?" asked Chauncey.

"Good point," answered Dale.

"Maybe because nothing is totally far-fetched at this point," said Professor Horace.

"Please continue," said Chauncey.

"Immediate results point to the possibility of a mutant hybrid lizard of some sort."

"Hold on, Dale!" snapped Professor Horace. "Let's not get too far ahead of ourselves!"

"He could be onto something," said Chauncey. "I may not have the background in this line of work that you guys do but we can't sugarcoat what's going on. What I've seen and been through, and trust me I haven't told you everything, we need to prepare for the worst-case scenario."

"And how do you propose we do that?"

"Well Stanley, obviously we work with what we have so far and keep running tests and researching everything. Dale, I'm sure coming directly from the Pentagon there are tricks of the trade the Professor and I don't know about. I haven't reported to anyone, not even my boss Triple B, what happened in my bedroom. You know as well as I do there's always some kind of physical evidence left behind at a crime scene no matter how well you've covered things up."

"In most cases, yes," said Dale. "That's the way it's supposed to be, unless they decide differently."

"Who are 'They'...in you circle I mean?" asked Chauncey.

"The folks at the top," answered Dale. "The guys I answer to at the Pentagon. I am part of 'They' to an extent."

"Tell me more."

"There's plenty of technology authorized by the Government the public doesn't know about. I'll doubt you're surprised by that working in law enforcement all these years, who isn't in this day and age? But if 'They' don't want any physical evidence found at a crime scene, no trace whatsoever, 'They' can make it happen, trust me on that one."

"What if I call Triple B right now...?"

"You'll be wasting your time. The stuff I used no one will find a damn thing."

This just keeps getting better and better.

"So the snake encounter didn't happen?" asked Chauncey.

"That's right," answered Dale. "It stays between us. The only other people who know anything answer to me, Hank and Kelly. Once I return what we collected The Powers That Be decide what to do with it, most likely store it somewhere and never be looked at again. If word does get out to the public it will become a myth or mystery at best like Area 51."

"What about Ali? She knows quite a bit she helped me clean shit up for God's sake!"

"She can talk all she wants. Even if she talks to your boss or goes to the press it won't do any good. The top CSI folks in the state can come in and no one will find shit. I hope your girlfriend's not a big gossiper."

"No."

"Good for you, both of you. If she told everyone she knew in Prime she'd be written off as a lunatic. Especially after local CSI folks are convinced there was nothing present to begin with."

Chauncey glanced at Professor Horace who nodded in agreement.

"He's right," added Professor Horace. "If I went public with this stuff I'd be written off as a crackpot scientist and my position here at Prime State University will be gone. If I'm lucky Widen Labs would let me work at a different facility in another state if I agree to change my name. I'd be better off getting into the Witness Protection Program."

"Who do you think has better benefits?" asked Dale.

"I don't know, Dale. I've never worked directly for the man that I'm aware of, never met him. Unless certain people at Widen Labs qualify for a similar position, women included. Jane Newton raises some eyebrows. That's for sure."

"Do you think she'd get your gig here if anything happened to you?" asked Chauncey.

"Anything's possible," answered Professor Horace. "Widen Labs are The Powers That Be in Prime. If they want to make something to happen they will. They are 'They' around here."

After the confirmation about what the local version of 'They' was everyone stayed quiet for a moment. Chauncey looked over at Dale, just now taking notice of his casual attire, specifically a grey t-shirt, blue jeans, and a worn out dark red baseball cap with no logo on it. Perhaps he didn't want anyone to know which team he was rooting for, if any. He could've been wearing the same outfit underneath the white coveralls he had on the other day, not that it really mattered. What did seem a bit off, however, was having the same dark sunglasses on as before. It was nighttime and Professor Horace's lab wasn't brightly lit, so what's the deal?

"Do you always wear sunglasses at night?" asked Chauncey.

"Not always but quite often," replied Dale. "I can assure you it has nothing to do with Corey Hart."

"I didn't think so, what's the deal?"

"They're prescription glasses, that's all."

"Not the first time I've heard that one. But it looked like your assistants were wearing the exact same ones, is it the same deal with them as well?"

"Not that I know of unless they say otherwise, which they haven't."

Another moment of silence occurred. There wasn't anything particularly awkward about it, but Chauncey felt the need to break the ice again.

"Does everything stay on a 'need to know' basis?" he asked. "Even with your closest partners, possibly good friends?"

"Not everything," replied Dale.

"But lots of things I'll bet."

"You got that right."

"I hear you."

The Detective came up with the most important inquiry as quickly as possible.

"Does it have anything to do with what you've been exposed to?" asked Chauncey.

"Like what?"

"I don't know. Various chemicals you worked with? Going as far back to when you were an exterminator?"

"Not that I know of," replied Dale.

Anything's possible.

CHAPTER 24

I⊤ was late the next morning, a little after 11 am. Chauncey pulled into his usual parking space after returning from Cameron's Coffee Café. Nothing unusual seemed out of place as Mrs. Watson's car was also parked in her usual spot and could assume she was most likely engaging in some quiet indoor activity. Unless she was out with her new electrician friend Oliver Wood but he doubted that. Too early in the day to get together if Mr. Wood had to work, but anything's possible.

The Detective's meeting with Prime State University's one and only Professor Horace along with the Pentagon's Prodigy Dale Shusterman was fresh on the mind. It didn't bother him to think of Dale like that. Not because he thought the guy was extraordinarily gifted but for being honest about the Government's deceit. That may sound contradictory but it provided relief in an investigation where he needed as many people as possible working on the same side striving toward the same goal.

Chauncey shut off the engine and turned his head right.

The dog rested quietly in the passenger seat since they departed earlier. He'd spent about an hour at Cameron's Coffee Café chilling over a cup of regular coffee contemplating last night's conversation in the Widen Science Building at Prime State University specifically in Professor Horace's lab without trying to get too deep into thought over it. Thank God he decided against taking another look at the snakelike abomination he'd blown to bits, if that was an accurate way to describe it.

Forget it, he thought, don't think about the gory details.

As he opened the driver's side door Lady's head popped up, anticipating getting out of the car. It was the most excitement he'd seen in her all morning, which was fine after everything happening recently.

What next?

"Hopefully very little," Chauncey told himself glancing over at Lady again.

Moments later the mailman pulled up next to him. Chauncey didn't have to get out of the car or turn his head quickly to receive a very friendly greeting.

"Top 'o the morning to you!" said the mailman, first name being Ronan, who sported jet-black hair, a thick moustache and an Irish accent to top everything off. This lifted Chauncey's spirits in seconds.

"How goes it Ronan?" asked Chauncey, smiling instantly. "I don't usually hear such a typical phrase like that from you when we see each other.

"Well, it's late in the morning. If you take that literally it's the top o' the morning, so it's appropriate!"

"This is true. What have you got today?"

"I got nothing for your landlady but I got a couple of things for you and Ali's name is on one of them. I know she don't live here but I don't worry about that anymore, here you go."

Three things Ronan handed over to Chauncey. One

piece of mail from Prime Electric, a utility bill no doubt and the other in his name and a return address with a post office box number, probably a bank statement. No big deal. Last but not least was a parcel from NetFlix, the one with Ali's name on it.

"She'll be happy to see this," said Chauncey. "I'm pretty sure it's the next volume of episodes of Stephen King's Stranger Things she ordered."

The Detective took a few seconds to open it and peak inside to make sure. His suspicions were correct.

"That it is," he said.

"You liking it so far?" asked Ronan.

"From what I recall I got into it. The story took place in the 80s so you didn't see cell phones or anything."

"A period piece, huh?" asked Ronan, chuckling.

"You could say that," answered Chauncey.

"Isn't Winona Ryder in it?"

"Yeah, she actually did a really good job, too. Now that you mention it I'm looking forward to see what she'll be like in these newer ones."

"Does she still look good in her mid-forties?"

"I think so, but I've always had a soft spot for her."

"Don't we all?" asked Ronan.

"Probably," said Chauncey.

"Let me know what you think of it."

"If I find the first batch of discs I'll let you borrow them."

"That's sounds like a good deal to me!"

"Alright, talk to you later."

Ronan nodded then backed out of the space he was parked in, a real easy stop for him today since he didn't have to get out of the vehicle. Chauncey was OK with that and there's no crime in liking your mailman.

The Detective decided he had everything in order and got out of the car and headed up the walkway to the door. Nothing seemed out of the ordinary which prompted him to take the keys out of his pocket, the same set he'd put in his pockets only moments ago as old habits die hard, only needing to fiddle with them very quickly to find the right one to enter into the lock. Turning the key to the right created the usual clicking sound, as always the door opened a few inches, maybe five or six, not that Chauncey thought about it. Very little strength was required to push it all the way open which suited him fine. He made his way into the kitchen and immediately saw a white envelope on the counter only a few inches away from the sink. He thought Ali might have left a sweet little note for him, but the moment he set his eyes on it he instantly dropped the keys and the mail, barely hearing the sound from the impact when they hit the floor.

The two words handwritten on the envelope in large letters naturally spooked him: LOVE LINK. Nearly a minute would pass before he picked it up and opened it. He slowly unfolded the white piece of paper and miraculously kept calm placing it down on the counter.

I am your Venomous Valentine,
I hope you feel my sting crawl up your spine.
As the poison runs through your veins,
I hope it reaches your brain making you insane.

I know life's a bitch but you scratch my itch,
As a result there is no glitch,
But don't ever think we'll get hitched,
With or without you I'll be rich.

Now don't tell me to watch what I say,
I'm the one you betrayed,
You should leave your heart on a shelf,
Then simply go and fuck yourself!

Chauncey froze. Not exactly Shakespeare but this definitely made his skin crawl. Whoever's responsible for the three murders here in Prime paid him a visit, was it a coincidence that he wasn't home? Suddenly he went into panic mode, he left someone behind!

"Lady!" he exclaimed.

He turned his head to the right and the window by the front door shattered into pieces. He felt a massive force of nature push up against him. That was the only way to describe it. The unknown pressure nearly caused him to lose balance and keel over. The lack of sound after the glass breaking made it more frightening. But seconds later he faintly heard car tires skidding then speeding off.

Chauncey found himself in a kind of blank zone mentally for a minute or so before coming to grips with what had just occurred. Then complete coherence returned and, without any hesitation, he dashed toward the door. He couldn't remember opening the thing, much less if he'd shut it on the way out. Next he found himself on the walkway by the bottom of the stairs and quickly glimpsing out at the road spotting a set of tire tracks, which meant he wasn't just hearing things. A bit of a relief but the window shattering was far worse in this particular experience but none of this mattered as he ran down the walkway to get to his car. Within seconds he collided into something, or someone to be specific.

It was Oliver Wood.

Chauncey landed face down on top of Mrs. Watson's friend the electrician. He could see the poor guy was disoriented looking straight in the eyes.

"What the...hell?!" exclaimed Mr. Wood.

"My God!" said Chauncey. "Are you alright?"

"I think so. What the hell are you trying to do? Run the Prime Marathon or score a touchdown?"

"Neither! I didn't see you!"

"You have got to be kidding! You were looking right at

me from the beginning to the end of this damn walkway! Did collision course enter your mind at all?"

Oliver was right. Chauncey had run down the entire walkway without realizing it. He wasn't expecting another visit from the electrician so it made sense that the poor guy was at the beginning of the walkway and here to see Mrs. Watson. Chauncey slowly got back on his feet. Oliver did the same immediately after.

"The dog's waiting for you," said Oliver.

"What?" Chauncey asked.

"She barked at me when I pulled up. I saw her in the driver's seat. Is she taking lessons?"

Chauncey quickly maneuvered around Oliver Wood and made his way over to the car. As he reached the driver's side door the window was open and little Lady Jane was sitting in his usual spot with the typical relaxed stare she often had. Hopefully she was unfazed and with any luck completely unaware of what occurred moments ago. She'd heard plenty of cars burn rubber before but everything else could be left out of the equation as far as Chauncey was concerned. He extended his right hand to pat her on the head able to breathe a sigh of relief.

"Thank God," he muttered while looking into the dog's eyes.

Something he did not say too often.

CHAPTER 25

THE DETECTIVE WASTED NO TIME inviting his two most trusted constituents, Professor Horace and Dale Shusterman, back out to his residence again. He reached Professor Horace, who he now felt comfortable enough to call Stan on the first try feeling grateful he didn't have to text or leave a message. He and Dale were making small talk on the walkway outside his front door about the Love Link poem he'd discovered earlier while Stan checked out the tire tracks on the road.

"I don't know if this person just has a bad sense of humor or in need of better inspiration," said Dale.

"Like a creative writing course?" Chauncey asked.

"Maybe," answered Dale.

"I'm pretty sure Prime State University offers it, they might have it available as a degree program."

"In this day and age most likely, Stan might know off the top of his head."

As soon as Dale finished that last sentence Stan had walked across the tiny front lawn and stood in front of the two of them.

"Did you find out anything?" asked Chauncey.

"It was a 1973 Corvette Stingray with BF Goodrich raised white letter radial tires," confirmed Stan.

"I had no idea you knew cars so well!"

"I don't."

"What do you mean?"

"That one in particular I do even drove it once myself."

The conversation stopped temporarily, almost abruptly. Several more seconds would pass before someone finally broke the ice.

"You're shitting me," said Dale.

"No I'm not," responded Stan.

"Who does it belong to?"

"Jane Newton."

The conversation stopped again. This time very abruptly. No one knew what to say after hearing that. Stan sounded uneasy with that particular answer. Yet without hesitation Chauncey handed the note over with the Venomous Valentine poem. He briefly held up the envelope it came in which had Love Link written on it to confirm the connection.

"Is that her writing?" asked Chauncey.

"You better believe it," stated Stan.

"Do you think she's behind all of this?" asked Dale.

"Possibly," said Stan, slowly but reluctantly, not sure if he could believe it himself.

A cell phone rang, specifically Chauncey's. He pulled it out of his right pocket and glanced at the caller ID before answering.

It was Triple B.

"What's up?" he asked.

"I'm on Route 21," said Triple B.

"What are you doing there?"

"We found a mail truck stopped in the breakdown lane. The carrier's dead. It's a mess, Chauncey. His name is Ronan..."

"I'll be right there!"

The Detective ended the conversation that instant. He looked up at Stan and Dale to break the news.

"What's going on?" asked Stan.

"I think Jane Newton killed my mailman," he answered.

"Where'd this happen?"

"Right on Route 21 according to my boss!"

"We should all go," suggested Dale.

"We can take my car," said Stan.

"Alright," agreed Chauncey. "Just give me a minute to get ready and we can go!"

"We'll start it up and wait for you then."

"That works for me!"

Chauncey rushed back inside to get his jacket. It was placed on one of the chairs at the kitchen table. He wasted no time putting it on then put a call through to Ali. She was probably in the middle of an aerobics class and couldn't be reached. He left a very brief message:

"Honey, it's me! I'm heading to Route 21 to meet Triple B! There's been an accident! Well, not exactly. Anyway, I'm going to leave the dog with Mrs. Watson. The window's shattered! I'll tell you about it later."

He ended the call and placed the phone down on the kitchen table. By that time Lady had wandered over and lay down in front of him. He wasted no time picking her up and headed back outside.

"I'll bet both Mrs. Watson and Oliver Wood will enjoy your company," he told her.

Chauncey walked about halfway down the walkway then up the stairs to his landlady's entrance. He knocked on the door and within seconds was greeted by both Mrs. Watson and Mr. Wood!

"Can you take her until Ali comes home?" he asked. "I can't leave her by herself on short notice."

"Of course," said Mrs. Watson.

"She looks like a Muppet," said Mr. Wood.

"What are you talking about?" Chauncey asked.

"The way you're holding the dog," he added.

"Right!" stated Chauncey, ending the conversation. He put Lady down and she quickly went inside Mrs. Watson's place. That went a lot smoother then he'd anticipated. Mrs. Watson and Oliver Wood smiled and slowly closed the door. His attention turned to the sound of a car engine which prompted him to rush downstairs and head toward the end of the walkway. The vehicle in question was a black Lincoln Town Car parked in the very last space with Stan behind the wheel and Dale sitting in the back.

"I'm sure you don't have a problem riding shotgun?" asked Dale as he poked his head outside the right rear passenger window.

"Not at all," responded Chauncey, who immediately opened the front right passenger door and got inside.

"I'll bet you haven't seen one of these in a long time!" added Stan.

"You're right about that! Do you think we'll be able to catch up to a Corvette if we have to?"

"I've made a few modifications. On a vehicle like this no one would expect it."

"That's a good point. It kind of makes me think of a Hearst. It would fit in at Montrose Morgue!"

"All we need now is The Tall Man from Phantasm!" added Dale.

"How fitting!" Chauncey exclaimed.

He couldn't complain about a guy came all the way from the Pentagon and knew some horror movie trivia. Who wouldn't love The Tall Man? However, they might be on their way to encounter something far worse.

Is that possible?

They were about to find out.

Stan put the vehicle in reverse and backed out of the

parking space. He immediately put it in drive and heading to Main Street in Downtown Prime. Most people who live around here know that's the easiest way to get to Route 21. It would be dark soon. The only problem might be the rush hour traffic. But that wasn't a big issue even when Prime State University students returned for the spring semester, which they had. Chauncey hadn't really noticed. He still felt relieved that school wasn't in session when Roy Cumberland's murder took place on campus. He was curious if anyone from the school newspaper looked into it. Not likely. Too much time passed and it had all the coverage it would get. Not to mention the Dean, Administrators, and all the big shots Widen Corporation want the story buried as quickly as possible. The death of Roy Cumberland had not been confirmed or denied as a murder. Not to the press! He still didn't want to go public with the Love Links either. If he had his way he wouldn't deal with the press period.

Then there's John Walsh on America's Most Wanted.

Concentrate you idiot!

I'm glad I'm not driving, he thought.

"I'm sure we won't have any trouble spotting them," said Stan.

"Huh?" asked Chauncey.

"They're on Route 21, right? Not off one of the exits?"

"That's right as far as I know."

Another minute passed before they reached Main Street in Downtown Prime. Nothing seemed out of the ordinary cruising just slightly above the speed limit. The three of them wanted to reach their destination as quickly as possible without attracting too much attention. The last thing they needed to do was cause an accident or get stopped by the police on their way to a crime scene, especially one involving a murder!

Chauncey stayed in a world of his own riding shotgun. He kept his head up and looked forward but being so used to driving out to a crime scene every time he got a call from Triple B this felt foreign to him. He barely noticed when they got onto Route 21.

It didn't matter.

What he saw next would change all of that.

CHAPTER 26

Chauncey hadn't paid attention to how far down Route 21 they'd gone. But just by making a glance to the right something caught the eye immediately. A mail truck stopped in the breakdown lane with its right front tire slightly off the pavement. Stan slowed down considerably but before enough time passed to park directly behind it Chauncey would spot the top half of a human head with very distinguished black hair sticking out the driver's side window. A grim reminder of what Triple B told him already. But he couldn't believe it until now. This one would take a long time to accept, Ali as well.

Ronan was dead.

The Detective could barely see a blue Toyota Corolla parked in front of the mail truck halfway off the breakdown onto the grass which he recognized as Triple B's. Moments after stepping out of Stan's black Lincoln Town Car Triple B appeared before his eyes after walking over on the grass by the right side of the mail truck, probably to avoid oncoming traffic. A smart move, however very few vehicles had passed by them so far, somewhat surprising considering the time. It was still light out, but Chauncey knew that traffic would increase rapidly very quickly. The sight he saw right away would convince anyone to slow down and take a closer look, but this wouldn't cause an ordinary traffic jam.

Something far worse: Gridlock.

Stan and Dale had gotten out of the vehicle by the time Triple B was standing in front of Chauncey shaking his hand. The two of them nodded immediately afterwards hoping to extend some kind of introduction. Triple B would take enough time to glance at each of them individually.

"Professor Horace and Dale Shusterman," said Chauncey.

"That's what I thought," said Triple B.

"Where is everybody?"

"I haven't called it in yet. I wanted you to see it first."

"Why?"

"I figured you especially with your present company might be able to determine right away if there's a connection."

"What have you got so far?" asked Stan.

"A couple of gunshot wounds to start with," confirmed Triple B. "But there's more."

"More of what exactly?" asked Dale.

"I don't know. Chauncey, it might be a good thing these two are here with you. All I can tell you is the full name's Ronan O'Hara. He's got a bullet in the chest and another one in the upper right side of the neck he would've died seconds after receiving the latter."

"The neck wound?" asked Chauncey.

"Yeah," stated Triple B.

"Hopefully he got that one first and with everything else he never knew what hit him."

"You might be onto something."

"What do you mean?"

"See for yourselves!"

Triple B stepped back on the grass and walked over to the right side door of the mail truck, which was wide open. Chauncey followed with Stan and Dale directly behind him. Triple B moved a few steps back so Chauncey could get a full view inside. He was already horrified and saddened by what little he saw only moments ago knowing this was his favorite mailman. There was no surprise with what he expected to see: a massive amount of blood flowing out from the bullet wounds in the chest and the upper right side of the neck. The worst part, however, was that the poor soul's eyes were wide open. Ronan O'Hara was the last guy this should have happened to, in his mind at least.

"He didn't deserve to die this way," said Chauncey.

"You know him?" asked Triple B.

"He was my mailman, great guy."

"I'm sorry."

Chauncey leaned in to take a closer look, specifically in the upper neck area. As he suspected there were no marks, no calling cards found, no Love Links here.

There didn't need to be.

He received that back home long before Triple B got in touch with him. Stan and Dale stood behind Chauncey, one looking over each shoulder to get a better view inside.

"Come over here, Chauncey," said Triple B.

The Detective followed his boss to the front of the vehicle, what used to be Ronan O'Hara's mail truck. It might as well be a coffin at this point. Who in their right mind would want to drive it now?

Then again, in Prime you never know.

Chauncey hadn't paid attention to how much further ahead Triple B had parked his vehicle, the blue Toyota Corolla, from Ronan's mail truck, at least twelve maybe fifteen feet along with it being halfway on the grass off the breakdown lane. He looked down at the pavement which prompted Chauncey to do the same.

Someone burned rubber to get the hell out of there leaving very distinct tire tracks. Ones Chauncey had never seen before and he'd seen many, yet immediately suspected what kind they were and who made them. Luckily the gentleman who was gracious enough to escort him to this particular destination would be able to provide those answers. But before anything more was said Triple B had one more thing to add:

"Some calls came in about a red Corvette Stingray stopped on the side of the road," said Triple B.

"You're right about that," added Stan.

"Where are you when I need you?" asked Chauncey, turning his head back to find Stan looking over his shoulder...again!

"Right here!" confirmed Stan enthusiastically.

"Right answer," added Triple B. "You sure about that?"

"Damn straight," said Stan. "There the exact same ones I saw in front of your house, Chauncey."

Everyone stayed quiet for another minute or so until all four of them had gathered in front of the mail truck to view tire tracks only a Corvette Stingray can make according to Professor Stanley Horace, an expert in Herpetology along with this particular automobile in question.

"Ronan was the type of guy to give the shirt off his back for you," said Chauncey. "Probably thought she'd broken down, got a flat tire or something and didn't like seeing her stranded."

"She?" inquired Triple B.

"What?"

"How do you know?"

"We think it's an inside job, kind of."

"Inside job?" asked Triple B. "Who's involved?"

"The one and only Widen Labs," added Stan.

Everyone kept quiet for a moment. Chauncey's boss wanted more answers, so he had to break the ice by asking more questions.

"Your own people Professor Horace?" he asked.

"That's right," said Stan.

"At least one in particular," added Chauncey.

"And who might that be?" inquired Triple B.

"Jane Newton," confirmed Stan. "She's kind of my go-to gal going back and forth from Widen Labs to Prime State University. Her main thing is working for the company but while on campus she more or less answers to me."

"I'm aware of that. Chauncey and I got the info we needed early on thanks to Sergeant Matheson."

"I like him a lot," said Stan.

"You do? I'll put in a good word for you."

"Thanks."

Another moment of silence took place, if you will, until Detective Chauncey Winfield broke the ice again.

"What now?" he asked.

"You've seen everything you needed to see here, right?" said Triple B. "I'm going to call this one in and start the paperwork, the necessary formalities."

"Formalities," said Chauncey. "Where would we be without them?"

"Welcome to life at the Pentagon," added Dale.

"No thanks," chimed in Stan. "I'd rather hold out for tenure at Prime State University."

"Good idea."

"Time to track down a certain Corvette?" asked Chauncey.

"You got that right," answered Stan.

"Do you really think we can catch up to it in a Lincoln Town Car?"

"It's got a few surprises in it. I'd rather not take the time to explain anything to you. Bottom line it picks up speed a lot quicker than most other cars similar in appearance. You wouldn't believe what this thing can outrun. I had engineers at Widen Labs make a few modifications, alright?"

"As long as it goes faster than a Hearst," added Dale. "Then again, with all the bad shit The Tall Man did with his wheels in the Phantasm movies we shouldn't have any problem doing good shit with your car, Stan."

"Thanks Dale," said Stan.

"The Tall Man?" asked Triple B.

"That's right," said Chauncey.

"What's he talking about?"

"Remember Phantasm?"

"A little bit."

"That's all you need to know. Don't worry about it."

"I'll talk to you later."

Triple B took a cell phone out of his pocket ready to call in a homicide. Chauncey, Stan, and Dale made their way back to Stan's Lincoln Town Car. The three of them got inside taking the same spots as before. Stan behind the wheel, Chauncey in the right front passenger side and Dale in the back but sat more in the middle this time around. Stan immediately started the engine and sped off right away, creating the sound of tires skidding but only slightly. Not nearly as loud as a 1973 Corvette Stingray nor would it leave the kind of skid marks, even if an attempt had been made to peel out!

About a minute passed before one of them broke the ice.

This time it was Dale with questions Chauncey had planned to ask.

"Do you really think we stand a chance going up against the Corvette in this thing?" he inquired.

"Anything is possible," answered Stan.

"That doesn't sound very promising. What else can you tell us about it?"

"Have you ever seen the movie Corvette Summer?" asked Stan.

"I think so."

"I have," said Chauncey. "Mark Hamill and Annie Potts were in it his first role in 1978 after Star Wars and way before she did Ghostbusters and Designing Women. I take it Jane Newton's car is the exact same model?"

"More than that," said Stan. "It's the exact same car."

"You're shitting me."

"I'm not. She bought it from a private collector a few years ago."

"How much did she pay for it?"

"I have no idea."

"She makes a decent enough salary at Widen Labs to be able to do that?" asked Dale. "I'm working for the wrong people!"

"How much does she make?" asked Chauncey.

"At this point I have no idea," said Stan. "I know her starting pay was in the six figures when she came in. I'd assume it's in the upper six figures by now. But that's considered privileged information at best for my ears. Since I'm primarily employed by Prime State University thanks to Widen Labs I'm still tied to them as well but to a lesser extent. I still receive a paycheck from them so they can use my services if needed, it's called a retainer."

"A retainer?" asked Dale. "Is that in the six figure range?"

"Not even close. Prime State University pays me pretty good, not as much if I stayed full-time at Widen Labs bit I have a more independence with my own lab..."

"What I saw of it," interrupted Chauncey. "I have to say it's definitely intriguing. It's bit eerie being left alone in there but it's quite something for a lab in a school in a city as low key as Prime is!"

"It's definitely not MIT or UCLA but it serves its purpose."

"And you honestly don't mind the cut in pay?"

"Like I said, Chauncey, independence is a big thing for me and despite getting an opportunity to become Professor Horace due to fascism you don't feel the grip of that particular f-word as much when you're teaching students about science instead of being stuck in a lab in a corporation day and night answering to the suits every five minutes who only care about results!"

"Instant gratification," added Dale.

We're definitely on the same level, thought Chauncey.

CHAPTER 27

CHAUNCEY, STAN, AND DALE quickly made their way down Route 21. The amount of traffic coming from the opposite direction increased dramatically. Not surprising considering the time. None of them were about to check their watches but just by looking straight ahead it was obviously approaching dusk very rapidly. Keep your eyes on the road and you'll still know the difference between the darkness and the light and whatever occurs in between the two. In another minute or so they reached the exit that would take them to Hobson Road. At this point you'd think Chauncey would know the exit number right off the top of his head. But living and traveling in the same area for such a long time he just didn't think about it.

The Detective really needed to cut himself some slack. Who wouldn't be distraught after finding their favorite mailman in all of Prime shot to death on the side of the road? He could always plug in a GPS or look up Mapquest on his phone if he absolutely needed to be detail-oriented with every aspect of this case. But as Roscoe P. Coltrane on the Dukes of Hazzard would declare at this moment they were definitely in 'Hot Pursuit' chasing after Jane Newton. Of course Chauncey knew this scenario was far more legitimate than a TV show's depiction of small-town cops with nothing better to do but pull people over thanks to phony or altered speed traps. He was just glad he lived in the city of Prime where law enforcement had better things to do most of the time.

Once the Lincoln Town Car reached the end of the ramp Stan turned right onto Hobson Road. Chauncey already knew what their destination was. No other reason to come down here except when you're chasing a fugitive. Of course it would be nice if they could get John Walsh on the phone. Then again, Triple B was still at the crime scene looking after poor Ronan and only called it in minutes ago. Chances are not a single police cruiser had arrived yet.

Hopefully rush hour traffic wouldn't be too bad.

"Where are we headed?" asked Chauncey.

"Into the Badlands," answered Stan.

The Detective knew the answer. He just wanted to make sure they were on the same page.

"Chase Conservation Land," he reiterated.

"When was the last time anyone called it that?"

"Never," he answered.

"What are you guys talking about?" asked Dale.

"I forgot you're not from around here," said Stan.

"I've been around these parts a few times."

"Done a lot of sightseeing?" asked Chauncey.

"Not really except for Prime State and Widen Labs."

"I went to Widen Labs for the first time recently to see none other than the lovely lady were chasing after right now. That place is a trip in and of itself."

The Detective wasn't about to mention the trip he

had after leaving Widen Labs after having the meeting with the one and only Jane Newton where they shared his favorite drink: coffee. Not yet. Who knows what she put in it? Out of the three of them inside this black Lincoln Town Car Professor Stanley Horace is the one who could probably figure that out. However, Chauncey did not want to ask about that just yet. He was not in the best state of mind despite being stone cold sober.

He decided something needed to be done in order to get the thought process reorganized. It started with a spontaneous random comparison right off the top of his head, specifically with two of the murder victims.

"Been thinking," said Chauncey.

"About what?" asked Stan remaining calm.

"The woman found here, Stacy O' Connell, an ex-employee of Widen Labs was from Ireland, right?"

"What about it?"

"My friend the mailman who just got shot to death, his name was Ronan O'Hara, all Irish all the time!"

"What are you saying?" inquired Dale, getting curious about where the conversation was going.

"Yeah, what are you saying?" asked Stan. "So we've got four murders, two of them happened to be Irish. Are you trying to tell us Jane Newton has a bias toward killing people who are Irish on behalf of Widen Corporation?"

"Of course not," said Chauncey.

"What made you think of it, then?"

"Just thinking out loud, sometimes making comparisons like that, matching up little things as simple as ethnicity will help me get the wheels in my head turning again. It helps me reorganize a bit."

"I hear you," said Stan. "That helped me back when I was an undergraduate. Matching up the simplest things could get the brain stirring enough to make it easier to remember the complicated shit. It did a lot of good when test time came!"

"I figured you'd be smart enough to know everything related to reptiles off the top of your head," said Chauncey.

"I know quite a bit, Detective. But why do you think we have textbooks and notes scattered all over the fucking place! Did you honestly think I had all the answers when you brought in that thing to my lab in garbage bags?"

"Sorry about that."

"Don't be, this is a new experience for all of us."

"Thanks."

"You're telling me!" added Dale.

As soon as those last words were spoken it became pitch black outside. It made sense with it being the winter time and it would be a while before the clocks changed for the spring season. The Detective just hoped a full moon wouldn't be out tonight.

"I don't need to be superstitious at a time like this," he told himself.

"What's that?" asked Stan.

"Never mind," he said.

"Are you sure?"

"Yeah, I think so."

Chauncey knew it wasn't smart to just blurt out shit like that, but with it being such bizarre circumstances the three of them were in at the moment who could blame him? However, as a Detective he needed to be much more aware of his actions.

Only two more minutes would pass before arriving at their destination.

For Chauncey, it felt like an eternity. He had a sinking feeling in his stomach that Stan and Dale felt the same way. But he didn't dare ask them if that was the case.

Stan slowed down and pulled his black Lincoln Town Car into the open area by the swamp, very close to the same spot where poor Stacy O'Connell's body had been discovered. The place was big enough to be a parking lot which made it easy for Chauncey, Triple B, Frosty, and EMT guys like Lurch and Colin to be there simultaneously. In many ways it was the perfect place for a crime scene to be, but Chauncey couldn't imagine a proposal ever being submitted to the city to turn it into a parking lot. Anyone so much as suggesting pavement be put down sounded unusual. No one in their right mind would stop there anyway. He'd never heard about anybody venturing out there to go fishing, not even the Weekend Warrior types in the National Guard either. If they did, chances are they never came out.

Stan stopped the car, put it in park and turned the lights off but left the engine running. It wasn't loud at all, which Chauncey thought was a good thing. He didn't feel a need to mention it, but knew the time was right to discuss a game plan.

"Where do you think she is?" he asked.

"I don't know," said Stan. "But it won't be long, she'll make her presence known, I'm sure of that."

"You think we should just wait?"

"For now, yeah," said Stan.

Chauncey turned his head right to look out the passenger side window, eyes focused back on Hobson Road. He sensed something. Somehow he knew another vehicle was approaching. He couldn't hear an engine, he felt vibrations. It didn't make any sense, but he paid close attention. A red 1973 Corvette Stingray arrived, slowly coming down Hobson Road before coming to a complete stop. The weirdest thing about this was the lights were turned off the whole time, but he could see it as clear as day despite being pitch black outside.

The driver turned the lights on allowing Chauncey, Stan, and Dale to determine Jane Newton was behind the wheel. They didn't expect it to be anyone else, but confirmation was very reassuring. She pressed her foot all the way down on the gas pedal. That exact moment music started playing. So loud if Chauncey didn't know better he'd think they were listening to the same music on the radio in the car the three of them were sitting in right now.

The scariest part for him occurred the moment he heard the thundering sound of the drums in the introduction of the song. He recognized it right away. The song was Let's Go by Montrose, the first track off the 1976 album Jump On It.

Dale spoke up first.

"We might as well be listening to that in here!" he shouted.

"You're telling me!" added Chauncey. "Man I have this CD around somewhere!"

"You know what this is?" asked Stan.

"You bet! This is Let's Go by Montrose!"

"Like Montrose Morgue?"

"That's right," he said. "But the two are not connected in any way I assure you!"

"I didn't think so," said Stan. "But this could help us."

"Are you talking about Ronnie Montrose the guitar player?" asked Dale.

"Yeah," answered Chauncey.

"Didn't Sammy Hagar have something to do with him?"

"He sang on the first two studio albums. It was the start of his recording career. What you're hearing now comes from the fourth album. A guy named Bob James did the vocals on this one."

"Isn't there also a jazz musician with that name?" asked Stan.

"Yeah," said Chauncey. "But there's no connection between the two."

When Chauncey spoke those last words Jane Newton pressed her foot all the way down on the gas pedal again and put the car in first gear then sped off. This time the screeching of the tires was so loud for a split second it drowned out the music completely, not that any of them would make a mental note of it. Nor would they be surprised if there were skid marks twice as long as the ones she'd made in front of his house earlier today.

This scenario prompted Stan to follow suit. He pressed his foot down on the gas pedal of the Lincoln Town Car and sped out on the dirt they were parked on. No chance of leaving the kind of skid marks found on the pavement ahead of them and the vehicle fishtailed slightly after just a short distance but he regained control quickly. By the time they reached Hobson Road one glance in the rearview mirror showed the massive cloud of dust, or dirt created. Charlie Brown's buddy Pig Pen couldn't compete with this! Trying to imagine what it would've looked like while it was still light out wasn't difficult. If that were the case one of them could've filmed it with a camera on a cell phone and posted it on YouTube. Then again, Chauncey was able to see the Corvette Stingray very clearly.

Stan picked up speed very quickly. It wasn't long before they reached the exit to put them back on Route 21. He looked over at Chauncey for advice.

"You think we should get back on the highway?" asked Stan.

"She'll avoid it at all costs," answered Chauncey. "There's already a major crime scene which she created. That car stands out so easily. The traffic has accumulated in both directions by now. Unless she wants a massive police chase but I'll bet her instincts are telling her to fly solo."

"Her car's got wings?" asked Dale.

"I doubt it," said Chauncey. "Unless you know something we don't."

"Not so far."

All that changed when a bright light shined through

the rear window. At first they thought Jane Newton was behind them but quickly determined it came from above along with the loud sound of a propeller as well, obviously a helicopter.

Chauncey thought it was one of his guys doing surveillance on the way to the crime scene on Route 21.

"I didn't think they'd be out here this soon," he said.

"It's one of ours," said Stan.

"What do you mean?"

"That's a Widen chopper!"

"Are you sure?"

"Trust me I know! I can recognize the sound of one of those instantly!"

The bright light shining through the rear window vanished as quickly as it appeared. The pilot turned it off. Another minute passed before the Widen chopper flew away indicated by the sound of the propeller slowly fading. It remained high enough in the air allowing them to be able to hear themselves speak.

The Detective had a lot of questions.

"What's their angle, Stan?" asked Chauncey.

"What do you mean?" said Stan, answering the question with a question.

"Are they in on it?"

"I'm not sure. But I hear what you're saying."

"Are you sure?"

"They know something! That's the best answer I have!"

"Sorry," he said.

Chauncey didn't mean to get the poor guy riled up behind the wheel. He was pretty sure Stan wouldn't accuse him of that. But he wasn't trying to pour gasoline on the fire, so to speak.

Immediately after passing the exit to get back on Route 21, Stan picked up speed again with Chauncey and Dale taking notice of it right away. Not that either one of them would mention it. Chauncey was definitely taken by surprise. He started leaning over to check the speedometer when they caught up with Jane Newton in the Stingray, which he again could see clear as day. Part of him didn't want to know why.

"You've definitely modified this thing a bit," he said.

"I told you so," Stan responded.

"What do we do?"

"I don't know, not yet."

"Maybe a Jewish Viking would help?"

"What the hell are you talking about?" asked Dale.

"I was about to say the same fucking thing," added Stan.

"Forget it," said Chauncey. "It's just my sense of humor."

"Come on Jewish Vikings?" asked Stan.

"Inquiring minds want to know," added Dale, sarcastically.

"Keep in mind we're not from the National Enquirer either!"

"Alright," said Chauncey. "It's just something I call my dog once in a while. Do you want the long story?"

"Not now," said Stan.

"Shut up for a minute!" snapped Dale.

"What is it?" asked Chauncey.

"Look over on the driver's side."

Chauncey and Stan focused as best as they could on the front left side of the vehicle they were now tailing behind, obviously the 1973 Corvette Stingray. Chauncey wouldn't be able to get this one out of his head for a long time. In some ways that excited him knowing the origin behind it, luckily he never got too caught up in the 'fanboy' mentality. He honestly couldn't remember if that was one or two words.

He can't think about that right now.

"I see something," said Chauncey.

They could see Jane Newton's left hand sticking

outside the driver's side window holding an unidentified object.

"What is that?" asked Stan.

"I have a bad feeling about this!" said Chauncey.

"Cut to the RIGHT!" shouted Dale.

"What for?" asked Stan.

"Just do it!"

Stan quickly turned the wheel to the right. He slowed down a bit too, but not much. If he'd accelerated he would've been directly beside Jane Newton, giving her the opportunity to use her firearm. After seeing what she did to Chauncey's friend the mailman Ronan O'Hara he didn't want to set it up and cause them to meet the same fate. Next he heard the sound of metal clanking on the pavement, seconds later there was a massive explosion. He slammed on the brakes and came to a screeching halt. They felt that along with the impact of the explosion. Luckily they were far enough away not to be physically harmed at all.

"What was that?" asked Stan.

"A mini-bomb," confirmed Dale.

"Seriously?" inquired Chauncey.

"Damn straight! I got one on me!"

"You're fucking kidding me! No one in Prime who works in law enforcement is authorized to own explosives like that!"

"I came straight from the Pentagon, remember? I don't work for the local police. I told you before, I've got access to stuff most people don't."

"I remember, like the cops around here won't find a trace of evidence left of that snakelike thing that was in my bedroom. Am I still following you?"

"You're right on the money!"

"It wasn't the brightest move to slam on the brakes like that, right?" asked Stan.

"No," replied Dale.

"I'm sorry."

"I was pretty sure we'd be far enough away by the time the bitch dropped it."

"That makes one of us!" said Chauncey.

"That's why I told the Professor here to cut to the right," he added. "Slowing down wasn't a bad move, either."

"Are you sure about that?"

"I didn't have my seatbelt on! I could've gone flying through the windshield!"

They kept quiet for a few minutes. Absorbing sighs of relief after what just happened. They had to think of something.

"So what do we do?" asked Chauncey.

Stan pulled the car over to the side of the road and turned the lights off. Definitely a good start, and there's no point in chasing after her if she plans on dropping more mini-bombs on the road.

"We wait," said Stan.

"Obviously," added Dale.

"She'll come back this way soon. She recognized us, at least my car. I have a feeling she'll go back to where she came from."

"The Badlands?" asked Chauncey.

"Yeah," answered Stan, in a quieter tone.

"Why?"

"She's part of it, whatever their working on back at Widen Corporation. She's not only running experiments, she's also a part of them."

"Do you know how crazy that sounds?"

"Does it really surprise you with everything you've seen so far? Detective, you're hearing it from me! Professor Horace, a guy who's technically on the inside! I come from Widen Corporation!"

"You're right," said Chauncey. "It shouldn't surprise me but it does."

"Whatever happens," said Dale. "I don't know. Let's not tell ourselves it can't get any worse. I'm just trying to be realistic, this is fucking insane!"

Another moment of silence, if you will, occurred between the three of them.

At least they weren't at each other throats.

With what they were up against, that was the last thing they needed.

Off in the distance was the sound of a revving engine, which could only come from a certain 1973 Corvette Stingray. Stan rolled the driver's side window down all the way to hear it more clearly. Chauncey took notice of the fact that it had to be done manually.

How old was this Lincoln Town Car?

The driver claimed to have made some 'modifications' to it yet didn't specify exactly what.

He had to admit it picked up speed rather quickly, very handy if you're pursuing a Corvette Stingray.

However, something else caught his ear.

The same intro to the song she blasted earlier! Let's Go by Montrose. The thundering drums played by Denny Carmassi, who later on pounded the skins with Ann and Nancy Wilson in Heart. What amazed him more was the fact that he heard that long before seeing the headlights far off in the distance.

Is it supposed to work that way?

Chauncey estimated the distance to be at least a quarter of a mile between them and the oncoming vehicle, no need to specify at this point, heading in their direction. What kind of a stereo system did she have in that thing? The sound of the engine and the music of Montrose seemed to balance out the closer she got, whether that made sense or not was another matter altogether. It felt like an eternity waiting for her to get there. Not that they had seriously considered the possibility of her stopping to chat. Most people who drop mini-bombs in the middle of the road knowing someone is following them are not concerned about their social skills.

The Detective thought the moment would never come for Jane Newton to arrive happened. However she passed by them so fast by the time they looked back she was already long gone. Not so much as a glimpse of the taillights. That didn't stop Stan from switching the lights on in his vehicle again then turning it around and heading back the way they came down Hobson Road toward the Badlands. He picked up speed rather quickly. Chauncey didn't check how fast he was going, instead deciding to have faith that he would get them where they needed to be.

The sound of the Corvette engine and the music of Montrose ceased to exist. Chauncey could not recall if he had heard either of those things when Jane Newton zipped by them only a minute ago. Perhaps somehow she modified her vehicle to temporarily break the sound barrier. Nothing should surprise him at this point in the investigation. Maybe he had gotten so scatterbrained it altered his senses along with some aftereffects of whatever was in that coffee she gave him. He chose the latter theory, but hoped everything was out of his system.

It didn't take long to catch up with Jane Newton again. This time Stan kept a reasonable distance behind her. What that might be Chauncey wouldn't put any thought toward. Of course he heard Let's Go by Montrose loud and clear in his ears and could only wonder how much more he and the Venomous Valentine would've hit it off during their original meeting had they learned about their similar taste in music, making him grateful to be involved with Ali for such a long time.

She might've spared him from the spiked coffee.

Wishful thinking, he realized.

The Detective's train of thought got interrupted when Stan took his right hand off the steering wheel and pressed a button on a fancy car stereo which had internet and satellite connections.

There was far more to it than that.

A female voice came on:

"Subject: Music. Please Enter."

"Do your thing, Detective," said Stan.

"What thing?" he asked.

"Tell it everything you know, the song, the group, who's in the band, any information off the top of your head!"

"Why?"

"Trust me on this one, okay?"

"Let's Go by Montrose with Ronnie Montrose on the guitar, Bob James is singing, I think bass is by someone named Randy Jo Hobbs, Jim Alcivar keyboards and the drummer's Denny Car..."

"Information: Processed. Thank you," responded the female voice, hearing the mechanical tone much clearer.

"What is it taking a request?" asked Dale.

"We hear the song loud and clear already!" added Chauncey.

"Nothing like that," said Stan. "It's not tuned in to a regular satellite radio. This thing is connected to a computer system from Widen Corporation.......and so is Jane Newton!"

"So what's going to happen?" asked Chauncey.

"A program is installed to jam certain frequencies."

"What? The volume will go way down on her stereo? I have to admit it's too loud even for me and I love Montrose!"

The Detective was not taking Professor Stanley Horace very seriously, he was about to learn a thing or two.

"It can do better than that," said Stan. "It will slow her

down, maybe stop her!"

"Say what?" asked Dale, laughing slightly. "That sounds like something out of a comic book! A lame one! You didn't see stupid shit like that on Knight Rider! And that goes way back."

"Tell me about it," added Chauncey.

"Watch and learn, my friends."

Stan pressed a finger on the same button for the second time. Chauncey looked at the tiny 2 x 3 inch monitor above it. Normally he wouldn't have expected to see anything on it except for a radio station number but after what just occurred which permitted him to verbally submit information about the music of Montrose nothing should surprise him.

Again with the female mechanical voice:

"Widen Corporation: Employee Extensions A to Z."

What was spoken also appeared on the monitor.

"Christ!" snapped Chauncey. "I went through this on my own computer system trying to get Jane Newton's extension. That thing is so damn slow!"

"It's cool," said Stan. "This won't take as long, just got to go through a quick formality getting this thing started."

"Formalities," said Dale. "There's plenty of that shit back at the Pentagon."

"And in law enforcement," added Chauncey.

"Here too obviously," said Stan, sarcastically. "Now shut up for a minute! It's almost ready!"

"Select letter, then name," it spoke.

That voice which Chauncey now recognized as the same one he heard when he tried to get in touch with Jane Newton the first time around.

He didn't get that option originally, so there's a good chance of picking up speed. He didn't even want to find out fast they were going.

"N," said Stan. "Newton."

"The extension is 978!" Chauncey blurted out.

The Detective knew he got carried away. Now he felt slightly embarrassed.

"Sorry," he said, in a quieter tone.

Stan didn't respond right away. Chauncey turned his head to look for a glare in the eyes.

There was none.

"I trusted her, she trusted me," said Stan. "She may still trust me."

"Come on, Stan," said Chauncey. "She knows who we are."

"I know."

"She knows it's you behind the wheel. She knows your car, right?"

"Of course she does."

"She dropped the bomb on you! Think about it."

"He's right," said Dale.

Professor Stanley Horace knew that, all too well. But it still didn't sink in entirely.

Intuition told him it will only get worse, time to do what he had to do. One more push on that button will do it.

"Let's just hope this works," he said.

"You mean you don't know?" asked Chauncey.

"There's a first time for everything."

"I'll trust you now, even if she doesn't."

"Same here," added Dale.

"Thanks," said Stan, pushing the button. "I mean it."

Within seconds, Let's Go by Montrose would stop altogether. Chauncey wished he paid attention to how close it was to the end of the song. Hearing the introduction of the drums twice convinced him she was playing the song over and over again.

Not a bad choice driving in a fast car.

If only it was under better circumstances.

Immediately she slowed down to nearly half the

speed she'd been going. Now she stood a better chance of complying to posted speed limit, not that anybody bothered to check. Regardless, they knew neither the State Troopers nor one of Prime's police cruisers would catch up to her right away.

That job had fallen on them.

"Can we expect anything else?" asked Chauncey.

"Just wait," answered Stan.

Another minute or so passed and she slowed down way more than expected, far below the posted speed limit. At the most maybe twenty miles per hour, Stan made sure to stay considerably further behind. At this point tailgating will only provide a brief glimpse of another mini-bomb obviously targeted at them. He wasn't going to make it any easier for her to blow them to Smithereens.

I don't want to win the love of A Girl Like You, he thought.

He wasn't about to mention that to either Chauncey or Dale, though they probably felt the same way. The Detective would've picked up on the reference right away.

No doubt about it.

Now the inevitable moment had arrived.

They were back at the Badlands.

Stan came to a complete stop while Jane Newton drove down to the far end and pulled in. Much to his surprise, she immediately shut the engine off.

What was she planning to do?

Stan decided to pull in right where the parking area began, if you could call it that. He estimated the place had enough room for at least forty vehicles, maybe more. He seriously doubted the day would ever come. Of course depending how events unfold tonight the Badlands might turn into a haunted historical landmark.

"Let's play it safe staying on the opposite end," he

suggested.

"Good idea," said Chauncey.

Stan shut off the engine then looked behind him.

"Dale," he said. "Stay in the car for now, she's met Chauncey and knows me. She might get rattled seeing somebody she doesn't recognize."

"Like a snake?" asked Chauncey, and not joking either.

"Anything is possible."

"Alright," said Dale.

The Detective and Stan made the first move by getting out of the black Lincoln Town Car. They both made their way to the front and stood about ten feet from the vehicle. Jane Newton leaped out of the driver's seat of her 1973 Corvette Stingray and miraculously landed on her feet. How that was possible no one could fathom, the scariest part seeing it done so gracefully. Chauncey compared it to either a deer or a gazelle, but what stood before them could never capture the beauty or innocence of those creatures. She took a few steps forward and stared them right in the eye. She wore all white except for black boots and her hair slicked back perfectly. The clothing reminded him of Samurai warrior-types seen in Kung Fu flicks and Anime stuff. If her look was legitimate or exploitative he couldn't say. Chauncey knew better than to label or stereotype someone or something by what he saw on TV. He may love his movies but that is best left for entertainment purposes.

"Dale's right," said Chauncey.

"How so?" asked Stan.

"It would be a lot better if this came out of a comic book!"

Another crazy source of material besides movies or cartoons, he didn't plan to catch up on reruns of Knight Rider anytime soon either.

Jane Newton kept her eyes focused on Chauncey and Stan. If this was a staring contest she would win by intimidation and the look on her face was unrecognizable. Stan had worked with her for a number of years now. Not the same person he once counted on as a trusted colleague. Her eyes changed, somehow able to look more reptilian.

Had she experimented on herself?

Next she raised both arms up and reached for objects behind her back. Chauncey thought she might be carrying Samurai swords as weapons. But what could she do standing so far away? She had to be a hundred feet away from them, did she somehow possess an ability to throw those things far enough to slice through their flesh?

Nothing should surprise him anymore.

Chauncey was about to go for his gun, but before he had a chance to do that he saw what they were up against. Jane Newton revealed what she had reached for, and it wasn't Samurai swords!

She was holding semiautomatic rifles in each hand and aimed them directly at Chauncey and Stan. For a split second they froze like deer in headlights until Dale rolled down the rear window and popped his head out to get their attention.

"HIT THE DECK!" he shouted.

More like hit the dirt. Chauncey and Stan both dropped face first to the ground and the sound of gunfire rang in their ears. They had no idea for how long, probably a few seconds but it felt like an eternity. Luckily the bullets had flown way over their heads thanks to Dale Shusterman.

The Detective wasn't sure what was louder: the gunshots or the music of Montrose.

If he had a choice it would be the latter. He would rather risk losing some hearing listening to rock and roll than be permanently crippled or killed in the line of fire.

Chauncey was thankful he didn't hit any pavement when he dropped. He assumed Stan felt the same way. Who wouldn't? He'd pushed his nose in the dirt and the pressure was excruciating, even if it had only been a few seconds. Luckily there'd been no heavy rain throughout the day or he'd be eating mud. Literally! He slowly lifted his head up and looked straight ahead. So did Stan. They set their eyes on what they saw before: Jane Newton standing tall with semiautomatic rifles in each hand. Neither of them knew what their next move should be. They heard a car door open and close.

Dale decided he wanted in.

"Crazy bitch!" he shouted. "Is this your idea of a welcome wagon? You're way behind the times! That shit may fly in some old Western but not here!"

Jane Newton turned her head slightly to the left and glared at Dale. She aimed the weapon in her right hand and started firing. The bullets hit his right leg inches below the kneecap. Everything happened so fast he didn't react right away. No shouting out at the top of his lungs despite the sudden severe pain. He couldn't recall the number of shots fired or how many bullets he'd been hit by.

Dale collapsed and dropped to the ground. He felt no control throughout his entire body. A strange euphoria came over him which lasted very briefly and unsure how to describe it. Next he went into a trancelike state. For some reason that prompted him to look up and set his eyes back on Jane Newton, still standing in the same spot.

He heard a very quiet, echoing voice.

"Dale."

That was all he could hear. But he'd instantly recognized it as Professor Stanley Horace.

As he continued to keep his eyes on Jane Newton he had also taken notice of some changes. Snake like eye slits with no color in the pupils or white for that matter.

Her eyes were now black.

And could be seen as clear as day.

How Dale saw this was beyond his comprehension especially considering the darkness and distance. Somehow he sensed it. Her cheekbones looked scaly, almost lizard-like. Most people would dismiss it as wrinkles from aging, but he knew otherwise. At first it might look like lacerations or scarring, but not the case. Next her noise slowly sank in, almost disappearing. Very strange not being very large to begin with, and the nostrils could still be seen clearly. While all this took place her skin gradually turned from a typical white flesh color to a light shade of green. Now he believed he was hallucinating.

The look on her face was so frightening it made the Rodian creature Greedo in Star Wars look like a harmless possum.

As he waited for more bullets to be fired at him, ideally just one in the head to be taken out instantly, Jane Newton very slowly opened her mouth. With no way of anticipating what she might say he simply expected the worst. He figured if he was lucky he would receive a quick goodbye and that would be it.

This could be the end of Dale Shusterman.

Not the case.

Instead he laid his eyes on a sharp tongue, almost lizard-like in appearance but resembling who knows what kind of species. If she'd been part of an experiment connected to Widen Corporation, hybrid. An indescribable scream came out of her mouth, the sound at a decibel so loud and far stronger than the sound of the engine in her 1973 Corvette Stingray as well as the music of Montrose she'd blasted cruising fast and furious back and forth on Hobson Road. It even surpassed the explosion of the mini-bomb she dropped.

Now that's frightening.

Vibrations rang through the air and on the ground flowing through his body. Chauncey and Stan have to be experiencing the same thing, but right now there was no way of asking them.

When the screaming stopped he instantly felt wide awake, a moment of clarity. He watched what he considered a human hybrid named Jane Newton turn to her right and make her way toward the swamp, marching gracefully to a small opening of water a short distance from where former Widen Corporation employee Stacy O'Connell's body was discovered. The area was surrounded by a multitude of trees, marshes, grass, bushes and countless other kinds of vegetation and wildlife.

Despite being called Chase Conservation Land no one really knew what was out there.

It was a place to disappear.

She dropped her weapons on the ground then slowly set foot into the swamp, vanishing in a matter of seconds.

Jane Newton now resided in the Badlands.

Dale turned his head left to find Chauncey and Stan standing beside him.

"You alright?" asked Stan.

Before he could answer an extreme amount of pain emerged all of a sudden. It felt like he was burning. Obviously the result of the bullet wounds in the right leg.

"I'll call for help," said Chauncey.

The Detective reached into his jacket pocket for his cell phone. He rummaged his hand through for a couple of seconds with no luck but grasped what felt like an envelope of some sort. He didn't bother to take it out, not what he needed right now.

Did he leave the phone in Stan's car?

Within seconds he remembered.

"Shit!" he shouted.

"What's the matter?" asked Stan.

"I left my phone on the kitchen table at home!"

"Alright, take it easy. Mine's in the car."

"Wait," said Dale.

Without hesitating, Dale reached into the right pocket in the pants he was wearing. He tried not to think about the fact that his right leg was wounded, yanking his cell phone out right away then handed it to Chauncey.

The fire was excruciating.

"Are there any first-aid supplies in the car?" asked Chauncey.

"No," said Stan.

The Detective decided to call Triple B first who was nearby on Route 21 taking care of business with Ronan, now deceased. It took a minute to remember his boss's number, but it came to him. Triple B and Ali's were the ones he called most. He started to dial and looked down and Dale, who eyes were focused on the Corvette Stingray.

"Nice pair of wheels, huh?" he asked, hoping to keep the guy distracted from such severe pain.

"You're telling me," said Dale. "Do you think she'll come back for it?"

"That's a good question," added Stan.

Immediately after that comment the answer came.

The red 1973 Corvette Stingray erupted before their eyes into a massive explosion. The sudden sound of the blast and the flames was both blinding and deafening. No fire, ashes, or debris came near them but the heat was unbearable. Dale felt it right away. The burning sensation in his right leg had increased more than ever. Far worse compared to what they were all witnessing. Chauncey could tell the poor guy was hurting.

No first aid supplies.

They had to do something.

"Let's move him," said Chauncey.

"Where?" asked Stan.

"Out of sight from that," he answered, motioning to

what was left of the Corvette Stingray, now up in flames. "Nothing got close to us but the heat's murder on that leg!"

"We'll bring him over there," said Stan, pointing to the front of his vehicle where he and Chauncey were standing earlier. They both got down on their knees with Chauncey getting behind Dale's back and Stan by the feet.

"Be careful handling the right leg!"

"You think?!" snapped Dale, understandably so.

"Have some faith in me," said Stan. "I do have a PhD, right? I know a little about being a doctor, even if I'm not a physician."

"Sorry."

"It's all good, man."

Dale closed his eyes and took a deep breath the moment they grabbed a hold of him. He didn't want to see what Stan was doing knowing he was already in shock, making the predicament he was in worse. But how could it be? He now sensed he was in front of his friend's Lincoln Town Car expecting to be put down. However, they carried him slightly further to get behind the left side of the vehicle in the space between the left front tire and the driver's side door. A lot of room there, and the heat from the explosion had all but vanished. The pain in his leg from the bullets still inflicted him big time but he could feel a difference compared to before.

Now back to business.

"Hey," said Chauncey, catching his breath. "You think she rigged the car with some kind of self-destruct device?"

"Of course," said Stan, very confidently.

"I know one thing," added Dale. "She had the same type of explosive built into her engine. The mini-bomb she dropped on the road earlier, it's the exact same thing."

"Are you sure?" asked Chauncey.

"Trust me I know enough about this stuff," said Dale. "I got one of those things in my backpack in the backseat, remember?"

"Let's not worry about that now," said Stan.

"Don't say anything," said Chauncey. "When help gets here neither one of you knows about a mini-bomb in the backseat. They won't search the car. The three of us were together when we saw my boss on Route 21. Don't mention that she dropped one of them on the road earlier. Dynamite's not in your vocabulary, Dale. The same goes for you, Stan. The only explosion you guys saw was a red 1973 Corvette Stingray going up in flames!"

Stan nodded then they both looked down at Dale.

"Yeah," said Dale, in a very weak tone and slowly raising his right hand in the air to gives thumbs up, then dropped it ten times faster.

Out of nowhere Chauncey could hear a low and somewhat mechanical sounding male voice.

"Hello? Hello?" it spoke, barely audible.

He looked down at his right hand and had instant recall. It came from the cell phone he borrowed from Dale, forgetting he finished dialing Triple B's number before lowering his hand down when all hell broke loose. Actually, hell had been breaking loose for quite a while at this point. But with Jane Newton, his self-proclaimed Venomous Valentine, her car going up in flames was the tip of an iceberg.

What a shame contradictory analogies like that can't change the circumstances.

The Detective put the phone up to his right ear.

"What's up, Triple B?"

"I was about to say the same thing," replied Triple B. "Didn't recognize the number. We got the area closed off as a crime scene up here, lucky we didn't stop traffic for very long."

"Guess what? You're about to have another crime scene on your hands down here at the swamp."

"The Badlands, I take it?"

"You got that right! Send everything you got! When they see your number they'll know it's legit!"

"Right, I'll head down there right now."

"Thanks."

Chauncey ended the call and handed the phone back to Dale, who looked like he was going to lose consciousness.

The sound of a helicopter was not far off in the distance. Now way it could be a rescue unit sent out by law enforcement from the city of Prime, impossible to get here that fast if Triple B was calling for help this very second. It had to be the same chopper from Widen Corporation that flew above them earlier.

The aircraft slowly emerged above them coming from the direction of the swamp Jane Newton had disappeared into only minutes ago. When the spotlight shined down on them again it was far brighter than it had been while flying overhead earlier on Hobson Road. Chauncey, Stan, and Dale could barely read the small print on the bottom rear end of the chopper:

Widen - 978.

Immediately afterwards they became completely blinded by the light altogether, then instantly the chopper disappeared. Much faster than it had arrived, leaving them unable to determine which direction it flew off in. Of course being disoriented by all of this didn't help either.

Dale could no longer keep his eyes open.

The faint sound of sirens off in the distance was the last thing he heard.

CHAPTER 28

ABOUT TWENTY MINUTES HAD PASSED since Chauncey called Triple B and everything was falling into place. Four fire engines surrounded the once precious 1973 Corvette Stingray that went up in flames. If a mini-bomb had been installed into the engine chances are nothing would be salvageable. Even though he'd made it loud and clear to both Stan and Dale not to mention anything about explosives it is because they wouldn't need to. Living in an era with a massive amount of technology in use for crimes of all types it wouldn't take long for Fire Chief Fernandez and company to determine the cause of the explosion. And if anything gets discovered on Hobson Road from the car chase earlier in the evening let those guys ask about it first.

Play dumb for now.

That might change the more he talks to Triple B about what happened. No one would believe him that Jane Newton turned into some type of lizard creature. Even someone like Professor Horace who's got a PhD in Herpetology would get written off as a lunatic. Dale Shusterman reports directly to Washington D.C. and wouldn't be permitted to say anything to law enforcement in Prime except for speeches constructed by superiors at the Pentagon. However, Chauncey had a feeling the poor guy would keep quiet about it.

When an ambulance arrived Chauncey waved his right hand in the air and directed them to get up as close as possible to Stan's Lincoln Town Car, as expected Lurch and Colin got out.

"Get a stretcher!" he told them. "It's kind of tricky he's lying down on the other side of the vehicle there's some really bad bullet wounds in the right leg. I don't think he's conscious either so we can't wait on this."

"Alright," said Colin.

"You got it," added Lurch.

Without hesitating the two of them headed toward the back of the ambulance, opened the doors and pulled out a stretcher per Chauncey's instructions. The Detective lead them around the front of Stan's vehicle by the driver's side where Dale was laying, obviously in a lot of pain with plenty of blood soaking through the right leg of his black jeans.

"He's hurt bad," said Colin.

"We had no first aid supplies of any kind," said Chauncey.

"We thought it'd be best to bring him back here as far away from the fire as possible," added Stan.

"Then that's all you could do," said Lurch.

"Good to hear, Lurch," said Chauncey. "Sorry, I meant to say Zack!"

"Don't sweat it."

Chauncey and Stan could barely hear some groaning out of Dale's mouth. Hopefully, regaining consciousness, even if it's just a little bit, is a good sign.

"Do you think he'll be alright?" asked Stan.

"Yeah, seriously," added Chauncey.

"I think so," said Lurch. "Frosty probably has both of your numbers on speed-dial we'll keep him posted."

"When Dale comes around," said Chauncey. "Don't mention anything about Montrose Morgue right away."

"Why?" asked Colin.

"He might think he's among the living dead with everything we went through tonight!" said Stan.

"Damn straight," added Chauncey.

Not the smartest things to say at this point, but neither one of them revealed any unusual or specific occurrences throughout the day and night. They didn't even want to mention the little note, or Love Link perhaps, that Jane Newton had left for Chauncey at his place earlier.

Chauncey and Stan stepped back to allow Colin and Lurch to conduct the duties of Emergency Medical Technicians. They had to trust someone eventually. Hell, these guys have to think quicker than the doctors back at the hospitals. Stan caught a glimpse of his friend's eyes opening, just briefly, while being rolled back to the ambulance.

He'll be alright.

"Chauncey!" called Triple B, who'd been hanging with Fire Chief Fernandez the whole time.

"What's up?" yelled out Chauncey.

"Ali called. She's on her way here!"

He wanted to shout out to his boss to call back and demand that she doesn't. But he wasn't in the frame of mind to argue with anybody right now. He waited while Triple B walked over to chat more.

The Detective decided to break the ice upon arrival.

"How's it looking over there?" he asked.

"I'll bet that was a really nice car," answered Triple B. "And not enough emphasis on the 'Was' part."

"You're right about that!"

"Was Jane Newton the one who drove it last?"

"Damn straight."

"So all that's left are her charred remains?"

"You won't find anything," said Stan. "She took off into the swamp."

"Is he serious?" asked Triple B, looking over at Chauncey.

"She also shot up Dale Shusterman's leg for her encore, you'll find her weapons over there," confirmed Chauncey.

The Detective pointed toward the small body of water Jane Newton wandered into. Barely able to see where she dropped the two semiautomatic rifles. Not bad considering how dark it had gotten outside.

"That's where we found the second victim," said Triple B. "What was her name? Stacy O'Connell, right?"

"More or less," said Chauncey.

Three police cruisers pulled in with blue lights on and sirens blaring. Triple B waved at them and marched in the direction where the guns were located. It wouldn't take long to close off the area as another crime scene. At some point a police chopper might fly over the swamp to do surveillance but Chauncey wouldn't bet on it.

The Badlands is the place to disappear.

Next pulled in a black four door Plymouth Breeze and that could only be one person: Ali. Definitely a sight for sore eyes for Detective Chauncey Winfield even if he didn't want her to come down here, maybe it was a good thing he forgot his phone.

She immediately spotted both him and Stan then drove up where the Lincoln Town Car was parked. Chauncey made his way over to the driver's side door as she rolled the window down.

"This is not the safest place to be right now," he stated, trying to be firm but couldn't help smiling a little.

"You left your phone on the kitchen table," she said.

"I know. There's a first time for everything, isn't there?"

"I guess so. That's why I called Triple B on it to see if he knew where you were hoping you were safe!"

At that moment Triple B came back to talk.

"I think we'll be here a while," he said.

"Just like I thought," said Chauncey. "It's going to be one of those nights."

"Go home and relax for a while."

"What.......seriously?"

"It'll take some time for us to go over everything here, could be all night. I'll call you in a few hours."

"OK by me!"

Triple B nodded and headed back over to where the police cruisers had parked. Chauncey looked over at Stan who was slowly walking toward him.

"You stopped her by playing music," said Chauncey.

"That's right," said Stan.

"How's that even possible?"

"Trade secrets my friend."

The Detective smiled as they shook hands. He walked around the front of Ali's car and got inside. As soon as he turned to say something a little fuzzy canine head poked its head between them. The dog had been chilling in the backseat and he had no idea.

"You got her before coming out here?" he asked, feeling his mood increase by volumes.

"Of course," said Ali. "I couldn't leave her behind knowing she was worried about you!"

"I'll bet she was all smiles and had her paws up on you the moment Mrs. Watson opened the door!"

"Damn straight!"

Chauncey instinctively reached into his right jacket pocket for the envelope he felt in there earlier having a funny feeling what it might be. A holiday card for his girlfriend he'd forgotten about. It didn't happen very often but definitely more than once, and she could probably recall the number of times it occurred.

No matter.

He pulled it out and quickly glimpsed at the envelope which had Ali written on the front. Without hesitating he handed it to her.

"How many times is it now?" he asked.

"Not that many I assure you," she responded.

"So it's still the thought that counts?"

"Of course!" she stated, smiling.

She quickly opened the envelope and took the card out which caught her eye immediately.

"Where did you have the photo done?" she asked, astonished.

"What are you talking about?" he inquired, a bit confused.

She held the card up to show him the picture on the front which looked a lot like Lady for sure and that's why he got it.

"I bought that one, seriously," he said.

"Could've fooled me," she told him.

She opened the card up and read what he wrote inside:

"Hap-B Valentine's Day, with plenty of Love from Chauncey and Lady!" she stated.

"Wow! I got it that long ago? I guess it's kind of appropriate for this time of year."

"Are you kidding? It's not even Groundhog Day yet!"

"That's right it's still January, but were near the end of it."

"It's the 29th, I think."

"Close enough, right?"

"Of course, it's the thought that counts."

Ali put the card down then slowly backed up and turned around then put the car in drive and got back onto Hobson Road. Chauncey didn't pay much attention to how long it took for them to arrive at the exit for Route 21. As they headed up the ramp he opened the glove compartment and discovered some CDs he'd left in there. Surprisingly, he came across Montrose's Jump On It! Track 1 was Let's Go, a song he'd heard more than enough of chasing after Jane Newton tonight! But that wouldn't stop him from enjoying everything else on it. He was just glad to find something he wouldn't get tired of listening to right away. If you were lucky some stuff from the first CD Sammy Hagar sang on might be on the radio occasionally but that's it.

Chauncey barely noticed getting onto Route 21. He was just relieved he could go home for now. A minute or two passed before they started another conversation.

"I saw something on the way down here," said Ali.

"What?" Chauncey asked.

"We just passed by it, on the other side of the road, it looked like an accident. There was a mail truck. I thought it was Ronan's, some police cruisers and an ambulance. Did that have anything to do with what happened tonight?"

"Sort of," he responded, slowly and reluctant.

"The car on fire down at the swamp looked intense, made me think of something like The Fast and the Furious."

Chauncey couldn't respond right away. He didn't want to just blurt out what happened to their favorite Irish mailman.

"I wish it had been that fun," he told her "Wouldn't mind if Vin Diesel had been there as well. I'll tell you everything when we get back."

He looked down and saw little Lady Jane Spitz still snuggled in the same spot between the two front seats, anticipating her next move an attempt to climb forward into his lap.

"Hey Thundermutt!" he said. "The power of a Jewish

Viking would've been helpful tonight, but I'm glad you sat this one out."

Chauncey looked forward feasting his eyes on the Montrose CD. He opened the case, took the disc out and inserted it into Ali's player. A quick glance determined the stereo had already been set to CD mode. Neither of them listened to music on the radio often. He pressed the 'forward' button to start at track 2. He looked up and saw they were passing by the Woodward Hotel, easily seen while driving down Route 21. Chauncey spotted a woman, standing statuesque with skin so pale it glowed. She had a deadly stare, and he felt a piercing sensation. The name Stacy O' Connell entered his mind again but then it hit him:

Jane Doe.

Track 2 started, the song began:

"What Are You Waiting For?"

To
Mary Deon
(February 11, 1955 – April 27, 2017)
I am forever grateful I got to say goodbye to you.
Even though I didn't know it would be for the last time.

And
Max Fleming
(December 22, 1993 – September 7, 2017)

For Rob, Jack, and Ben.

www.ingramcontent.com/pod-product-compliance
Lightning Source LLC
Chambersburg PA
CBHW020233260626
47156CB00002B/661